)st

(USA Today)

JENNIFER PROBST

"Probst nails it, pun intended and acknowledged, with this sassy and sexy tale."
— Alice Clayton, *USA Today* bestselling author
of *Wallbanger* and *Rusty Nailed*

"A fantastic, sexy contemporary romance with captivating characters, witty dialogue, and some whimsical magic. . . . A winner and a must-read!"
— *Harlequin Junkie*

"Bestseller Probst creates a likeable cast [and] refreshing female friendships."
— *Publishers Weekly*

"This book is full of emotion and heart. . . . 5 stars!"
— *Sizzling Book Club*

Turn the page for more sensational acclaim!

Searching for Someday is . . .

"A refreshing, lighthearted read with adorable characters and a fantastic classic love story."

—*Miss Construed's Reviews*

"The perfect blend of romance, humor, family, friendship, sex, and man or woman's best friend. You will laugh, cry, smile, and enjoy every moment. . . . I didn't want the story to end. *Searching for Someday* earns a perfect 5-star rating!"

—*Bookish Temptations*

"What do you get when you throw in some quirky characters, a hot and steamy love/hate relationship, a little magic, and a dog named Robert? The answer is a few enjoyable hours of reading this adorable book. Who doesn't love a good romance?"

—*TwinSpin Reviews*

"Delightfully romantic and fun. . . . Probst is one of the best contemporary authors!"

—*Under the Covers*

The Marriage Bargain   *The Marriage Trap*
The Marriage Mistake   *The Marriage Merger*

Don't miss the bestselling series "destined to steal your heart" (Lori Wilde)—the **Marriage to a Billionaire** novels from Jennifer Probst!

"Nonstop sexual tension crackles off the page. . . . It will hook you and leave you begging for more!"

—Laura Kaye, *New York Times* bestselling author
of *One Night with a Hero*

"A beautiful story with characters that will stay with you forever."

—Candace Havens, bestselling author
of *Take It Like a Vamp*

"Jennifer Probst is an amazing author."

—*Fresh Fiction*

"Fiery and wild . . . it goes straight to your heart."

—*Maldivian Book Reviewers*

"Witty, sweet, and sexy . . . very enjoyable."

—*Bookish Temptations*

"Jennifer Probst is . . . one of my favorite authors!"

—Susan Meier, author of
Nanny for the Millionaire's Twins

"Breath-catching romance."

—Catherine Bybee, *New York Times*
bestselling author

ALSO BY JENNIFER PROBST

The Searching For Series
Searching for Someday

The Marriage to a Billionaire Series
The Marriage Bargain

The Marriage Trap

The Marriage Mistake

The Marriage Merger

searching for perfect
a novel

JENNIFER PROBST

Pocket Books

New York   London   Toronto   Sydney   New Delhi

Pocket Books
A Division of Simon & Schuster, Inc.
1230 Avenue of the Americas
New York, NY 10020

This book is a work of fiction. Any references to historical events, real people, or real places are used fictitiously. Other names, characters, places, and events are products of the author's imagination, and any resemblance to actual events or places or persons, living or dead, is entirely coincidental.

First Pocket Books paperback edition May 2014

POCKET and colophon are registered trademarks of Simon & Schuster, Inc.

For information about special discounts for bulk purchases, please contact Simon & Schuster Special Sales at 1-866-506-1949 or business@simonandschuster.com.

The Simon & Schuster Speakers Bureau can bring authors to your live event. For more information or to book an event contact the Simon & Schuster Speakers Bureau at 1-866-248-3049 or visit our website at www.simonspeakers.com.

Manufactured in the United States of America

10 9 8 7 6 5 4 3 2 1

ISBN 978-1-4767-4495-7
ISBN 978-1-4767-4498-8 (ebook)

"The thing that is really hard, and really amazing, is giving up on being perfect and beginning the work of becoming yourself."

—Anna Quindlen

This book is dedicated to all my readers who have inspired me, supported me, loved my books, and made me want to do better. And for anyone who needs to believe they are worthy . . . of love, forgiveness, success, friendship, or happiness.

You are.

searching for perfect

one

NATHAN ELLISON RAYMOND Dunkle couldn't catch a break.

He raced out of his lab, late again, his mind a bit foggy from an intense brainstorming session in the pursuit of a groundbreaking physics formula to transform advanced propulsion. He eased his Tesla through crowds of city traffic and tried not to panic. This event could be the turning point in his life, and he refused to miss it. What if his future wife was there right now, meeting some other man because he was stuck at work? Again.

Ned clamped down on his impatience and moved another few inches. He was tired of his social life revolving around his lab partner, Wayne, and his brother, Connor. Ever since he left NASA to dedicate his time to getting the private sector into space travel, his days had melded together in a long line of formulas and research. The weekly golf trips with his friends fell apart. His dating life, slow to begin with, ground to a big fat zero. Three months ago, he had celebrated his thirty-second birthday and realized he had no one to invite over. A small cake appeared in the lab and after Wayne hummed a few bars of *Happy Birthday*, they got back to work.

Pathetic.

That's when he made his decision to change.

Ned pulled into the city limits welcoming visitors to Verily and perused the street for a space. The brightly lit shops lining the sidewalk overlooked the Hudson River and gave off a quaint charm that embraced visitors, bringing them into the fold of the welcoming area. His brother had laughed when he told him about the upcoming speed-dating mixer, but Connor didn't believe in settling down with one woman. Years of watching his brother date endlessly with no commitment in sight depressed him. The whole catch-and-release repetition just seemed . . . empty.

Ned craved a real connection with a woman, someone he could share his life with. He had no interest in bar hopping or bed hopping. Marriage equaled all the things he lacked: comfort, sex, and companionship. Once Ned made decisions, he dedicated all of his time and energy into the steps needed to reach his goal, and this newest idea was no exception. After six weeks of intense research, he was ready.

He pulled into a space and turned off the ignition. Grabbing a pack of breath mints from the glove compartment, he popped one in his mouth, and wiped his hands down his khaki pants. Crap. He'd forgotten to change out of his white coat, and the coffee stain from this morning was prominently placed on his chest. He spit on his finger and tried to scrub the fabric, but the brown splotch only worsened. Could he take the coat off entirely? He yanked one shoulder down and spotted the wrinkled cotton shirt crushed underneath. Nah, leave it on. The hell with it. He didn't want a woman who only cared about clothes or appearances anyway.

He pushed his glasses up his nose and peered into the driver's side mirror. The healthy brown glow he'd hoped to sport had gone horribly wrong. Damn bronzer. Golf season hadn't started yet, and his white skin had thrown him into a panic this morning. He knew women liked the beachy look, so he bought the self-tanner at lunch and applied it at work. He'd followed the instructions perfectly, but instead of a sunkissed glow, he got carrot orange. Ned rubbed at his face frantically and tried to move the color around. It wasn't that bad. Wayne had just glanced over at Nate after lunch, and when pressed, said he looked fine. Of course, he'd been wrapped up in the velocity testing, so maybe he hadn't really studied him.

Holding back a groan, he got out of the car and headed toward the restaurant called Cosmos. At least the mixer wasn't in a bar. He hurried his pace, tripped over the uneven sidewalk, and finally found his destination. The warm air hit him full force, with the delicious scents of garlic, tomato, and fresh bread. The restaurant was decorated in tasteful Tuscan colors, and soft lighting dimly illuminated various tables in the main room. Timers sat on each table, and people mingled with drinks and appetizers in hand.

Ned froze.

He fought the urge to turn around and walk back out, but he wasn't a failure, and he didn't intend to start now. He'd studied for this. It was his moment.

"May I help you?"

He looked down, and a young girl holding a clipboard smiled up at him. "Yes. Ned Dunkle. I signed up."

"Of course." She crossed his name off and gave him a ticket. "Welcome to our speed-dating mixer at Kinnections. You have just enough time to get a drink at the bar. Here's your number. You'll be starting with table nine. Five minutes maximum at each table, and here's a sheet with all the participants. If you like someone, note down the name, and at the end of the mixer, we'll introduce the people who are interested in each other."

"Great." He took the ticket into his sweaty hand and fought his way to the bar. Laughter and easy conversation drifted around him, along with the musky scent of perfume and something stronger. Was that him? He ducked his head and did a quick sniff. Oh yeah, way too much cologne. He'd liked the scent at home, but now he felt lost in the piney, woodsy tones it promised on the label. Oh, well. No one would notice.

He scanned his surroundings and got into game mode. That's when he saw her.

Perfection.

The woman moved across the room, practically

shimmering with energy and poise. Stopping now and then to chat with different people, she claimed the attention of male and female participants alike. Her whiskey gold eyes dominated her face, and thick, wavy hair tumbled past her shoulders in a deep caramel color. Her hot pink suit matched her nails. But his attention kept getting dragged to her shoes. Four-inch heels, open toe, pink with silver rhinestones. The silver-cuffed toe ring only emphasized her bubblegum-colored toenails.

She clearly was the type of woman who got any man she desired, owned her sexuality, and called the shots. Her husky laugh vibrated in his ears, dove into his gut, and squeezed. It was a sound full of life and the potential for fun. A wave of longing hit him, and he tamped down a laugh. Yeah, right. Not in this lifetime. Still, if she were involved in the speed-dating event, he'd be able to meet and talk to her for five minutes. That alone would make the whole evening worthwhile.

Not that he wanted a woman who was just beautiful. He learned that lesson well and didn't need a repeat. Not in this lifetime.

A buzzer sounded, and everyone ran to their tables.

Showtime.

He headed toward number nine and settled down with a glass of house wine he didn't like but was easy for the bartender to make. His normal drink usually took too much time to explain. A petite blonde slid into the seat, glanced up, and did a tiny recoil. He tried not to rub his face and make the orange more noticeable.

The timer chirped.

"Hi, I'm Naomi."

He took a deep breath. "Hi, Naomi. My name is Ned."

"Hi, Ned. So, what do you do?"

"Umm, I'm an aerospace engineer."

"Oh, like planes? Do you own a plane?"

He shook his head. "No, rockets."

Her eyes widened in excitement. "You own a real rocket ship?"

"No, no. I work on rocket ships. Well, I work on prototypes. Research stuff. I don't own one."

"Oh." She looked disappointed. "I like to fly places. How about a jet? Do you own one of those?"

He tried to focus, but the conversation was heading into twilight zone territory and a full minute hadn't even gone by. "Uh, I'm sorry, I don't. I have a car."

She lit up. "I love hot cars. Lamborghinis, Ferraris, Hummers. Did you see that movie *The Fast and the Furious*? They had some really hot cars."

"No, I missed out on that film."

"Do you smell that?" She crinkled her nose and glanced around. "Is that cologne?"

"I guess some guy put on too much."

"Ick, I hate when that happens."

"Me, too."

Unfortunately, she refocused on the original bizarre conversation. "A man's car tells a lot about him. People cite that horoscope junk all the time, but they don't realize that the choice of vehicle really defines a person."

"I don't think I realized how important it was."

"What type of car do you drive, Ned?"

"A Tesla. It won the award for the safest car in America and has zero emissions. The cutting edge of efficiency and cost savings."

She sighed. "I drive a Mitsubishi convertible Eclipse in cherry red. I don't think I can date or respect a man who drives an economy vehicle. We just won't have the compatible energy needed in a relationship, especially in the bedroom." She gave him a sunny smile. "Nice to meet you, though."

Ding.

Already a little shaken, Ned rose and made his way to the next table. A tall brunette with glasses studied him carefully and waited for the timer to begin. "I'm Sandra. I'm an elementary school teacher, divorced, no children, and live by myself."

Ned relaxed when she paused. This, he could handle. An intelligent, direct conversation to discover if there was any chemistry or connection. "Hi, I'm Ned. I work as an engineer and I've never been married."

"Do you have issues?"

He laughed, enjoying her sense of humor, and then realized she was frowning at him and dead serious. "Oh. Probably. Doesn't everyone have issues?"

"I don't. You have a stain on your shirt."

He swiped at it and blocked it with his arm. "Sorry. I was rushing out of the lab and running late."

She pointed a finger at him. "You're a workaholic."

He shifted in his chair. "I do work a lot, but I'm looking to change that. Do you—do you enjoy your job?"

"Not really. The Common Core stuff wrecked everything, the sixth graders are hormonal and impossible to control, and they want to take away most of our benefits."

"I'm sorry. Are you thinking of switching careers?"

"In this economy?" She looked at him as if his lab coat had suddenly caught fire. "No way. I have to deal with it, so I made a schedule to keep conflict to a minimum. Get pregnant in eighteen months so I can extend my leave to a full year. Have the second child exactly fourteen months later, so they're close in age. But I don't want to deal with any workaholics. My father was one, and my parents ended up divorced. Have you always been selfish?"

"Huh? No, if I had a family, I wouldn't work as much. Let me ask you—"

"Sorry, I'm not taking a risk with you. I think our time is up."

Ding.

At table eleven, he knocked over his partner's cocktail and stained her pretty red dress. At table twelve, he met a catalog model who dismissed him immediately and gave him a lecture on the perils of skin cancer from sunbathing. He drained his bad wine, but there was no time to get another because those five minutes dragged on endlessly and melded into another session more horrifying than the last.

Finally, at table fifteen, he scored.

Debra had a sweet smile, long red hair, and a milky white complexion. He introduced himself. "It's lovely to meet you, Ned. Meeting people is so hard nowadays, we're reduced to embarrassing ways to find one another."

His shoulders relaxed slightly. "Yes, I agree. Though I'm surprised you would have any problems."

She laughed and ducked her head. "Thanks. So, instead of asking a bunch of inane questions for five minutes, I composed a few fun ways to see what personality types we are."

"Very creative." He'd read about this in *Cosmopolitan* magazine and completed dozens of surveys regarding the type of man women truly craved. His skin tingled with excitement. "Ask away."

"Wonderful!" She drew out a stack of index cards and shot him a playful expression. "Question one, what type of first date would you take me on to impress me?"

Yes. He knew this one cold. He tried to keep the triumph out of his face. "I'd take you to the New York Public Library in Manhattan and find out what type of books you like to read. Then have a picnic in the park afterward."

Disappointment gleamed in her brown eyes. "Oh.

A library is free, Ned. And a picnic is cheap. No limo? Broadway play? How about the revolving restaurant on top of the Marriott Marquis? Are you afraid to spend money on a woman?"

What was she talking about? *Cosmo* always said a man needed to be romantic. Unique. Money didn't impress; thoughtfulness and originality did. "Sorry, I wasn't thinking. How about your next question?"

She perked back up and slid to her next note card. "If you were to compliment one part of me, what would that be?"

This one he knew! *Marie Claire* talked about it constantly. "Your smile," he said.

Her lower lip kicked out. "Are you kidding me? Do I work out at the gym twenty-four-seven so you can comment on my teeth?"

His ears roaring, he blinked in sheer confusion. This could not be happening. The last time he took Connor's advice and commented on a woman's body, he'd gotten a drink thrown in his face. "I didn't think women liked when men did that."

She rolled her eyes. "That's ridiculous, we live for it."

Ned made a mental note to go back to bodily compliments. "Do I get one more shot?"

"Last one. This is the most important. If we got in a fight, how would you apologize?"

Finally. There was no way to get this one wrong. "I'd tell you straight out I was sorry and that I'd work on fixing what I can so we don't have the same issue in the future." Hello, *Self* magazine. Communication and stating a verbal apology was a number one priority with women.

Debra stuffed her cards into her purse and gave him a look. "Why the hell would I care if you're sorry? Actions speak louder than words. I want jewelry. Sorry, Ned, you're just not for me."

Ding.

By the time he hit table twenty, he was aggravated, tired, thirsty, and disillusioned. Most cared about his appearance, money, or man toys, and all he wanted to do was get serious and leave all the junk behind. Despite weeks of reading women's magazines, he'd flunked every five-minute session.

Finally, he reached the last date. The woman seemed nice enough, but he'd been here before. No more. This time, he was running the date his way.

"Hi, I'm Bernadette."

He leaned forward, placed his elbows on the table, and narrowed his gaze. "Hi, I'm Ned. When will you be ready to be married and have kids?"

The woman jerked back. She seemed shocked, but he bet she was just pretending. He hadn't met a female without an agenda this whole night. "Umm, I'm not sure. I want to be in love with the right person. Then marriage and kids can come later."

Hmm, good answer. Ned raised the stakes. "How long? A month? Two? You're already past thirty, and statistics show once your eggs reach thirty-five, your fertility starts declining, and chances of a healthy baby decrease by forty percent."

Was that a moan? He was only citing statistics straight from *Glamour* or *Self*. He forgot which one. Her lower lip trembled but he had her full attention. "I'm only twenty-nine," the woman whispered.

"Right on the precipice. I would rethink your plan if you want to birth at least two children. You do want children, right?"

Another small moan. "Yes, I've always dreamed of having children."

Finally. A woman who knew what she wanted. He relaxed. "Me, too. I think we have similar philosophies. It's been a tough night, but I'm glad we finally met. I think I'm supposed to wait till the end, but since this worked out so well, how about dinner Friday night?"

Ding.

The woman pressed a trembling hand to her mouth. She blinked rapidly. Were those tears? What was going on?

He opened his mouth to question her, but a vision in hot pink swarmed into his line of sight.

Dream woman.

She was even more stunning close up. Her lips held just a touch of glossy moisture, and his nostrils kicked in at the scent of sandalwood and cinnamon. She laid a hand on Bernadette's arm and whispered something in her ear. Bernadette nodded, swiped at her eyes, and stood up. Dream woman patted her back, pointed her in the other direction, and watched her walk away.

"Hey, we were setting up a date."

Dream woman swung around and met his gaze head on.

He stilled. Those golden eyes sucked him in deep and held on tight. He struggled for breath, entranced by the white-hot heat and fury beating from her in waves. Deliberately, she placed her palms flat on the table and leaned in.

"I want to talk to you."

His spirits perked up. "Great. Did the clock start?"

"Forget the clock. I need to finish up a few things and then I'd like to have a chat. I'll meet you at the diner next door in ten minutes."

No way. She was interested in him? Odd, she looked a bit intense for having just asked him out, but he'd go anywhere with her. Maybe this horrific night would turn out alright. "Don't I need to fill out my request sheet first?"

Was it possible she looked even more furious? Her expression fascinated him, all sharp angles and soft skin. Funny, if you took away each of her features, it seemed as if her face was too big for her body, but when put together, she had movie-star looks. Like Julia Roberts. A long, gazelle-like structure, highly cut cheekbones, thick brows, huge eyes. "I'm sure that sheet won't be needed. I'll see you at the diner."

She pulled back, swiveled on her four-inch pink heels, and disappeared into the crowd.

Ned dumped the sheet. Other than Bernadette, the event had been a bust. But his date with Dream Woman was everything he'd hoped for. Who needed long term if he could enjoy her for one perfect night? He'd have just enough time to pop another breath mint and rub a tissue over his orange face to see if he could lighten it up.

Ned headed toward the diner.

two

KENNEDY SIPPED HER coffee and studied the walking disaster across the table.

It took a while to calm down her client, but she'd convinced poor Bernadette that the man was joking and then hooked her up with Brian, who'd been making moony eyes at her all night. Speed-dating events were a bit . . . touchy. Some clients loved the quick pace and even quicker decision making. Many thrived on sheer dating stress and adrenaline, rising to the top and scoring the best overall first impression.

Others tanked.

Like this guy.

She took her time and let him stew. He probably thought he was going to score with her, but she had a completely different intention for this meeting. As the top recruiter and makeover expert at the Kinnections matchmaking agency, she'd come across various types of men and learned the fine art of patience. She helped them find true love by using a mixture of encouragement, motivation, empathy, and teaching behavior modification.

But this bozo had broken all the rules, and she wasn't allowing him back into society without an attempt to protect future women. The harsh lights of the diner emphasized the garish tone to his skin. Dear God, he was a living Dorito. He waited patiently for her to speak, but she noticed he grabbed a few napkins to wipe down the white Formica counter before settling his elbows on the edge. Great, a germaphobe to boot. "What's your name?" she asked.

"Ned."

"Hi, Ned, I'm Kennedy. Can I ask you a question?"

"You can ask me anything."

"What did you hope to accomplish tonight?"

He blinked behind thick black-framed glasses. Usually, she loved a good designer frame with a funky style, but these were just wrong. Oversize, squared, they dominated his face and swallowed his eyes. "I don't understand. I'm looking to meet a woman who's right for me."

"I see. Do you usually approach strange women with the same questions you fired off at Bernadette?"

His unibrow hiked up alarmingly, scaring her. Her fingers itched for a wax strip. "I was getting to know her. I thought we were connecting."

She tapped a nail against the chipped mug. "You thought you were connecting? You insulted her, zapped her confidence, and instilled a fear of being alone and childless for the rest of her life. Did you honestly consider that meeting a success?"

He jerked back and shook his head in confusion. "No, I didn't mean to do that. I was being direct."

"Age and weight are two sacred items never to be

discussed. They're the Holy Grail of silence, Ned. Didn't you know that?"

He ran his fingers through his hair. The shaggy brown strands hung almost to his shoulders and covered most of his face. Kennedy wondered if he ever visited a hair salon. There was no cut or attempt at a fashionable style. He reminded her of a neglected sheepdog. "Yes, of course, I know about that. I completely forgot because I was upset. I dealt with twenty sessions of torture by women who only focused on money, date destinations, or how many planes I owned."

"You own a plane?"

"No, that's the point! I thought the goal of this thing was to find a woman with similar philosophies, but all they cared about was money."

She studied him more closely. He seemed genuinely upset and didn't give off the creepoid vibe she expected to find. His orange hands wrapped around his coffee mug as if seeking comfort. The white lab coat looked ridiculous paired with pants straight from the eighties. A shiny khaki material that hung loose on his hips and displayed no pockets or discernible form. The large, smeared coffee spot in the middle of his chest reminded her of the barking stain commercial. This man needed to carry a tube of Tide to Go.

But it was the pocket protector that gave it away.

Oh yeah. Major nerd. From the glasses to the clothes to the poor social conversation, this man screamed, Help me. Could he be genuine? Curiosity piqued. "What are you looking for? To get laid? A few dates?"

He straightened his shoulders. A loose thread dangled from the lab coat. "I want to find a wife."

"Why?"

He never flinched. Just met her gaze with a directness that surprised her. "I'm tired of being alone. My career has come first for the past decade. I'm not interested in a parade of women who aren't interested in settling down. I want a family. Companionship. Is that too much to ask?"

He put down the coffee and flexed his fingers. She noticed his nails were bitten to the max. Frustration shot from him in waves. It was rare to discover a man so focused on marriage. Normally, she'd do a victory dance and sign the guy up for Kinnections on the spot. Too bad he didn't seem to have a clue. Maybe he just needed some advice.

"There's nothing wrong with that goal, but people need a bit of the dance first. A hint of flirtation. A give-and-take of conversation to build trust. That leads to a first real date."

"I know. I prepared for this."

She raised a brow. "You're orange, dude."

"I tried to use bronzer to get the beach look. I figured women liked it."

"You have a coffee stain on your shirt, you're wearing a lab coat, you haven't cut your hair since 2000, and I feel like I just got dragged into the woods and buried under a flock of pine trees to die. Is that your cologne?"

He gave up and began picking at his nail. "It's proven women are susceptible to the emotional power of scents. A leisurely walk in nature evokes feelings of happiness."

"Not with half a bottle. I'm experiencing more of a horrific run through the forest while a deadly black bear chases me."

"I overshot. I had to work late. Besides, I don't want a woman who believes clothes or looks are important."

Kennedy sighed. "Clothes *are* important. A first impression gives you the opportunity to show the other person you care. You don't need to sport Calvin Klein, but clean, pressed, and at your best increases your chances to meet the right person."

"I tried." His eyes lit up. "Would you like to go to dinner Friday night?"

"No."

"You didn't ask me here for a date, did you? You wanted to kick my ass."

She smothered a laugh. It was a shame. Good intentions in a male were gold, especially one who truly wanted to find love and didn't want to hide behind casual sex and a few good times.

Unless . . .

The idea took root, flowered, and exploded into full-bloom roses. Unless she took him under her wing. Taught him how to interact with women. Gave him a makeover. Coached him to close a first meeting to a real date instead of waffling in the shark-infested waters with no help. A surge of excitement tingled in her blood, something she hadn't experienced in a long time. Possibility.

She ached to transform him.

She was damn good at her job, and had numerous solid matches to back up her confidence. Lately, she'd wondered if she was going through a slump. Nothing excited her anymore. Her own dates were commonplace and led down an endless path of disappointment. The lovers she took to bed were satisfying for an hour or two, but in the harsh morning light, she felt no need to keep them around. Her career was satisfying, but she hadn't done anything spectacular or out of the box lately. She was stuck, while everyone around her seemed to be moving forward at a rapid pace. Most of her close friends were engaged or involved in permanent relationships. Usually she adored the dating scene with the lure of the unknown and expanse of possibility spread before her. But she had struggled with burnout lately, and began spending most of her hours at Kinnections or hanging with girlfriends.

But this man presented a true challenge.

Kennedy switched gears and downshifted into business mode. First, she needed more information before making the commitment. He remained ultra still in the chair, no fidgeting or impatient movements. Definitely a desk jockey. "What's your full name?"

"Nathan Ellison Raymond Dunkle."

Fascinating. This just kept getting better and better. "You got stuck with a real doozy, Ned."

His face remained deadly serious. "I know. If my mother was still around we'd sit down and have a conversation regarding her original intentions."

"You know if you put the R in, you come up with NERD."

The unibrow lifted again. "If you think you're being clever, I'll have you know that even the junior high jocks figured that out pretty quickly. You'll have to work much harder to impress me."

Kennedy fought a smile. Good. He had a sense of humor buried under all that intelligence. You couldn't teach a person that part, you either owned the trait or not. Definitely raw material to extricate and polish. "Touché. And what do you do?"

"I'm an aerospace engineer."

She pressed her finger against her lips and pondered the amazing scene unfolding before her. Did this get any better? "You're a rocket scientist."

Impatience simmered from his frame, though he remained still. "Yes, that's what an aerospace engineer is. But we don't call ourselves rocket scientists any longer. It's outdated."

Her gaze fell to the pocket protector and his outfit. "I apologize."

His demeanor shifted, and he gazed at her with sudden suspicion. "What is it you really want? I apologized for how I came across to Bernadette. You don't want to date me. Why am I still here?"

Kennedy tried very hard not to lick her lips and ask for a cup of cream. A nerdy, rich rocket scientist who wanted to get married and meet his match. This was her swan song—her Eliza Doolittle—her crowning achievement and challenge of a lifetime.

"I have a deal to offer."

"What type of deal?"

She smiled. "The deal of a lifetime. I'm going to get you everything you've ever wanted. I'm going to find you the woman of your dreams. All you need to do is listen."

He blinked. Pondered. And leaned forward.

Gotcha.

He stopped picking his nails and studied her with a razor-sharp gaze. "How? Who are you?"

"Kennedy Ashe. I run the Kinnections matchmaking agency with two of my partners. We structured the speed-dating event for our clients tonight, but we're also looking to expand. Our focus is to match couples for long-term relationships. Our statistics are quite impressive, and I can give you plenty of information to sort through. You strike me as a numbers person. Results. Correct?"

The big picture seemed to click into place. He pushed his glasses back up his nose. "You ran the event? You're a saleswoman."

"Recruiter. I have a proposition for you, Ned. I'd like to help find your wife."

Disappointment flickered over his features. She watched his shoulders sag. "I see. You want to sign me as a client to your matchmaking agency. How much?"

Giddiness swept through her. His doubtful, accusing stare confirmed his sharp intelligence. This was going to be fun. "Ah, you think I'm a hustler, don't you? Think I want to take a huge deposit, promise you the world, and walk away, right?"

"It did cross my mind."

"I'd be disappointed in you if it didn't. I think I can help you. My main role in Kinnections is to take the clients and give them the tools to meet and connect with the opposite sex. People have issues. The world is hard, especially meeting new people. Sometimes, people need to learn to get past some of their social barriers in order to present themselves at their best."

An unruly snort burst from his lips. "Oh, I see. You want me to lie and pretend I'm someone else in order to get the girl. That'll never work."

"Why not?"

"Because it's a mirage. I can't change who I am at the core. I don't want to."

"Neither do I. Look, if you don't get a chance for a woman to see who you really are, you're never going to find the woman of your dreams. I'm not going to change the person you are—I have no need to. But I will work on some simple surface things in order for you to have more opportunities. First impressions are critical. I'm talking about a bit of polish. A little refining in social conversation. Make sense?"

He scratched his head. The shaggy hair parted, then

fell back around his face like a curtain. "What's in this for you?"

"Job satisfaction. If I succeed, maybe more business for Kinnections. And an opportunity to help. That's it."

"How much?"

"One thousand is the initial sign-up fee. It includes counseling, makeovers, and two dates."

"And if I agree?"

She sensed surrender, but it needed to be on her terms. He was a project that would take up all her time and energy. "If you agree, I'll find your match. But you'll have to put yourself completely in my hands."

"How long is the contract?"

"One year. Of course, if you don't see results or aren't satisfied, you can leave anytime less your initial deposit. It's all explained in the contract."

"How do we begin?"

She whipped out her cell phone. "Give me your email and I'll send over the contract with some other information. As soon as you've made your decision, let me know. We'll schedule the initial consultation and take it from there."

He recited his email. Her nails clicked as she typed it in her phone.

"Why me?"

She looked up. His raw question hit her gut, and emotion rushed out. Wasn't it hard enough to go out there, again and again, and fail? To believe there really is someone just for you? This man, in his botched clothes and oversize glasses and orange skin, wanted to believe. He was her greatest test yet and would confirm her belief in happy-ever-afters.

At least, for some people.

Her voice vibrated with determination. "Because I believe there's someone perfect for everyone. And I want to help you find her."

He stared at her for a long time, probing her face in utter stillness. Then he nodded. "Okay."

"Look over the contract. If you agree to the terms, call me, and I'll get you in this week for a formal consultation. I'm looking forward to working with you." She took the last gulp of coffee and reached for her purse to throw money down.

His hand shot out and grabbed her wrist. "I got it."

His grip was snug. She expected soft, damp hands, but they were firm and deliciously warm. She drew back quickly. "Thanks. I'll be waiting for your call."

She slid out of the booth and walked out of the diner. Her step was light as she made her way to her car, and the brisk March wind seemed full of possibilities.

three

KENNEDY LOOKED UP as her two friends and business partners rushed into her office. "What's up? Did the quarterly profit statements come in?"

Kate looked about to burst with excitement. "Better."

"Did Arilyn finally sleep with the FedEx guy?"

Arilyn shook her strawberry hip-length hair in mock seriousness. "His package is much smaller than that of the man I'm currently seeing, thank you very much."

Kennedy laughed. "Spill."

Kate clapped her hands together. "Jane and Tim are getting married!"

Kennedy jumped from the chair and shared in a screaming group hug. Jane was a client of Kinnections who'd struggled to meet the right man. They all had worked with her to increase her confidence, tweak her appearance, and find her a match. Of course, when Jane's older brother, Slade, threatened to expose the company as a fraud in an effort to protect his sister, Kate took him on as a client, ready to prove the agency's validity.

She did. And they fell in love with each other in the process, and were now engaged to be married. Now that his sister was also happy, it only made the upcoming wedding that much sweeter. Of course, it didn't hurt that Kate, the main owner and founder of Kinnections, possessed a special "touch" that allowed her to sense when a true soul connection existed between two people—her unique ability had allowed her to truly believe that Slade was the right one and had helped to set up Jane and Tim as well.

Ken paused in the middle of the hug. "Can we use this in our advertising? It's brilliant. Brother and sister matched by Kinnections—double wedding. Get your match on!"

Kate and Arilyn looked at her. Then shook their heads. "No way. This celebration is private," Kate said. "Of course, it'll go into the statistics, which means two more weddings. We're coming close to stellar numbers now, so that should make you happy."

Ken stuck out her bottom lip. The pout always worked with men. They told her it was sexy and irresistible. "I won't use names. We'd be missing out on a fortune and the chance to blow that ridiculous Bravo show away. Who needs a millionaire when you can find love with the boy next door?"

Arilyn gave a delicate snort. "Not gonna happen. And you may need another move. The sulky-lip thing is way overdone. Maybe bite it? That's in all the erotic romance novels."

Ken rolled her eyes. "I'm not a cliché, A, and it hasn't failed me yet. Oh, fine, forget the advertising. I'm still thrilled for you and Jane."

Kate grinned. "Girls' night out? Mugs?"

"Absolutely. How about Friday night? Tear Genevieve away from her man, and we'll make it a celebration. I can't believe we have three engagements in our group." An odd emotion clawed at her gut, but she smothered it. She wasn't interested in marriage anyway. She bored quickly, and as far as she could tell, no man would be able to tie her down. But her friends deserved every ounce of happiness, and damned if she wasn't going to support them.

"Done." Kate took in Kennedy's no-nonsense black Chanel suit. "Do you have a client?"

A twinge of excitement coursed through her. "Yes, he should be here soon. This one's a true challenge. I'm taking him on."

Kate cocked her head. "Hmm, you haven't worked with a new client in a while, especially a male. Is he hot?"

She grinned. "Nope. He's a wreck. Isn't it great?"

Arilyn sighed. She was the resident counselor and computer programmer for Kinnections. "I'll clear my schedule."

"I'm going to recruit all of you for this one."

"What's he like?"

Kennedy almost bounced up and down with sheer excitement. "Three words. My. Fair. Lady."

Kate gasped. "No way!"

Even Arilyn looked a bit buzzed instead of meditative. "How bad? Like guttersnipe bad?"

"Yes. Picture this. Nerd heaven. Big bulky glasses. Shaggy dog hair. Walmart clothes. And orange skin from a botched self-tanner."

Kate seemed to calculate the items on the list with glee. "Appearance only?"

"Much worse. He told Bernadette at the speed-dating event that she was nearing thirty and her eggs were getting old. Then asked her on a date."

Arilyn winced. "Poor Bernadette. Did she cry?"

"Almost, but I saved the whole thing. Took Mr. Geek to the diner to whip his ass, then discovered he had no clue what was going on. He wants to find a wife and has no idea how to do it. I absolutely had to have him."

"What are you going to do first?" Kate asked. "Hair, right? A good haircut fixes everything."

Arilyn shook her head. "Can't do a thing if his skin is orange. Are we talking peach tinted?"

The bell on the door tinkled. They all turned and looked.

Ned stood in the doorway. He wore his lab coat, baggy tweed pants, and his trusty pocket protector. His shoes looked almost orthopedic, with a thick sole. He'd also done something strange with his hair. Instead of hanging in his face, he'd slicked back the edges with a pound of hair gel until he was sporting a kind of half-assed psycho Mohawk. She wondered if a category five hurricane could move a strand.

"Hey." He paused, waiting for them to speak, but it took them a minute to get over the hairstyle. "I'm Ned."

Kate broke the dead silence and launched into hostess mode. "Welcome to Kinnections, Ned. We're so happy to have you here. I'm Kate, Kennedy's partner."

Arilyn shook her head and came out of her trance. "I'm Arilyn; I do the therapy and computer programming. It's nice to meet you."

His hand went to check on his hair, which of course hadn't budged an inch. "Thanks."

Kennedy cleared her throat. "New hairstyle?"

He gave a half grin. "Yeah, you said it looked disheveled, so I figured I'd neaten it up. Do you like it?"

She shared a look with her friends. "No. But we'll fix it."

Kate kept a smile pasted on her face and whispered under her breath. "The hair should be first."

Arilyn leaned into the tight circle. "Are you kidding me? He's completely orange. You have to take him to Ming."

Kate shuddered. "God, are you sure? Is he that far gone? He may never come back if we sic Ming on him."

Kennedy sighed. "We have no choice, the pigment is completely discolored."

Arilyn took a sniff. "What's that smell? I feel like I stepped into an ocean and drowned."

Kennedy lowered her voice. "Last time it was the

woodsy pine. He has no idea how much cologne to use."

"Hello? I'm standing right here. I can hear everything you're saying, even if you think you're whispering," Ned said, sounding a little peeved.

Arilyn clucked her tongue. "We apologize, Ned. We have your best interests at heart."

Kate nodded. "Kennedy will take great care of you, and we'll be here if you need anything."

"Let's go into the consulting room," she said. "See you later, guys."

They said an enthusiastic good-bye, and she led Ned into the purple room. Her files, contract, and notes were already on the small table clad in a neat leather binder. The purple, soft-cushioned chairs set off a thick carpet, deep wood accents, and watercolors on the cream walls. A unique rock garden trickled out a stream of water and gently bubbled, a soothing background for sharing dreams and desires. The room was designed to inspire openness and trust, a complete feng shui heaven created by Arilyn, whose love for yoga, meditation, and all mystical universe stuff helped balance out Kate's hard-core workaholic ways and Kennedy's own drive to command a room socially and increase their clientele.

She motioned for him to sit. "Why don't you get comfortable? I went over your initial questionnaire, but my first step is to have a confidential chat so I can get an idea of the ideal women to match you with. Then we'll decide what works best."

"No more speed dating."

She grinned. "I agree. But we have tons of options." He settled against the purple cushions. "I got you a bottle of water. Would you like coffee or tea instead?"

"No, water's fine, thanks."

She crossed her legs and glanced at his papers. "Why don't we start with your job? You have an impressive résumé. NASA?"

"Worked there for a number of years. Then transferred into the private sector. Sector Space X is a new company targeting the niche market of spacecraft for the civilian. I'm currently studying advanced propulsion."

"What makes the rocket go off, right?"

"Correct. Of course, the new Vortex engine uses gel-propellant, which is quite fascinating, but I'm currently analyzing a more efficient yet controversial method."

Kennedy wanted to ask more details about his work, but that wasn't the focus of the meeting. She'd always been interested by mechanics, though she had no talent for it herself. The moment she looked at how something worked, it broke. Still, there was something kind of sexy about a man who figured stuff out, and she needed to reveal more of that up front to keep a woman hooked. She made another note.

"You have a perfect body. Do you work out often?"

Her pen stilled. "Did you just comment on my *body*?"

Ned frowned. "No offense. I just wanted to give you a compliment."

The flattering aspect of the remark was lost amid its complete rudeness. She leaned forward and shot him a warning look. "Rule number one: there will be no questions, statements, or verbal thoughts expressed about any part of a woman's body. Understood?"

"Why?"

"Women are extremely conscious of being objectified. Most of us have self-esteem issues and don't need to be reminded of our weaknesses."

He shoved his fingers in his hair, but they got caught in the gel from hell. "Dammit, that's what *Cosmopolitan* said! I followed it to the letter, and a woman at the speed-dating event said women love getting remarks about their bodies. Said she didn't work out at the gym just so I could comment on her smile."

She smothered a sigh. Poor thing. Mixed social signals could blast a man to pieces, especially someone like this guy. "*Cosmopolitan* is correct. That woman is a rarity."

"I don't know. My brother says women love when men focus on their bodies. Says if you compliment their breasts, ass, or mouth, it's a sure sign of scoring."

Kennedy stiffened as the memories poured in. Huddling by the lockers, afraid to go into the hallway where he was waiting for her. The laughs and shoves and insults of "fat girl" that echoed in her ears long into the night. Her breasts had been larger than most because of her weight, and those dirty stares and grabby hands still held the power to nauseate her. She sternly reminded herself that that was all in the past, breathed in, and refocused. This man genuinely had no clue about how to talk to women, and this was where the real work started. She bet no one had ever bothered to take the time to try to educate him.

"Your brother is wrong, Ned. Very wrong. The best way to make a woman happy is to compliment her intelligence. Her sense of humor. The sparkle in her eyes or the sweetness of her smile. The kindness of a gesture. We want to be valued beyond the physical, and then we feel safe enough to open up."

He seemed to watch her with a burning focus that radiated through the thick lenses of his glasses and pierced her soul. An image of Clark Kent skittered in her vision. Geeky, clumsy, socially awkward, but underneath, hotness galore. And she could do it; she sensed a wealth of appeal behind his veneer that she ached to unearth. But none of it would occur if he were stuck on how women needed to be treated and didn't want to change. She waited for his answer and sensed it was a turning point.

"I understand. That makes sense. That's what the consensus of magazines stated."

"Magazines?"

"Yes. When I decided it was time to get serious about a relationship, I studied every cultural aspect to get an idea of what women wanted and expected from a man."

Her eyes widened. "So, you read *Cosmopolitan*. What else?"

He ticked them off on his fingers. "*Marie Claire*, *Self*, *Glamour*, *Oprah*, and *Men's Health*. I read all the articles and took the surveys. That's why I'm so frustrated. I keep getting different reactions that just don't follow the format."

Damn, had she ever met a man who tried so hard in his hunt for a wife? Her heart softened. She had to give him credit. He may be a hot mess, but he had the right intentions. "That's what I'm here for. I'll help you figure it out. Let's talk about your family. Is your brother married?"

"Oh, no, he's not interested in settling down. Says there are too many women out there to restrict himself."

Uh-oh. An older brother giving bad advice was a nightmare. "I see. Are you two close?"

"Yes, we live together now. He raised me when our mother took off. Dad was too overwrought to deal with us, so my brother took over." She noticed he told the facts calmly, as if giving a PowerPoint presentation. A twinge tightened her chest. She bet his brilliance had always set him apart from the crowd, and a supportive, loving mother could have helped.

"I'm sorry."

His shoulders lifted. "No need. We turned out fine. Could've been a lot worse."

He meant it. Many men either buried the past or used it as a crutch to explain away bad behavior. Ned accepted his circumstances and moved on. Admiration cut through her. Yes, he possessed character. She could work with that.

"How about past relationships?"

He shrugged. "Not many to talk about. I graduated early, got recruited by NASA, and worked nonstop for a number of years. Went out a bit here and there but rarely got past the third date or so. Most women were bored by my career once they discovered I wasn't an astronaut. Now that I'm back in New York, it took me a while to get settled. I moved in with my brother and delved into a new project, so I haven't had the chance to meet someone yet."

She struggled with the urge to ask him about his sexual past, then scratched it off the list. Too personal for now. She doubted he was a virgin, but it sounded as if his bedroom antics had been . . . limited.

"I'm not a virgin."

Kennedy couldn't remember the last time she had blushed, and swore this wouldn't be the first. "I didn't ask."

His lips twisted in a self-deprecating smile. "I heard your thoughts loud enough. I've had sexual experiences. They just usually lead to a parting of ways because of our lifestyle differences. If I felt lacking in that department, I'd find a way to fix it."

Her nerves tingled. Odd to hear a man talk so honestly about sex in a way that wasn't defensive. She bet he'd be open to all sorts of suggestions with one simple focus: a woman's pleasure. Like he attacked his job and his life, the bedroom would only be another obstacle he wanted to overcome. She scribbled on her notepad and cleared her throat.

"Understood. Let's talk a bit about women. I made note of your survey answers. You don't seem to have many strict requirements. Are you open to ethnicity? Age? Backgrounds? What type of woman do you imagine sharing your future with?"

"Anyone."

Kennedy stared at him. She'd counseled hundreds of men, and there was always a list. A type. Someone to avoid at all costs. "You're willing to date anyone? There must be a few qualities you want in your wife."

He picked at his nails, seemed to catch himself, and rested them on the arms of the chair. "Of course. I can waste our time giving you an inventory of qualities that each person dreams of in a soul-mate. Generosity, humor, attractiveness, intelligence, sexual chemistry. They won't mean a thing until I meet her, though, will they? If I love her, I'm willing to compromise. I want to share my life and have a family. So my true answer remains. I am open to anyone. I just need to find her."

Odd, the way he communicated made perfect sense. There would never be any guessing with this man, and no games. Direct, honest, unflinching. She just needed to find him a female who owned the same type of qualities, or one who was the complete opposite. Either he'd get along best with similar types, or he'd need the balance of contradiction.

Definitely a mixer. Targeted, maybe four to five women of all types, a melting pot he'd be able to delve into. But it wouldn't work until she made some major changes on the outside.

Ken smiled. "I think that was a great answer."

"Then why does that expression on your face make me nervous?"

She laughed. "I told you I'm not looking to change who you are, but I need to tweak the surface. For the next two weeks, I'll be attached to your side. Other than work, we'll be spending evenings together, and weekends. When I feel you're ready, I'll schedule the first mixer. Is that agreeable?"

The unibrow lowered. "What are you going to do to me?"

Her palms literally itched, a sure sign of success. She lowered her voice.

"Everything."

NED ALMOST JERKED IN his seat from that husky, sexy spill of voice. Like velvet and gravel mixed together. The word drilled in his brain over and over, bringing up an array of delicious images.

Yep. She was a definite distraction.

He pegged her for a major flirt, but he didn't think she realized what she'd just done to him. Probably looked at him more like an amoeba in her scientific experiment. Her black pencil skirt emphasized the toned muscles in her legs, which were a deep golden brown. The snug jacket cut over the natural fullness of her breasts and lifted them up like a present. Today, she wore a glittery silver ankle bracelet with tiny charm things. As she shook her leg, they tinkled and brought attention to the strappy platform sandals no woman should be wearing in the cool March weather. A natural sultriness radiated around her figure, and though she obviously knew how to use it, Ned figured that most of the time she had no clue how insanely attractive she was. Something seemed to hold her back, as if she hid a big secret at her core. Would be interesting to explore those limits and see inside. But that wouldn't happen in his lifetime.

She was already looking back down at her papers. Dismissed, without a thought what that husky voice could do to a man. "Let's talk about your hobbies outside of work. I see you golf."

She uttered that word with pure disdain. He itched to show her the excitement of the subtlety and mental challenge of the sport, but obviously, she was more of a baseball or football fan. "Yes. I golf."

Her gaze probed under the cotton fabric of his lab coat to get an idea of his biceps. He may not have a killer body, but he wasn't soft. He ate healthy, golfed, and did regular crunches to keep his abdomen tight. Irritation bristled. What would it feel like to be a man she lusted after? Those gorgeous eyes reminded him of a sleek, strong lioness, pure gold shot with a touch of amber. Fogged with desire, he bet they'd get soft and sleepy. Maybe she bit and sucked her lower lip, which had a natural pout. She was probably trained to know exactly how to elicit a man's response, down to the last detail. She was so out of his league, it was like Butch Harmon versus Happy Gilmore. Ned shifted in his chair and tried to refocus. Golf.

"Golf is good. Anything else?"

He pulled back his shoulders. "Books."

She scribbled something. "Reading is a definite plus. What were the last three books you read?"

"*The Kama Sutra. The Claiming of Sleeping Beauty. Fifty Shades of Grey.*"

The pen stilled. Her mouth opened, and her tongue slid over her lower lip. Ah yes, he'd finally elicited a feminine reaction. He tamped the flood of satisfaction. She was his matchmaker, intent on finding him his soul-mate. No reason to muddy the waters by crushing on her like a schoolboy. Still, he enjoyed the dilation of her pupils as she processed his statement. "Interesting. More research?"

"Yes. Research." Once he got a woman into bed, he intended to keep her there. Part of his study to understand women included a range of erotic novels and how-to manuals to guarantee perfect sexual stamina and performance.

She regained her composure and clasped her hands together, index fingers touching. Her nails were dark purple today. An intricate silver ring flashed in the light. He wondered if she had a lover. He wondered if she had many.

"I'd like to change your name to Nate."

He waited a beat. "My name is Nathaniel. My nickname is Ned."

She seemed to choose her words carefully. "Ned evokes a certain image. Think of this as a reinvention. Since your birth name is so beautiful, I think we should go back to Nate as a nickname."

Ned analyzed her statement. He'd always preferred his real name, but the kids in school hadn't let him use it. They loved to torture him, calling him "Ned the Nerd." He never thought of taking back his birth name after high school and claiming it for his own. He nodded. "A good idea. Nate it is."

She smiled. Her front tooth was slightly crooked, which only made her even more appealing and emphasized her hot pink lips. She was so very . . . colorful. "Wonderful. I think that wraps up most of my questions, so I can begin working on some initial matches. I'd like to start tomorrow evening at six. Meet me at the following address." She handed over a business card. It held an address, phone number, and the word MING.

"Who's Ming?"

"A miracle worker. I know you have a demanding work schedule, but I'll need you to have open availability after work for the next two weeks."

Could he do this? Put himself in the hands of a stranger and trust her to find him happiness?

Yes. He hadn't come this far to quit now. If he kept his focus, it would all be worth it.

"Okay."

Her smile grew, and he admitted he'd do just about anything to see it again. She was a definite witch, with her apparent power to spellbind him with a single gesture or facial expression. "Great. Trust me, and I'll take you all the way."

The innuendo almost made him groan. But he refused to go down on the first round. He dropped his voice and pretended to be in control.

"I'm looking forward to it, Kennedy."

He caught a flare of unease in her eyes, before smoothing back to her polished social director demeanor. But Nate suspected there was a lot more to her beneath her surface. And he wanted to find out just what those layers held. Maybe he'd even show this beautiful woman a lot more than she ever suspected.

Maybe.

He stood. "I'll see you tomorrow at six." He left without looking back, wondering how it would all turn out.

four

NATE EYED THE bright red door with suspicion, but his eager guide for the evening gave him no time to think. Just pushed him through until he popped into an empty waiting room. The lights were dim, and there was only one large counter set up. No magazines, no water, no snacks. When he'd first heard he was going to a spa, he figured a little pampering couldn't be so bad. Images of hot towels, long fragrant massages, and a beautiful woman rubbing his feet flickered in his head. But this was a dump.

Located on the edge of Verily, hidden up a steep hill, there seemed to be neither foot traffic nor pedestrians. Just a broken-down building with a bright red door. Elizabeth Arden it was not. How did this place get clients?

Kennedy motioned for him to take a seat as she walked up to the desk. The woman frowned at her instead of giving her a welcoming smile and launched into a tirade in heavily accented Chinese. Kennedy listened, nodded a lot, and basically seemed to try to suck up to her. What type of establishment was this? If this was the type of business Kinnections patronized, he may have made a terrible mistake.

Kennedy did a slight bow and returned. Sweat beaded her brow. "Thank God. Ming will see us."

"Who is this person? There's no customer service. No nice amenities. And they seem rude. We should leave."

She dropped her voice to a fierce hiss. "You do not make any negative comments. One complaint and we'll get thrown out. Ming is the best, and she'll return you back to normal. Above normal, actually. You'll never be the same."

His unease grew. He pulled at his lab coat and noticed the new stain of mustard on his lapel from eating lunch at his desk. Again. It had been hell getting out on time, but he was looking forward to beginning his journey toward his future wife. Who would've thought it would begin in a crappy underground dungeon with a woman named Ming?

"What is she going to do to me?"

Kennedy pointed a finger at him. "Whatever she wants. You need to follow all her instructions exactly. This is very important."

"I'm not stupid."

"No, but you like to argue, and that will get us thrown out."

He had no time to respond. The door behind the desk swung open without a sound. He caught an impression of an elfin figure dressed in a Japanese robe, shrouded in shadow. One long, bony finger drifted out and beckoned him forward.

"Go," Kennedy whispered.

Crap, why was he scared? A little old lady couldn't hurt him, and if he didn't like anything, he'd just walk out, no matter what Kennedy said. He straightened his shoulders and stepped through the door.

She led him down a dim hallway. The small woman moved lightning fast, practically floating over the ground as they turned right and made their way deeper into a maze of unending hallways. He itched to throw bread crumbs or mark a wall to find his way back, but there was no time. He stumbled twice just keeping up. Finally, she stopped and entered an unmarked door.

A long, flat limestone table took up the center of the room. Towels were placed around the site, and a luxurious open glass shower was set up in the corner. The walls were a pristine white and bare of decoration except for a few shelves that displayed an array of glass bottles. Music drifted softly from the speakers. He caught a flute, birdcalls, and the sound of rushing water. The air was moist and smelled of clean soap and the faintness of lavender. Ming headed toward a small bamboo-type desk with a large white basin and began prepping. Nate watched as she busied herself like a doctor preparing shots, lining up jumbo-size containers and pouring liquid in. Finally, she turned and faced him.

"You get naked."

"What?"

The top of her head didn't even hit his chest. Her bare feet peeked out from underneath the white robe that seemed to swallow her whole. Black hair was cropped close to her head, and her dark eyes snapped impatience and command. "I say get naked. Then lie on table."

Nate held on to his lab coat and shoved down the panic. Naked? In front of her? Hell, no. "Um, can I leave my T-shirt and boxers on? I'm not very comfortable removing all my clothes."

She spit in his direction. Sheer disgust marked her face. "You big baby? You no get naked for old woman? What you so afraid of?"

He jerked back. "I'm not scared! I just don't think I need to."

Ming took a step forward and wagged her finger in the air. "You orange. You look like carrot. I fix you, but you listen to me. Now get naked and lie on table on stomach."

Kennedy's words flashed in his mind. This was his first test. How could he fail already? And he *was* orange. Even Wayne agreed today that he should do something because it was distracting his concentration. He had hoped it would go away, but after four days, it still hadn't faded. Was he really nervous about a professional seeing him without clothes? No, he refused to let her win this round by acting like a child. Women did this stuff all the time, right?

"Fine." He took off all his clothes, folded them neatly, and placed them on an unoccupied shelf. The table was smooth and cool as he stretched out on his stomach, and his head was cushioned by a soft mat. He turned his head to the right, closed his eyes, and tried not to think of his naked ass up in the air for Ming to view.

He waited a while, breathing and listening to the flute, and began to relax. Steam began to rise up in the room and opened his pores. Maybe this wouldn't be too bad. A massage was something he really needed for his neck and back. Long hours spent stationary had tied him in knots. Maybe he'd even get in a bit of a nap. He figured—

"Aghgh!"

A mass of cold liquid was dumped on his back, trickling down his rear. Before he could process, a thousand stiff bristles worked its way over his skin, the rough back-and-forth motions scraping him and causing a mixture of tickling and pain, until he twisted around and batted it out of the way. "That hurts!"

"Be quiet."

He gasped. She scrubbed harder, completely disregarding his tiny yelps as she worked every inch of his skin, from the soles of his feet, ass, back, shoulders, and even his armpits. His skin tingled and burned, and the tiny beads of gel caused an abrasion that he swore would mark him for life. Dear God, he was going to have scars! She had no idea what she was doing, and seemed to even chuckle menacingly the few times he jumped and tried to wriggle away from the brush of doom.

The torture went on forever, until she muttered something and finally stopped. He dropped his head to the table and panted. Okay, he'd done it. The orange must be off. Maybe he'd get to recover and use that fabulous shower. The worst had to be behind him. He heard a few clicks, the drag of metal, and was just about to lift his head to see what was going on when the spray hit him.

The icy cold, bone-chilling spray, that is.

"Shit!" He jerked up, but she pushed him back down on the table with hard hands. The spray wasn't a gentle rain shower; it was more like a fire extinguisher filled with ice cubes hitting him at full power. He shivered under the stinging nettles and moaned softly under his breath. That's when he knew it was going to be a long night. She hosed him down thoroughly, not missing an inch, the intense pressure of the spray not allowing him any relief.

He slumped over when it finally stopped. He should get out of here. Walk away, call the Better Business Bureau, and bring her up on charges of assault. He thought of all the ways he'd get even with Ming while she clattered around behind him with something else, and he held his breath.

Ah. Warm, fragrant oil dribbled on his back and leaked over his spine. Heaven. His muscles finally relaxed. Maybe it was worth it to get to the good stuff? Nate imagined strong, nimble fingers working out the kinks in his lower back and neck and—

With a wild war cry, a hundred pounds of flesh slammed onto his back. In horror, he realized she'd jumped on top of him, and was stomping on his back with her bare feet.

"What are you doing?" he yelled, but she ignored him, doing some crazy dance routine and grinding her toes and soles of her feet into the sensitive skin of his ripped-up back. She worked her way up and down his body, her heels hard and demanding, twisting deep into different muscle knots until he bit his lip to keep from screaming in agony. Nate bit his tongue and silently cursed her and her children, prayed for revenge, and begged for mercy. He swore she wouldn't win, wouldn't break him. He'd survive this with his head held high and then he'd laugh at her for thinking she could destroy him.

As seconds turned to minutes, he got lost in a daze. Finally, she jumped gracefully off him, her robe flapping, and leaned over him. Her bright smile reminded him of the Joker from Batman before he struck. "Turn over."

He shook his head, which wobbled on his almost broken neck. "No, no turn over."

Ming cackled again, the wild gleam in her dark eyes scaring the crap out of him. "You big baby. I fix you. I do front now."

"No."

Her lips pulled back and she spit something out in Chinese.

"Fine! But I swear if you hurt me again, you will not get a tip!"

She helped roll him over. Nate looked at the ceiling with his most sensitive part out on display, ready to be tortured, and prayed for it to be over.

Time passed in a blur. When she jumped on his stomach, Nate was grateful she avoided his dick, which would probably never get an erection again after Ming was done with him. When she informed him there was to be one more round on each side, Nate gave up. He lost consciousness somewhere during the second round.

After his body, Ming moved to the head of the table and worked on his face. At least she couldn't jump on it. Still, her deft, firm fingers left no feature unexplored until his cheeks and jaws actually ached.

He was wrung out and exhausted when she finally allowed him to rise. He felt vulnerable, raw, and weak as a newborn kitten. He leaned a bit on her as she guided him into the shower and turned on the water. The hot spray was heaven, gentle and soothing, and she gave him a musky type of soap that lathered and wrapped him in bubbles. He took a long time in the shower and dried off with a fluffy towel. Ming came over and wrapped him in a terrycloth robe, tying the sash nice and tight, and led him to a small bench. He winced when she took a hairbrush, but she brushed back his long strands of hair from his forehead in long, soothing strokes that massaged his scalp. He relaxed into her ministrations. The music drifted over him, and no one spoke. When he finally opened his eyes, her face was right in front of him. She smiled, but this time it didn't strike him as evil.

"You good boy." She patted his cheek. "No more orange. You sit here a bit then come out when you ready."

She placed the brush down and left.

He had one last thought before he allowed himself to drift away for just one more minute.

Ming had definitely won.

NATE BIT INTO HIS cheeseburger and admitted that Mugs could be his new favorite place. The bar restaurant was casual, giving off a rustic appeal with wooden booths nicely offset by a large modern bar. The attached poolroom held tables, darts, and a variety of other fun games. The beer list was pretty damn impressive for a quaint town, where organic everything and chai lattes usually ruled. He swiped a fry in a pool of ketchup and savored the salty bite.

Kennedy had taken one look at his expression after Ming time and declared the need for food. He'd followed her back into Verily without protest, and after a cold microbrew and some red meat, the strange floaty bubbly feeling had finally popped.

"Why did you ask for a Clorox wipe for the tables?" she asked. "Didn't you trust them to clean it properly?"

He focused on his burger. "Waitresses get busy and don't bring a sterile cloth. Food slips off the plate and unconsciously you scoop it up, eat it, and come down with E. coli poisoning."

"You're a certified germaphobe, aren't you? How bad?"

"I'm not gonna do a Jack Nicholson imitation from *As Good as It Gets*, if that's what you're worried about. I just like to follow proper hygiene in bathrooms and public restaurants." He decided to change the subject rather than linger on another one of his issues. "That woman was horrible," he said. "Have you ever had a client sue because of her?"

She tossed him a smug smile. "They're too afraid to bring a lawsuit. Besides, Ming's the best. Look at yourself. Not a smidge of orange, and your skin is practically glowing with health. I bet your muscles feel like limp noodles, too."

"Not really." He ducked his head so she wouldn't see the lie reflected in his gaze. "But at least I look normal again."

They ate in silence for a bit, but a roar from outside made a few patrons look up. "Sounds like a storm out there."

"Yeah, we haven't had rain in a while."

A blob of ketchup fell on his pants to match the mustard on his lapel. He cursed his innate clumsiness and grabbed a few napkins. Kennedy pushed her lettuce around her plate. "What's the matter?"

"Nothing." Hmm, she looked cranky. Odd, she'd been fine till his burger arrived. As usual, he opened his mouth and his thoughts spilled out. "Why did you order that?"

She rolled her eyes. "Because it's healthy."

"Actually, too much roughage in the body can throw off your digestive system. Want a bite of my burger?" Her eyes lit up with sheer lust. Nate shifted in his seat. Damn, the woman was potent. He wondered what would happen if she ever looked at him like that. As if. "You probably need some protein."

Her fingers clenched her fork in a death grip. She took a dainty sip of water with lemon. "I have tuna as my protein."

He investigated the pile of lettuce and found a few dry pieces of fish scattered around. "Oh. No mayo?"

She glared.

"Are you one of those vegans? Or allergic to gluten or something?"

She stuck a leaf in her mouth and chewed. Nate felt sorry for her. Her usual vibrancy seemed to stagnate as soon as she got around food. As if her healthy choices sucked all the joy out of her. "No. I follow a strict balance to ensure good nutrition. Please don't tell me you eat like this normally?"

He finished his burger and swallowed it down with a sip of beer. "No. I don't mind eating healthy, as long as I allow myself a few vices. I try to stay away from fast food, but I'm a terrible cook, so I do eat out a lot. You don't need to diet."

A strange sound emitted from her lips. "I'm not on a diet."

A crucial piece of information danced around his consciousness. Something that would solve a bit of the puzzle that made up this woman. "Good. Your body is amazing."

Darkness stole over her features, seeming to capture her inner light momentarily. "Thanks."

He could tell she didn't believe it. Not one word.

And there was something bigger there, underneath, buried so deep he wondered if anyone had ever discovered it. Like a physics equation, she begged for a solution, and he longed to be the one to find it. Of course, that's why he sucked with people. He had no social filter and followed no rules. He dug until he hit dirt, by which point the person was usually so pissed at him he or she stalked off. Yep. He was a real winner.

"Do you ever let go and have something that's bad for you?"

She pulled those luscious lips back and snarled. "Why don't we move our attention from fries and concentrate on you? Now that you have the correct skin color again, we need to practice a bit on social conversation."

"Nothing wrong with getting to the heart of a person. It doesn't waste time." His damp hair kept sliding in his face, so he pulled a rubber band from his pocket protector and tied it quickly back.

"Initial trust is built from the first dialogue. You'll ruin it by mentioning sex, bodily parts, or making judgments on childbearing age, fear of commitment, or career choice."

He frowned. "What do I have left to talk about?"

She smiled. A tiny piece of green lettuce stood out within her incisor. Her lipstick had rubbed off from the napkin. A vibrant intensity beat from her figure in waves. Today she wore a black lace shirt, short red skirt, and red pumps. She'd shrugged off her red jacket and he spotted an upper arm bracelet. The gold cuff reminded him of something a slave girl would wear. He glimpsed the black matching lace of her bra peeking out. He'd read a story once where the hero sucked the heroine's nipples for an hour and made her come. Nate wondered if any of her lovers had ever treated her to such attention. Wondered if she'd be greedy, noisy, active. If she were his, he'd concentrate on wiping out every word in the English language from her mind so that she only moaned and whimpered his name.

His pants tightened to a painful degree. Down, boy. Never gonna happen in this lifetime. He had better get used to it. And stop reading those damn books.

"There are a million other topics to pick from," she said. "We'll practice now. Pretend we just met and decided to have dinner. What would you say to me?"

"You have a piece of lettuce stuck in your teeth."

She blanched, and then placed her tongue over her teeth and sucked hard. "Is it gone?"

Damn, she was hot. "Yes. Gone."

"Okay, that's what I mean. You definitely want to let a woman know if she has something on her that could embarrass her, but you need to learn subtlety. A touch of your napkin to your mouth. A gentle smile and a tap of your finger over your teeth."

He rolled his eyes. "Fine. But if I had something in my teeth or toilet paper stuck somewhere, don't waste my time. Tell me."

"Noted. Aren't you going to have the last few fries?"

"No, here." He pushed the plate across the table. "There's only three. Live a little."

She squirmed in her seat as if about to make the biggest decision of her life. Then palmed the three fries and began to nibble. The salt seemed to make her happy. A hazy glow of satisfaction came over her. Surrendering to her desires seemed to please her. Nate had a dozen other ways he'd like to make that look appear on her features, but he stopped himself from thinking about them—after all, she had flat-out refused to go out with him. Why would sleeping with him invoke any other response?

"Thanks," she said, gesturing toward the fries. "Back to role-play. We just sat down and ordered. Let's talk."

She sucked on the fry as if intent on getting every last taste of salt from the murdered potato. Unfortunately, the distraction of her pink tongue, crooked tooth, and long, tapered fingers slammed another type of image into his brain. What was up with him? He needed to get laid fast, or he was just going to humiliate himself with her for the long term. "Umm, do you live around here?"

"Manhattan. How about you?"

"Westchester. Umm, do you have any hobbies?"

She sucked harder. "Yeah, I go to the gym three times a week. How about you?"

"I enjoy golf."

"Oh, I've never played golf."

He straightened up in his chair. "The sport is the

perfect combination of skill and challenge. The swing is the key to success in the game, but it can be fine-tuned and changed to fit the individual. Tiger Woods actually spent more than a year completely redoing his swing in order to become a different type of golfer. Imagine the rush of watching the ball sail through the air and land perfectly on the green! Exciting, right?"

She finished the fries, and twirled her straw around in her glass. "Not really."

Nate glared. "I don't like this conversation. Let's just admit we're not suited for the long term."

"Right there!" She jumped from her seat and pointed her index finger at him. "That's where the breakdown occurs. You, Nate Dunkle, are a selfish conversationalist!"

He pushed his glasses up his nose. "What? I asked questions. She had no interest in me! She was bored by my explanation of golf."

"And so am I. That doesn't mean we couldn't be the perfect match. You just don't want to take the time and effort to dig deeper. You need to get out of your own ego and focus on her."

Irritation coursed through him. "You make me sound like an ass. I dig. I scored high on the surveys in *Cosmo*!"

She gave a snort. "Those surveys are fixed and give no helpful information. If a woman doesn't agree with what you say in the first five minutes, you declare her incompetent for a long-term relationship. She doesn't like golf. Big deal. How about asking what she does like and why? Don't you enjoy figuring things out at your job? People are the same. They're puzzles, made up of various pieces that need analyzing and understanding. You throw them away too easily if they don't fit your idea of what you want in a spouse, and you're going to regret it." Something flickered in her eyes. A memory? Was she talking about herself?

"Fine. Reset. But this time, just be you. Don't pretend to be someone else."

"I don't think—"

"I do." He studied her for a while. Took in her high forehead, the sweep of caramel-colored hair tumbling past her shoulders. Her face was a collection of interesting angles that fascinated him. Her pupils dilated as if his stare were an actual caress, and the color darkened to a deep whiskey. "What made you get into matchmaking?"

He waited her out. Finally, she gave up and took another sip of water. "Kate and Arilyn were my two best friends in college. After graduation, we went our separate ways for a while but ended up getting drunk one night and came up with the idea to start our own matchmaking agency. Kate is the overall director, Arilyn handles the computer stuff and counseling, and I do the recruitment and social events."

"Most drunken ideas are forgotten come morning."

The memory sparked a smile. "Not us. We nursed our hangovers and immediately began researching."

"Smart. It's hard to start a small business lately. Have you been successful?"

"Yep. Our marriage stats are increasing every day, and we're finally seeing a steady profit."

He smiled a bit at the raw pride in her voice. She had guts. Not many dove into the deep end, let alone swam without drowning. "Why Verily?"

"We didn't want to compete with the big agencies in Manhattan. Verily is unique enough to be small-town but cosmopolitan, and we cater to a specific demographic. Only ages twenty-five to forty."

"Interesting. That doesn't limit your customer base?"

"No, it was a risky move, but we wanted a certain niche. We studied that market and became known for our elite clientele."

"Millionaires only?"

She rolled her eyes. "You too? Has everyone seen that show? No, as long as you're happy in your chosen work and heading toward a goal, it's acceptable. Money isn't the target. Love is."

Nate loved the way she lit up when speaking about Kinnections. He adored confident women. Kennedy not only loved her job but she also served a higher purpose. She believed she was making the world a better place. Cliché, maybe. Sexy as hell, definitely.

"Have you taken on a client like me before? Worked with them so closely?"

"No, you're my first."

She stared back at him, and a crackle of awareness lit up the air. Her hand trembled around her glass, then steadied.

The anger he felt at her response took him by surprise. He sat across from a beautiful woman who was intelligent, funny, and out of his league. The words tumbled out of his mouth.

"Why? Because you feel sorry for me?"

Kennedy flinched as the thinly veiled accusation hit her ears. She studied Nate closely—brown eyes lit with fire, hidden behind those ridiculous glasses. A mustard stain prominently displayed on his lapel. The pocket protector with two perfectly sharpened pencils, a tiny notepad, and calculator wedged inside, screaming *The Big Bang Theory* meets *Revenge of the Nerds*. He sat in complete stillness and waited for her response.

A strange surge of emotions roared up from her gut. How odd. The way he looked at her, his gaze probing, urged her to tell the truth. She could pull a lot of stock answers from her arsenal and never let him get closer. But something had changed, and with his question demanded honesty. She struggled and tried to keep it light. "No, of course not."

"Bullshit." He leaned in, a touch of masculine temper giving him an edge she hadn't glimpsed before. "Am I just your little pet project to keep you from getting bored, Kennedy? A beauty-and-the-beast makeover special? Should I be grateful you picked me, shut my mouth, and just go with the program?"

"No!" Her blood heated at the attack, and she barely managed to stay in her chair. "I can't believe you would think so little of this whole process."

"I'm not a process."

"I know!"

"Stop giving me your standardized answers and tell me the truth. Why me?"

"Because I needed someone to believe in!"

His mouth opened and his eyes flared, and suddenly she felt smothered, as if he had wrapped his energy around her and squeezed. She tried to look away and break the intensity, but he didn't allow her, just slid his hand across the table and interweaved his fingers with hers.

"Thank you for telling me."

His thumb pressed into her palm. Her pulse picked up, yet her body felt sluggish. She shook her head and tried to figure out her reaction, but the waitress glided by, placed the check on the table, and mercifully, he released her hand.

"I gotta go," she said.

"Yeah, me, too. I'll walk you out." He put cash on the table and cut off her protest before she even opened her mouth. She allowed him to pay again, and they stepped out the side door near the parking lot.

Torrents of rain whipped in a fury, and the dark sky lit up with jagged streaks of lightning. She looked down at her high heels and held back a groan. Great. Good-bye, designer shoes. They'd be a muddy mess by the time she got to her car.

He stood with her on the edge of the sidewalk covered by the awning. "Better wait it out a bit," he shouted over the roar of the storm. "You'll get drenched, and we don't have an umbrella."

A pool of water dripped from the gutter and sprayed her in the face. She jumped back and yelped, but Nate had already pulled her closer to the door and blocked the brunt of the storm with his body. Her back pressed against the brick wall. The rain pounded the awning and she shivered from the damp. He quickly shrugged off his lab coat and tucked it around her, grabbing the sleeves in the front and dragging her close to his chest. The deliciousness of his body warmth enveloped her, and she softened against him.

"Better?"

"Yeah, thanks."

"I can't see a damn thing. Stupid glasses." He slid them off and stuck them in the pocket protector. "I'm sure it'll ease off in a minute. It's never this strong for too long."

"Probably."

He didn't smell of pine or ocean today. Instead, his natural male scent rose to her nostrils and swarmed her senses. Clean soap, rain, and a hint of some spice. Cloves? She tipped her chin up to compliment him on getting rid of the cologne, then froze.

His eyes weren't brown, as she had originally thought, but a deep moss green, with flecks of gold. With his hair pulled back, she noted the strong lines of his face, placed together in an almost beautiful symmetry she'd overlooked before. His lips were perfectly formed, the top a bit thinner and defined, the lower one generous and lush. His mouth looked soft. She wondered what his lips would feel like over hers.

"Ken?"

Her name ripped from those lips in a husky growl. She blinked and tried to find her footing, startled by his referring to her so intimately, but not entirely sure she minded. "Yeah?"

"What about us?"

Brain alert. She tried to break the weird spell, but he slid his hands up to cup her cheeks and thunder shook the ground, and somehow his body was pressed tight against hers. He engulfed her with a quiet, intense presence that demanded her response. As though on cue, her body lit up and begged for more. She grew damp between her thighs, and her nipples hardened to tight little points, and within those few seconds, she was completely turned on by her geek rocket scientist.

"There is no us. I'm your matchmaker."

Her victory of sane speech was short-lived. Those thumbs stroked under her jaw and began to trace the lines of her mouth. The fascinated, intense look on his face thrilled her. Had a man ever looked at her so . . . hungrily? As if he craved to feast on her for hours without end? A shiver bumped through her.

"Eliza and Professor Higgins hooked up at the end of the movie."

What was he talking about? Her heart beat so loudly she heard it over the raging storm. Oh, *My Fair Lady*. "You saw that movie?"

His mouth quirked. "Of course. I watched a bunch of so-called chick flicks and classic musicals to study the female mind and what she may find romantic."

Holy crap, she couldn't make him up if she tried. She dragged her tongue across her dry lips and watched his eyes light up with intent. Uh-oh. "They were terrible for each other. He didn't respect her enough."

"Yes, he did. Once she woke him up to the possibility of a match, he was done. He loved her from the first. He just didn't know it yet."

Oh, she was in trouble. She clawed for sanity, but his thumb pressed against her now damp lips and slipped inside just an inch to touch the tip of her tongue. The move was so damn sexy she forgot her clever response to his statement. She was an accomplished flirt, dated a wide variety of men, and knew every maneuver to block an unwanted kiss or touch like a black belt. Yet, here she stood outside of Mugs like a helpless virgin, waiting for him to do something she didn't want.

"Ken?"

"Huh?"

"I want to kiss you."

"Don't think that's a good idea."

"Agreed." He lowered his head so his breath struck her mouth. "Don't care."

His kiss broke all barriers without violence, urgency, or crazed passion. He simply claimed her mouth completely without question. His big hands cradled her face and his tongue slipped inside like he belonged there. Whisper-soft lips melded to hers and sipped at her essence, savoring every smooth thrust, exploring each hidden corner and bestowing sweet pleasure. She moaned under the sensual assault and asked for more. His fingers tangled in her hair and tipped her head farther back while he drank, tasted, demanded, gave. Her head spun and her knees weakened, and in that one moment, Kennedy fell completely under his spell.

He retreated slowly, nipping at her lower lip before pulling completely away.

Kennedy gripped his arms. Whoa.

Just . . . whoa.

Most men would've gone for the jugular and pushed past her temporary weakness to their advantage. Nate waited patiently while she got her bearings. He studied her face as if committing every feature and angle to memory, and once again she got the sensation of being wrapped in a cocoon of security and warmth. "You okay?"

"Yep. That was a mistake."

"We learn from lots of mistakes. Can we do it again?"

A tiny laugh escaped. The last of the fog drifted away, and the rain slowed to a lazy drizzle. Kennedy dug deep for composure. She fought the urge to duck her head, and instead met his heated gaze head-on. "No. I don't date clients."

"I'll quit Kinnections."

"Absolutely not. You don't want me, Nate. I don't do forever. I'm not looking for marriage or security or children right now. I just do . . . now."

"I like now."

A genuine smile curved her lips. She hadn't actually liked a man in a long, long time. She forgot how good it felt. "No. Sometimes the lines get blurred with matchmaking, but I won't let it happen again. We followed an impulse, but now it's over. And I'm going to find you a wife. Someone you can love forever. Someone perfect."

He seemed to analyze her words, picking them apart, studying, then sliding them all back into place to discover the full puzzle. Finally, he took a step back and nodded. "I won't push. I respect your decision. But I won't apologize."

"Good, I wouldn't want one." The heat surged again between them but she was prepared this time and able to ignore it. "The rain stopped. I better go. Don't forget to meet me at the salon tomorrow night. Six sharp. I emailed you the address."

"Okay. Good night."

He gave her freedom and she took it. By the time she reached her car and turned on the ignition, she looked back and he was gone. She made the short drive home and finally stepped into her trendy apartment. The silence soothed her raw nerves, and she went room by room, switching on the lights so there wasn't a slither of darkness. She kicked off her heels and dug her feet into the plush carpet. Rich wood floors were the new style, but she had no pets or children, and enjoyed the feeling of the cushioning on her bare feet. The deep vanilla cream matched the walls and contrasted nicely with the ice blue furnishings. She always enjoyed a clean, clutter-free environment, and structured the modern glass and cherry wood tables to balance the vivid watercolor paintings she preferred.

She grabbed a glass and filled it with water from the stainless steel fridge. She liked to cook when she had the time, and the bold steel blue granite counters, custom cabinets, and antique wine bar reflected the image and woman she always craved to be. Beautiful. Smart. In control.

Kennedy sipped her water and thought about Nate. Big mistake. It may have been the best kiss of her life, but she'd seriously overstepped her boundaries. Funny: she'd dated numerous men, slept with many, and never had the feeling one saw her clearly. The way Nate stared at her with unblinking eyes warned her of his intentions. His kiss allowed her to hold back nothing, like an unstoppable force urging her to surrender. He devoured her with his gaze and swallowed her whole. The real danger with Nate was in his ability to see beyond her surface polish to the truth.

A shiver worked down her spine. Silly, of course. He'd spot nothing she didn't want him to find. After all, her entire life was about remaking herself into the person she'd always dreamed to be. As if drawn there by a higher power, her gaze turned to meet her own in the silver heirloom mirror. She'd bought it for decoration, but it was her nemesis. A reminder. A warning.

"Hey, fat girl." The slithery whisper turned her stomach and chilled her blood. She looked around the empty hallways, but there was no one. She tried to take a few steps back, but the voice turned hard and mean. "Run from me now and I'll find you later. Then it'll be worse."

She swore she wouldn't cry or show fear. Heart pounding, she stepped into the staircase.

He smelled bad, of cigarettes and alcohol. He was a senior, got suspended a lot, but always seemed able to find her. "I have to go to the office. They're waiting for me."

Her voice trembled and he grinned. "Come here. Won't take long. Aww, did you get dressed up for me? Or are you trying to show off your big tits to catch a boy?"

Tears burned in the back of her throat. Her fingers clumsily tugged down her nice new blouse she'd saved up money for. She'd always loved clothes, and would pore over all the fashion magazines, marking her favorites. When she saw the top at the mall, she imagined how she'd look in the frothy, feminine creation. Black and lacey, extra long to hide her stomach, she thought she looked sexy. Now she watched the way he stared at her breasts and hated it. Her lower lip shook. "Leave me alone."

"Show me your tits and I will."

Horror flooded her. She turned to run, but he grabbed her wrist and twisted hard. His rancid breath hit her face. "I'm trying to help you, fat girl. You can't *get a boy when you're fat and ugly. But boys like tits and ass. The more you show them, the better they like you."* His other hand tugged at her neckline and tried to pull the elastic down. Humiliation writhed inside her, and his fingers were like cold, oily snakes against her skin. She gulped back the tears and pushed him away.

"Don't touch me!" He grabbed her breast and squeezed hard enough to make her sob, but she managed to push him away and stumble back. His low laugh echoed in her ears as she bent over to hide her chest and ran toward the girls' bathroom.

"See you later, fat girl. I'll be waiting . . ."

Kennedy shuddered, and slowly reached up to touch her face, reminding herself she was grown up. He had tortured her all year, until every morning she'd vomit, imagining what he'd try to do to her. The pushing and bullying and insults were nothing compared to the deathly stillness of the stairwell, either after school, or in between periods, or lunch. Then he began waiting for her after school, and nowhere was safe. No one ever helped her.

He'd forced her, over and over again, to humiliate herself in front of him under threats that it could get much worse if she didn't do exactly what he wanted. So she did. But it didn't matter.

Things got worse anyway.

How long did it take her to realize she began losing weight because she stopped eating? Food had always been a comfort, but now it was the enemy—the weapon used against her. She never voluntarily tried to lose the weight. Food slowly became something that would lead to more abuse and torture, so it was easy just to stop.

She embraced the empty ache in her body until it was the only feeling she was comfortable with. Maybe she'd become invisible, drifting away to a shimmer of her former self, finally safe from the boy and his crew.

Her mother celebrated Kennedy's loss of forty pounds, which hurt Kennedy the most—the knowledge her own mother would now parade her around to charity events and society friends, where before she pretended she didn't have a daughter. Every time Dad tried to get her to eat, her mother clucked her tongue and waved him away in dismissal. She even encouraged the starvation diet, insisting all women did it because the female body was their most powerful weapon. Not brains.

Her hand dropped from her face. Kennedy turned from her reflection and beat back the remnants of the past. She hated thinking about it, though her therapist always reminded her that scars were the sign of battles fought and won. Even wounds that couldn't be seen on the skin. Suddenly, the silence seemed deafening and full of low whispers. She grabbed the remote, and turned on the television, pumping up the volume. No more. She had worked hard to find a healthy balance and enjoy the body she now proudly owned. It had taken years to fight the demons and be able to see her actual reflection in the mirror, and not the distorted image of an overweight young girl. But the mirrors still mocked, taunted, screamed. She never knew when the woman in the mirror would appear disfigured. Fat. Alone.

The droning noise of a talk show soothed her ears. Kennedy finished her water and changed into her favorite hot pink pj set in comfy cotton. She laid her head on one of the plump pillows, closed her eyes, and slept with the lights on and television blaring.

Her last image was of Nate's face as he bent down to kiss her.

five

NATE WALKED INTO the living room and took in the scene before him. Beer bottles littered the tables. Some porno flick on the TV screen. An open bag of chips and Funyuns lay half-open on the couch among a bunch of crumbs. And his brother splayed out on the couch, feet propped up, one hand securely tucked into his underwear and cupping the family jewels.

"Hey, man. What's up?"

Nate nodded at Connor and automatically began cleaning up. Rolled up the open bags and securely closed them with a clip. Scooped up the empty bottles and tossed them in the recycling bin. "Nothing. Did you put out the garbage for tomorrow morning?"

"Nah, I forgot. How come you're so late? You score?" His brow wagged up and down like Groucho Marx. Usually, Nate would laugh. Tonight, annoyance flickered.

"Met with my matchmaker. I signed up at Kinnections, remember?"

"She hot?"

Yes. Nate shrugged. "Not really. Listen, I'll be late all week. Can you handle the garbage in the morning and get some groceries? We're running low."

"Sure, man, sure." A big-breasted blonde moaned and wiggled her hips on the screen. Distaste skimmed over Nate. Why did his brother's actions seem to get worse the older he got? It had been cool in high school. Acceptable in college. But now at thirty-six, it seemed . . . sad. "Wanna watch the movie with me?"

"No, thanks. I'm tired."

His brother pulled his hand from his boxers and climbed off the couch. They always joked that Connor got the physical genes in the family, and Nate had scored in the brains department. Nate topped six feet, but his brother towered over him and boasted a ton of muscle. He wore his blondish hair long and had encouraged Nate to go that route since he claimed women found it sexy. His eyesight was twenty-twenty and he'd been blessed with his mother's big hazel eyes and thick long lashes. Bastard. He'd dropped out of college to work construction, and made a decent living except in the winter months, when things got lean and mean. "You look different. Oh, you're not orange."

"Yeah, got some body scrub thing to remove it."

"Lame, bro. Don't lose the man gene."

"It was a very manly spa." He focused on setting the coffeepot to go off at exactly 5:45 a.m. and ignored his brother's look. Connor always knew when he lied.

"Hey, Ned, you got some extra money you can lend me for the week? The guys want to go out for a beer tomorrow night and I'm light."

He frowned. "I just lent you money last week."

Connor waved his other hand in the air. "Yeah, yeah, I'll catch up soon. I caught another construction job, so I'll be working extra. Also decided to go for the supervisor position. Been there the longest. What do you think?"

He glanced up from measuring perfect portions of coffee grounds. "Definitely go for it. You'd do well in management."

His brother lit up and again Nate acknowledged the guilt that flared up whenever he thought of the sacrifices Connor had made for him. College was expensive, even with scholarships, and after his parents pretty much orphaned them, Con worked three jobs to help Nate get to school and stay there.

"Yeah, I agree. Interviews start next week. But I got caught light after Stan's bachelor party. Too bad you couldn't go. The strippers were hot."

"Sorry I missed it."

"Guess getting people to Mars is more important, right?" He grinned, tipped back his beer, and finished it in one long swallow. "You got me, right?"

"Sure." He reached into his wallet, peeled off a few bills, and threw them on the table. "Listen, I changed my name back to Nate. No more Ned."

Connor laughed. "Why'd you do that? Everyone knows you as Ned."

"Let's just call it a new leaf. I'm making some changes so I can find a wife."

"Shiiiit, bro, I still don't know why you're stuck on

marriage. Once you screw them enough, you're done anyway. You hear me?"

Had his brother gotten cruder or was he just weary? "Just call me Nate, okay?"

"Sure, whatever you want. Just be careful with this matchmaking thing."

"Got it handled. I'm going to bed."

"'Night."

Nate left the kitchen. When his brother had first asked to become his roommate, he'd thought it'd be a blast. He enjoyed Connor's company and felt as if he owed him a great debt. His brother was, quite simply, his hero. Any other moody teen would've ditched his baby brother behind and taken care of himself. But Connor was the one who drove him to after-school science and math clubs. Protected him from the string of bullies ready to beat the shit out of him. Sat beside the bed quietly while Nate sobbed because the pain of his mother leaving was too much to bear, and the silence from his father cut his heart out.

But now they were grown up. He wanted a life for himself. A wife. Children. A dog. He loved his brother, but he was ready for him to move out. The few months originally promised had turned into a year, and Connor still made no attempt to get his own place. Nate's haven had become a frat house, where he was the maid, cook, and advisor for Connor and his construction crew. He had to talk to him soon. If he was serious about finding a wife, he couldn't bring her into this type of environment. Time his brother got his own place and moved out. It would be a good move for both of them.

Nate trudged to his room, stripped off his clothes, and got ready for bed. When he finally lay on top of the crisp white sheets, he thought of Kennedy. Thought of that one sweet, earth-shattering kiss he'd remember for the rest of his life. She tasted of salt, spice, and sin. He'd never wanted a woman as badly before and would have sold his research patent to China just for an opportunity to kiss her once more.

He stared up at the ceiling. The best part was that she had responded to him. Somehow, he'd gotten to her, and for that one moment, she belonged to him. But it was time to pull himself back from the abyss before the entire plan fell apart. He wanted a woman for a long-term relationship and didn't have the skills to scale maximum-security walls strategically built to keep out men with much more experience than him. If she were willing, he'd die trying to have her. But she wasn't. And the one thing he wasn't was stupid.

He would have to be very, very stupid to ever think Kennedy Ashe would want him for forever. She was too beautiful. Too perfect. And that, he knew, was a deadly combination.

It took a long time for sleep to come.

"NO. WAY."

Kennedy shared a glance with the stylist. The man arched a brow and pursed his lips in disapproval. Benny had a very large ego, well earned, and the idea that Nate didn't want to follow his instructions insulted him in all ways. Tall and lean, his dark hair was impeccably styled and touched with red to add depth, and a diamond winked in his left ear. He always wore black and manicured his nails; his nose was long with a slight hook that made turning it up at anyone who didn't suit him all the more easy. Like right now. She rested her hands on Nate's shoulders, covered by the plastic cape, and met his gaze in the mirror. "What's the real problem?"

"Are you kidding? You want to highlight my hair? Wax my face? Let me repeat myself. No. Way. I'm going home."

Benny threw up his hands. He spoke with a fake British accent, though Kennedy knew he was straight from the Bronx. "I cannot work under such conditions. I am an artist. I take your clients as a favor to you, but I will not be insulted."

"Listen, buddy, I read *Glamour*, and it specifically states that highlights need to be kept up every two weeks. I'm sure as hell not going to a salon on a regular basis, so you better rethink the plan."

Benny huffed. Then spoke with grudging approval. "He is right. I refuse to give highlights to someone who will not maintain."

Nate sat up taller and made a move to rise from his chair. "That's right. Now who's the expert? I'm outta here."

Benny curled his lip in disdain.

"Nate, please listen." Kennedy placed a light restraining hand on his arm, which immediately grabbed all of Nate's focus. "Benny is going to polish up your appearance to increase your natural confidence. You're not getting a fair shot with a lot of good women because you haven't taken the time to make a good first impression. I promise you it's not that dramatic a change."

"You want to cut off all my hair."

"Consider it shedding season and let's be done with this," the stylist sneered.

"Benny!"

Benny picked at a cuticle, already done with the whole episode. Nate glared and crossed his arms against his chest. Kennedy sighed internally. Ah, crap. Dealing with a man's appearance was always delicate, but especially one with so much work to do. Her fingers itched to uncover what she knew he was hiding: a certain geeky hotness that would intrigue women and find him love.

The unibrow rose. "How come this is all a one-way street? Why don't you trust me to tell you I'm fine the way I am? I refuse to be some blond-ass Twinkie."

She bit down on her lower lip to keep from laughing. Benny rolled his eyes. "As if," he muttered under his breath.

Nate jerked his head. "I heard that."

"Okay, listen, if you do this for me, I'll do something for you."

Benny looked interested. "I had no idea, darling."

Kennedy rolled her eyes. "Relax, Benny—I'm not

sleeping with him. But Nate, you can choose something that will stretch my boundaries. Even though
you're a client, I usually don't ask them to do anything
I wouldn't be willing to complete myself. Name it."

He feigned disinterest. "You're already beautiful."

A shot of female vanity and pride hit her. "Thank
you. Look, you won't get this opportunity again. Pick
something and I'll do it. The offer disappears in a minute."

"Let me teach you to golf."

She winced. Oh, this was bad. Being dragged out
on an endless lawn to smack a ball and walk eight
miles to do it again was *so* not on her bucket list. And
the outfits they wore were plain scary. Those awful
collared shirts and plaid pants above the ankle. She
once saw a golfer on TV wearing bright orange shorts
without even a hint of irony. Nightmare. Not to mention the droning on and on about handicaps and
strokes. "How about we bank the favor for now?
Think about it more in depth and come up with something you really want. Okay?" She used her best pout
and lowered her lids. Only once had a man told her
no when facing off against that particular expression.
She knew her odds were good.

His face turned stubborn. "No. Golf. And not just
once. I need a few sessions in order to teach you properly."

She shuddered. Analyzed the options for a way
out. Found none. She could threaten him, but he'd still
refuse and, without changing his appearance, she'd be

too behind the eight ball. Or golf ball. "Fine. You win. But no more bitching and giving Benny a headache. You follow our instructions. Deal?"

"Deal."

"Benny?"

The stylist ran his fingers through Nate's shaggy locks, a look of disgust on his face. "Deal. This is too horrific not to help with."

"Thanks."

She scrolled through her text messages and waited while Benny prepped a moisturizing treatment and began his magic. Kennedy sipped coffee, answered emails, and tried to ignore her client's grunts and groans of horror as the solution was rubbed into his scalp. Roughly. A razor edge was brought out from the drawer and a hot washcloth placed on his face. Suddenly, Benny gave a shout.

"My God, I am brilliant. This man needs scruff."

Kennedy walked over. Nate's voice was muffled under the cloth. "What?"

"Do you think he can pull it off?" she asked.

Benny tapped a finger over his chin and debated. "It's a gamble. If I do this correctly, he can become my greatest creation."

"I'm a fucking Frankenstein now? Get me out of here."

"Shush," Benny said.

"What the hell? I shave every day and now this is a problem?"

"Shush," Kennedy said. "Let him think."

Benny finally nodded. "We shall do it. But it must be delicate. I will set up the pattern but he must promise to follow it exactly. The hair growing in needs to be the right shape so he doesn't end up looking like a drug dealer gone bad."

Nate whipped off the cloth. "Drug dealer? No stubble, I'm an aerospace engineer."

Benny cocked his head. "Hmm, I'm making over a rocket scientist, huh? Not bad."

"Aerospace engineer."

"Shush," Kennedy and Benny said in unison.

Benny wielded the blade in warning. Nate settled back into his chair. Kennedy went back to work, content to let Benny work his magic.

"What are you putting on my eyes?" Kennedy pressed her lips together. Benny didn't answer, just applied the hot wax to the nightmare unibrow. "That's hot and sticky. What's going on?"

"Stop whining."

Kennedy swallowed a giggle and spoke up. "Benny needs to clean up your brows."

"They're eyebrows, for God's sakes. What can you do to them?"

Benny pressed the fabric down. And ripped it off. "Shit!"

"Stop being a baby. Women handle hard-core pain on a daily basis. Now hold still, I'm not finished."

"You ripped my hair off my face. I'm a guy."

"A hairy guy. You will need to wax regularly."

"Fuck you."

Kennedy held back a gasp. Interesting. Nate rarely cursed. Extreme pain pushed his societal limits. She wondered what else did, but then quickly shut down the thought.

An hour later, Ben revealed the finished cut, keeping Nate turned around so he wasn't able to peek at his reflection. An odd shiver coursed down her spine as she stared at the new and improved Nate Dunkle.

Oh. Yeah.

Frankenstein he was not. His dull brown hair now gleamed with health and shine, in a dusky golden brown that picked up the moss green in his eyes. The expert cut gave the front a bit of a wave that just brushed his brow. The back was a layered razor cut to shape his head and give him a touch of bad boy. The features of his face were finally revealed, and she admitted it had been a crime to cover them up with all that hair. She envisioned the way the dark stubble would edge his chiseled jaw and mouth, adding to the overall appeal. Her belly flipped over just once.

"You're looking at me funny. How bad is it?"

Kennedy smiled. "You look amazing. Turn around."

The chair swiveled. Those eyes widened as he took in the new cut. They both waited him out. Kennedy was getting used to his silences, and respected the way his mind processed every detail of the world around him.

"Not bad."

Benny sniffed. "As if. I am a master. We should have done this for a reality TV show. I would've been famous."

"As if," Nate muttered.

Kennedy gave him a glare in the mirror and hugged Benny. "You are a genius, thank you."

"For you, my love, anything. He must moisturize weekly and return to me every week until I am assured he can handle his stubble. Have you considered laser hair therapy for his back?"

"Hey, Ben, have you read the latest article in *Esquire* citing a diamond earring worn in the left ear gives off an air of desperation? How are you making out on the bar scene lately?"

The hooked nose turned up in its signature sign of disgust. "Stop being a mitch and get your ass out of my salon."

"A what? A mitch? What the hell is that?"

"A male bitch. Don't you get out enough? Learn the language."

Nate gaped. "That word doesn't exist and is not defined by Webster's."

"Live your life by Webster's standards and you'll miss out on everything. Wake up."

"I'm in some type of acid-tripped-up Wonderland. I can take care of my own stubble."

Benny dropped his voice. "Cross me once, my little aerospace engineer, and you shall live to regret it."

"Go ahead. Make my day."

Ken jumped in between them. "Bonding time is over! Let's go." She scrawled her name to the VISA sales slip, grabbed the moisturizer, and marched Nate out.

"How do you find these people? First Ming, then Benny. Who's next, the murderer from *Texas Chainsaw Massacre* to show me how to socialize properly?"

She clamped down another laugh and headed toward the car. "No, Kinnections will take care of that. The gym is next; I have something planned. You can meet me there Wednesday night. I'll text you the address."

Misery carved out his features. "Funny, suddenly having my hair ripped from my skin sounds like more fun."

"Don't be so dramatic. Is this your car?" She looked down at the super sleek black Tesla and gave him extra points. "Nice."

He practically beamed. "Thanks. Completely battery powered and emission free."

A smile tugged at her lips. "And it's pretty hot. So, I'll see you tomorrow?"

"Where are you going?"

She frowned. "Home."

"It's a beautiful night, you tortured me for hours, and I'm due a reward." Kennedy jumped off the curb. No way was she going through another stolen-kiss routine. The first one had almost ruined her. Nate laughed. "Relax. I'm not going to jump you. We're getting ice cream." He snagged her hand and led her down the sidewalk.

Shock kept her immobile for a while. "Ice cream? It's March. Ice cream is one of the most fattening treats a person can indulge in. Absolutely not. I'm avoiding dairy lately at all costs."

"And you're probably miserable. It's the last week in March and officially spring. Eating ice cream alone is a crime—you're coming with me. Consider it babysitting duty. You can watch me eat and make sure I don't get into any trouble."

A dozen protests fluttered through her mind, but he allowed her no time to voice them. The sun hung suspended over the line of the Hudson River, caught between day and evening, and threw the world into a rosy light that shimmered off the water. Her heels clicked on the pavement as he settled into a comfortable walking pace and began his way up Main Street. Shops began to turn on their silvery lights and displayed their wares proudly, ranging from pottery and sculpture to an array of cafés promising baked goods, fresh breads, and designer coffees. Kennedy relaxed and waved to Julia, the local librarian, and chatted a few seconds with old man Charlie, who sat on the same park bench beginning at five o'clock until his buddy Frank got off work and they marched to Mugs for their daily Coors Light cocktail. Emma stopped them to give Kennedy a special gluten-free dog treat for Kate's dog, Robert, to help test out the new samples from the Barking Dog Bakery. Nate seemed comfortable to hang out while she chatted. Emma shot them a curious look. She tried to tug her hand from his grip, but he held firm, so she gave up. When was the last time she strolled down the street hand in hand with a man? His fingers were warm and strong, and it was nice to pretend for a little while that she had a normal relationship like everyone else.

A group of boys flew past them on skateboards, chased by giggling girls. She suddenly realized he seemed to know the town well.

"I didn't know you were familiar with Verily."

"I'm not."

She swung her head around. His profile was strong and graceful in the dying sun, even marred by the horrible frames of his glasses. "Then how do you know there's an ice cream place open?"

"A quaint, artistic river town in New York on Main Street. Are you kidding? They always have ice cream."

She shook her head. "You didn't even have dinner yet."

"I'm a rebel."

Kennedy smiled.

They reached the small café, Xpressions, which boasted gourmet treats and homemade ice cream chock full of calories, fat, and deliciousness. Nate took his time picking out the flavor, requesting samples of the Raspberry Razzle and Chocolate Truffle. She thought about getting a fat-free frozen yogurt, but it was just too pathetic even to bother with. He turned to her with a serious frown. "If it was up to you, what flavor would you get?"

A bit of grumpiness overtook her. "Why get fruit in an ice cream? It's pointless."

He tapped the small plastic spoon against his mouth. "Brilliant theory. I'll take a double scoop, please. Chocolate Truffle and the Peanut Butter Bash."

Her stomach growled. She tried to remind herself that she had a perfectly proportioned piece of poached salmon and unbuttered green beans at home waiting for her. "Peanut butter is also high in fat. You just picked the two worst flavors to guarantee the clogging of arteries."

He gasped in mock horror. "Worse than the Cake Batter or Cookie Dough?"

"Fine. It's your funeral."

"Oh and on one of those homemade waffle cones, please. Sure you don't want one? They have frozen yogurt."

She glared. "No, thanks."

His face relaxed into the joy of a child as he attacked the ice cream cone, a bunch of napkins wrapped around the base. "Let's sit for a few minutes."

"I have to get home."

"Just a minute."

She huffed but led him to the carved bench by the dog park. They watched the dogs run and play in wild abandon, while they sat under a twisted elm tree. A man wrapped his arms around his lover and stole a kiss by the wire fence. Ken relaxed. She hadn't come out for a walk in a while. It was kind of nice to just sit and enjoy the sights of Verily.

"I love New York. Always amazed me you can hike the mountains, ride a horse, and see a Broadway play all within an hour of each other. Have you lived in Verily your whole life?" he asked.

"No, we all attended NYU and lived in Manhattan. Then Arilyn, Kate, and I visited for a weekend and fell in love. We decided to open Kinnections and settle here. How about you?"

He snorted around his ice cream. "I ended up in California at the Dryden Flight Research Center. My goal was always NASA, I just wasn't sure what base I'd end up with, but I'm a numbers guy. Always been fascinated by physics and the challenge of manipulating information and equations to increase efficiency. My teachers couldn't keep up with me, so it was only a matter of time before NASA came knocking. When it dismantled, the private sector exploded. I was able to come back to New York and enjoy working for a reclusive techno billionaire who wants to fiddle with space travel. But trust me, the astronauts and pilots are the ones who get the glory. And the girls."

She watched a trail of chocolate ice cream drip onto his spotless lab coat and smothered a laugh. He looked down and muttered a curse. "Damn, I almost got through the day without a stain. I'm running out of coats. Here, hold this."

He shoved the cone into her hands and tried to mop up the mess with the napkins. Kennedy stared at the gorgeous, shiny, drippy ice cream cone in front of her. Pieces of chocolate truffle peeked out from beneath. A chunk of peanut butter whispered her name. Sanity tugged at the fringes of her mind until a moan from Nate caught her off guard.

"What's the matter?"

"Stomachache," he said.

She raised a brow. "You think? Look at this monster. I warned you about dinner."

"You gotta finish it."

Her heart pounded and her palms began to sweat. "No! I can't eat this. I'll cut off five years of my life and gain ten pounds."

"Don't be so dramatic. I refuse to waste a good cone. I ate most of it, just have a little so I don't feel guilty."

"But I—"

"I had the top half of my face ripped off today. Eat the cone, Kennedy."

"Oh, for God's sake, fine." The first lick caused a tiny shudder of pleasure to explode along her nerve endings. "This is ridiculous. I didn't eat dinner either."

"Good, we'll be sick together."

The second bite almost put her into cardiac arrest. The third and it was all over.

She was so happy.

A whimper escaped, and she didn't care. She attacked the cone with more enthusiasm. After all, she was doing him a favor. "So, if you're studying propulsion, you're really dealing with velocity. Are you trying to manipulate the formula in order to reach higher efficiency?"

He jerked back and gave her an odd look. A warning bell sounded in her brain, but it was too muted from the sugar rush. He spoke very slowly, as if trying to balance his words, but his gaze shred her to pieces and seemed to rationalize every part. "Yes, but everything works together. In order to change the velocity, you need the right balance of impulse to propel momentum. The thrust equation depends on the mass flow through the engine and the exit velocity."

"Got it. Do you think the use of chemical rockets is the most efficient?"

Oh, God, the peanut butter hit the piece of truffle and exploded in her mouth like a double orgasm. She crossed her legs and squeezed tight, trying to get herself under control.

Nate cleared his throat. "No, I believe a nonchemical solution where an external source of electrical energy accelerates the propellant that provides the thrust is better. But if I reach a breakthrough on my research, the entire equation and use of the formula will change, which will give us another option." He suddenly seemed to notice Kennedy's enthusiasm for the ice cream cone and smiled. "It's really good, isn't it?"

"Yes, so good."

"You have some on your chin. Stay still." He reached over and dragged the napkin over her mouth, chin, and down her neck. She swirled her tongue around and around the cone and finally got to the crunchy part and took a bite. The crisp, warm wafer melted in her mouth. Heaven. Just one more bite and she'd throw the rest away. She'd eaten enough to make him happy.

"Funny, the way they break down the whole equation, huh?" she commented as she continued munching away. "It translates to people quite well. A person follows an impulse, which propels momentum and creates a change in life. But if one is too impulsive, the momentum could pick up too much speed and cause complete disaster. Life is a balance, I guess."

"But if one remains stagnant, and never follows an impulse, there is no rocket launch at all."

She ate the rest of the cone, and the sugar buzzed hot in her veins as happiness flooded through her. "Yes. I guess you're right. Unless you're very happy where you are, and then who needs a rocket ride?"

Suddenly, she looked up and found him closer than expected. He had slid over on the bench until his shoulder pressed into hers. His gaze studied her mouth, caressing her face, and the wave of his hair spilled over his brow, making her fingers crave to reach out and stroke the strands back. The ice cream high faded and was replaced by an electrical current based on pure, hot, no-holds-barred, down-and-dirty sex.

"Ken?"

"Yeah?" she squeaked.

The dogs barked. The clang of the gate opening and closing drifted in the air. The breeze tugged the strands of her hair and blew them wildly about. She caught the scent of mint, soap, and rich chocolate. Everything blurred and faded like a movie set gone dark. Nothing mattered except for the slow descent of his mouth toward hers.

"Promise me something."

Her body hummed and softened, ready to come out and play. Her core ached for his touch on her naked skin, his tongue back in her mouth, his voice whispering her name so sweetly, like nothing she'd ever heard in her life.

"What?" she whispered.

He pushed back her hair with a gentleness that contradicted the hot lust in his eyes.

"Always eat ice cream. It's a beautiful thing to watch."

She held her breath. Waited.

He clenched his jaw, muttered something under his breath, and rose from the chair. "Come on. I'll walk you to your car."

This time, he didn't take her hand. Stung but determined not to show it, Kennedy didn't let herself think of the loss of his touch or the kiss that hadn't occurred. They walked back in silence until they reached her vehicle.

"Good night, Ken. Drive safe."

He disappeared down the street, but she refused to look back.

Absolutely refused.

six

KENNEDY STUDIED HER client as he crossed the room. She'd texted him to meet her at the Tuck-N-Pack gym, but it took a few rounds back and forth to get him to agree. Guess working out wasn't his thing. His T-shirt and sweat shorts were the closest to normal clothes she'd seen him in. His legs held nice tone, and his six-foot frame wasn't overbearing and fit his body type nicely. His shoulders and biceps were pretty cut. Could he have possibly gotten those arms from golf? Nah, impossible: that was the wimpiest sport in the world and did nothing. Amazing how his whole persona changed with just a haircut, polish, and normal skin tone. Her Eliza was blooming in front of her eyes.

Kennedy had tossed and turned all night, thinking about that almost kiss, and finally came to a conclusion. Their relationship would now be strictly business. No ice cream cones, hand holding, or confessionals. It was perfectly normal to begin developing a bond when working so closely. Arilyn had struggled with the line many times; Kate had ended up with one of her clients, for crying out loud; and now it was her turn. But when morning finally came, and she climbed out of bed from a sleepless evening, she committed to the path. No more diversions.

He stopped and looked over his thick frames with pure suspicion. "Hey."

"Hi. How was work?"

"Wayne got blocked, so I had to talk him off the ledge."

"Your lab partner?"

"Yes. I hate these places. What idiot names a place the Tuck-N-Pack?"

"I thought it sounded creative. You seem cranky."

He glowered. Kennedy fought a smile. Her scientist looked kind of adorable with his newly waxed brows drawn down and his jaw clenched. "Let's get this over with. What are we doing? Weights? Bike? Treadmill? Or do you just want me to put you on my back while I do one hundred pushups for your entertainment?"

"Not today. You've got great biceps. And legs. Do you run?"

"No. It's from golf."

She snickered. "Yeah, right. We're taking a class today to stretch your boundaries. Have you ever danced?"

Something akin to horror flickered in his eyes. "Have you ever golfed?"

"Guess not. A man comfortable with dancing owns his body. Dancing brings grace, balance, and a certain sensuality. You live mostly in your head. You're missing a connection to your actual physical form, and I think this will do the trick. It's also a great workout."

His glasses slipped a few inches down his nose. He shoved them back. "What class is it?"

She turned on her heel and headed toward the smoked glass door in the back. Her fingers curled around the handle. "Zumba." With a grin, she opened the door and stepped through.

He froze to the spot and the door swung closed in his face. She waited, but he remained still, refusing to move. Kennedy held back a sigh and peeked back out. "Nate, trust me on this."

He waited a beat. Two. Then walked away. Kennedy leaped out in front of him. "Is there a problem?"

Nate lowered his voice to a dark hiss. "Do you know what gym class was like for me? I still have nightmares, and now you want to humiliate me in another group setting? Stomping around to a bunch of bad music with a cheerleader-type instructor is not my idea of a decent workout."

She jerked back. God, she hadn't anticipated his bringing up awful memories of high school gym. It seemed like they had suffered the same woes of adolescence—it had taken years before she'd been strong enough to go into a gym with her head held high and work out without wondering if she'd hear the chants of *fat girl*. She grabbed his hand and squeezed tight. "I'd never do anything to humiliate you. Never. Everything I do has a higher purpose, and that's to find you a wife, Nate. Your *wife*. I send all my clients to this gym, and no one judges them. Just try it with an open mind. Please."

She held her breath for his decision. An odd sort of heat flooded through her from the intense way he studied every inch of her face, as if probing beneath her skin to find all the stuff hidden. He had a way of making someone feel she was the most important person in the world under that stare.

"Are you sure Zumba will get me to my wife?"

"It's an important piece in the puzzle. Each step brings you to the next level."

He returned the pressure of her fingers. Funny, it was like they fit perfectly together. Almost like being home. The thought skittered through her, and she quickly tugged her hand away. Business. Just business.

"Fine. I'll try."

Giddiness flooded her. "Thank you. You won't regret it."

"I don't believe you, but I'll try anyway," he muttered.

She dragged him into the studio before he had time to change his mind.

The cool air hit her full force and pebbled goose bumps on her bare arms and legs. The room was half-full, and she guided him toward the back corner. Large screens were set up so the instructor could be viewed from every angle, and most of the students were warming up with gentle stretches. Nate crossed his arms in front of his chest and surveyed the room with disdain. She leaned over. "First off, no one's looking at you. No one cares. Try to let yourself go for once in your life and forget controlling the outcome. Don't rationalize the moves. Have some fun, and take an hour off from results."

He stiffened, but the perky brunette bounced to the center stage and spoke into her earpiece. "Is everyone ready to ZUMBA?"

The crowd roared. "Yes!"

"Well, let's turn it up, people!"

The music boomed from the walls and ceiling, wrapping them in a Latin-type rhythm that perked up the heartbeat and warmed the blood. Kennedy concentrated on their model, enjoying the back-and-forth steps of the warm-up, and watched Nate in the mirror under half-lidded eyes. He stomped back and forth with deliberate movements, his nose wrinkled in concentration. She knew it would be a big test for him to admit he may not get the steps, but it was important to dive beneath the control barrier he kept up. No woman wanted a perfectionist as a mate, or someone judgmental. She needed to scratch past his rigid mental structure and get him to *feel*.

The warm-up transitioned to grinding hip-hop. Kennedy missed many of the steps, but made up for it in enthusiasm and the swing of her hips. Another glance in the mirror showed the gleam of sweat on Nate's brow, the slip of his glasses down his nose, and the frustrated grimace of his lips. She almost caught the smoke from his head steaming out as he tried to mimic the instructor's rapid pace. As soon as he nailed one routine, she switched to another rocketing foot dance that seemed to have no rhyme or reason. It was exactly what Kennedy wanted him to experience.

"Let's work the hips, people! One, two, and three. Slide on four. Bump and grind, baby, that's what I'm talking about!"

Forty minutes into the class, Nate Ellison Raymond Dunkle surrendered.

It was a fascinating breakdown to watch. Kennedy knew the exact moment he decided he couldn't do it. No matter how hard he tried, the dance slipped away from him, always out of his grasp, leaving only the raw tempo of music, the scent of sweat, and the stamp of feet on the bare floors. The lights spun and threw him into a greenish silhouette.

Kennedy prided herself on breaking down the male species. Arilyn usually helped target the exact hurdle her prey needed in order to strip down boundaries. Kennedy wasn't educated as a counselor, but she enjoyed witnessing growth in a person. Lord knows she'd dealt with tons of angst in her own past. Still, pain built character. Growth helped love. Being stagnant and fearful only blocked any of the good vibes in a healthy relationship.

At least, that's what she always believed.

He stopped dancing. Stared at the move of bodies, flowing and ebbing, some in tempo and most not. She never stopped in her own routine. This was his journey, and his choice. She could only lead him in the right direction. Kennedy turned, bent, then did a rotation, a hip thrust that made her feel naughty and powerful. Again. And again.

Nate narrowed his gaze, taking in the scene, and did the one thing she'd swear the man was incapable of.

He danced.

He spun, lowered, rotated, and thrust. Worries over looking stupid, or not copying the exact movements, or the horror of his high school gym class all seemed to drift away. He missed most of the steps but never stopped. He gave up and gave in, and his body took over.

She couldn't tear her gaze from him in the mirror. His cotton shirt slipped up and she caught a glimpse of a nice rack of abs. The innate stillness he owned radiated outward into a flow of almost poetic grace, his feet sliding across the floor, his hips rocking with a power that left her a bit breathless. Like a caterpillar catching flight as a butterfly, in that instant he dove into the moment and owned it. An almost sexual energy emanated in waves and mixed with the earthy tempo, turning him into a man radiating sheer command. For one second, her skin tingled and her breath caught. For one second, she was completely and utterly attracted to him.

The music changed; slowed. Cool-down began, with gentle glides and simple arm movements. The moment passed and faded, already seeming like a weird dream. Class ended and students lingered to guzzle water, chat, and speak with the teacher. A proud grin curved her lips as she walked over to her profusely sweating client.

"What do you think?"

He adjusted his clothing, took a sip of water, and studied her over his glasses. "Tell me this is a one-shot deal."

She shook her head. "We Zumba every Monday, Wednesday, and Thursday. You'll enjoy it more each time."

"I think I'd rather see Benny or Ming." His gaze pierced hers. "Do you torture all the men at Kinnections before getting them their happy ever afters?"

She laughed. "Love and relationships are work. We always say learn to do the labor beforehand, and it will become a habit and lead to a more successful relationship."

He pondered the words and tilted his head. "Do you follow your own advice?"

The question took her off guard, but she made sure to recover quickly. "Yes. I've done a lot of hard work with myself. I think that's helped me form better relationships."

Nate nodded. "When was your last one?"

"My last what?"

"Long-term relationship."

Irritation bristled her nerves. She forced a casual smile. "Oh, not too long ago. But I'm ready and open for the next."

"You said you didn't do long term."

She took a slug of water so she didn't have to answer. He waited her out anyway, his gaze probing for truth. "Long term means something different to everyone. Yours is marriage. Mine is a few months."

Students chatted, mats were dragged out for the next class, and his voice reached her ears, deep and dark and caressing. "Maybe you deserve more."

She opened her mouth to set him straight, but a sweet, female voice interrupted. "Hi. Just wanted to welcome you to Zumba. It's so great to see a man here. Most don't have the guts."

Kennedy took in her high ponytail, bare midriff, and interested gaze. Whoa. She was really interested, her sly gaze sliding up and down his body. Fresh meat was always welcome at the gym. Nate didn't move. Didn't respond. Kennedy cleared her throat and bumped his shoulder. This was a perfect opportunity to watch him handle a first meet. Maybe he'd learned a few lessons from the disastrous speed dating and their time together. "Umm, Nate, I'll be right back."

She moved away to give them a bit of privacy, and fiddled with her iPhone. *Come on, dude, you can do this. Talk. Say anything. No, scratch that, say something that's not stupid.*

"Nice to meet you. My name is Nate."

Kennedy slumped with relief. Perfect. Maybe she should school him just to be direct from the get-go. No bad pick-up lines, body-related comments, or probing questions. Just direct information.

"I'm Heidi. Haven't seen you at the gym before. First time?"

"Yep, I'm a golfer, but figured I'd try something different. Hey, you have a great—"

Kennedy squeezed her phone in a death grip.

"Smile."

She let out her breath. He'd listened! Maybe this would be easier than she thought. Was he ready to be sent out? They had the wardrobe makeover coming up, and of course the role-play session with Arilyn and Kate, but she always saved that for last. A mixer would definitely work. Plenty of options.

"Thanks so much. I'm heading for a shake at the health bar. Wanna join me?"

"Sure." He glanced over at Kennedy. She gave him a subtle thumbs-up sign. He gave a slight nod in acceptance and began walking out. Their voices drifted through the room. "What do you do, Heidi?"

"I'm in school. Studying to be a nail technician."

"You need to go to college to learn how to paint nails?"

Heidi paused and swung her head around. "Nails are serious business. Why, what are you? A rocket scientist?"

He stiffened. Kennedy winced. Oh, no. No, no, no, no . . .

"Actually, an aerospace engineer. They don't call it rocket science anymore."

She cocked her head. "Are you serious, man?"

He gave her *the* look. Filled with derision and judgment. "Of course. Listen, I don't think this will work between us for a long-term relationship, but I'm completely open to having a short affair. What do you think?"

Ah, shit.

Heidi gasped. "You're an asshole." She stalked off, ponytail bouncing, and disappeared through the smoked-glass door.

Nate blinked. The lines of his face were stamped with complete surprise. He turned back to Kennedy with his palms upturned. "What did I do wrong?"

Okay, no mixer. Not for a while, anyway. Why the hell didn't he respect the woman's career path? Any work in this economy was a thing of pride. How dare he evaluate anyone's choices just because he was successful? Disappointment flooded her. She marched over and jabbed her finger against his chest. The scent of male sweat, cotton, and a hint of musk hit her nostrils. "Too many things to go over in a few minutes."

"I was honest and direct. Women appreciate that, right? I wasn't rejecting her, just changing the course, since I knew right away marriage was never going to happen."

"I don't want to hear it right now. Follow me."

She led him toward the back stairs. "Where are we going?"

"Out the side door. I think it would be best to avoid the shake bar until Heidi calms down. Don't you?"

He didn't answer. They popped out into the cool evening. She walked off her temper and into the diner where they had their first coffee date. Sliding into the red booth, she ordered a cup of black coffee.

"And you, sir?" the waitress asked.

"Do you serve humble pie? My gut is telling me I may need it for something."

"Excuse me?"

He waved a hand in the air. "Never mind. Tea with lemon, please. And a Clorox wipe."

The waitress shot him a look. "You kidding?"

"No." She rolled her eyes but returned with one, and he carefully wiped down the table. "The amount of germs at public eateries is staggering. Do you know many restaurants just use a wet cloth to wipe the tables clean after each patron? No soap or disinfectant."

Kennedy practically spit in fury and launched into her tirade. "Must be nice to make judgments on people who are trying to figure out what they want to do in life."

He blinked. "Huh?"

"Why do you think a nail technician is beneath you?"

He jerked from the direct hit. "I don't. I may not understand it, but I'm sure there's training involved. She said she needed schooling. It's honest work. That wasn't my problem."

"What was?"

"Connor said women in the beauty industry are unfaithful. I can't marry someone who won't be loyal."

She placed her palms flat on the table and leaned forward. "Wait. Your brother thinks all women who are cosmetologists or hairstylists will cheat?"

"Yes."

"For God's sake, why?"

The waitress plopped down their mugs. He took a moment to examine the rim of the cup for traces of lipstick before he seemed comfortable enough to take a sip. "He had a girlfriend once who worked at a beauty shop. She cheated on him and broke his heart. Later, he found out that all the women in the salon had encouraged her to do it. I've never seen him that upset over one woman before, and after that, he swore off any long-term relationships. Connor warned me never to get involved with anyone in the beauty industry."

Frustration steamed out of her ears. She opened her mouth, shut it, shook her head, and tried again. "Your brother had a bad experience with a specific woman—not everyone in the cosmetology world. How would you feel if I told you a rocket scientist—"

"Aerospace engineer."

"—aerospace engineer cheated on me and now I'd never even speak with anyone involved in the industry? Or anyone who taught physics? How would that make you feel to be judged right away without being assessed on your individual ethics?"

She pictured his mind completing a series of clicks as he processed the information. "I wouldn't like it."

"Exactly. A whole group shouldn't be punished for one person's wrong deeds."

"Agreed. It's just—" He broke off and sipped his tea. She waited, sensing something bigger beyond the unsaid words.

"What?"

"I don't want to hurt my brother. If I came home with a cosmetologist, it may bring up bad memories."

"Maybe he needs to work through it. You can't let your brother's issues keep you from opportunities that may work for you. That's not fair to anyone."

"I guess."

He drank his tea and grew pensive. She studied the graceful planes of his face and serious eyes while he pondered the liquid in his mug. It was a good time to back off, partly to keep her resolution to put some distance between them. She'd discovered his true motives, and though it didn't make what he had done right, she understood more now. The man needed major socialization, and she knew exactly what to do about it. But for now, the best thing was to leave. Pay for the coffee, wish him good night, and go home. They'd meet for the next round in the clear day with barriers resurrected.

Ah, hell. There was pain in his eyes, and her heart couldn't take it. "How old were you when your mom left?" she asked.

Most people wouldn't respond. Nate just told the truth. "Ten. I knew she was unhappy, because she cried a lot, and fought with my dad. My father worked construction like my brother, so we didn't have much. Mom liked pretty things. Clothes, jewelry, parties. She tried to drag Dad out a lot, but he only wanted to stay home in front of the television." He shrugged as if it didn't matter. Kennedy knew different. "I got up in the morning and she had her bags packed. Made me breakfast, and told me she was going on a trip for a while. Kissed my forehead. I was in a mood so I grumbled something at her and left for school. I never saw her again."

Her stomach tightened. She never understood why there was so much cruelty in the world, and why so many bad things happened to good people. "You don't blame yourself, do you?"

"Nah, she had one foot out the door a long time ago. I just regret not saying anything heartfelt or meaningful when I had the chance. My last memory of her is bacon and eggs frying, her black suitcase on the floor, and my own pissed-off resentment of having to go through another crappy school day while she goes off having fun."

"Your father didn't handle it well, I take it?"

"He had some sort of breakdown. Just withdrew into himself, became bitter, and forgot he had two sons left. We rarely saw him."

"Yeah," she said softly. "That pretty much sucks."

His lips quirked upward. "Good thing Arilyn is the counselor."

"Good thing. Did you ever think of trying to find your mom?"

"Don't want to. Connor and I don't need anyone else. That's why he warns me not to fall long term for a beautiful woman. Get in and get out, he says. He's afraid I'll get played and end up with someone like Mom."

The loose ends suddenly came together and created an intricate pattern that made sense. She swallowed past the tightness in her throat and the sudden urge to share. His loneliness emanated from him in waves, but the strength of his core touched her deep. Almost as if her soul-mate sat right across from her, waiting for her to reach across, take his hands, and tell him it would all be okay.

Fear slammed into her gut like a sucker punch, stealing her breath. What was she thinking? What was she doing? He was right: this was Arilyn's territory, and she had no right to strip him bare with no intention of helping or soothing his pain. Panic nipped at her like a puppy at her ankles. The air in the diner grew thick and stifling.

She had to go.

"Nate, I'm so sorry, I forgot I have to meet Kate tonight and I'm late."

"That's okay. Go ahead." Nate stayed sitting at the table, staring down unseeingly at his hands gripping his steaming mug.

She stood up, grabbed her Dooney & Bourke purse, and hesitated. "You deserve someone beautiful inside and out. And I promise you, I'm going to find her."

Kennedy rushed out the door. The word screamed in her mind like a mantra, roaring in her ears.

Coward.

NATE PAUSED AND RELISHED the moment. The first strong sign of spring had finally rolled in, and the air was ripe with promise. The mad sounds of chirping birds drifted in the breeze, and the trees sprouted rich and green from the bare bones of the nasty March madness. The west course of Westchester Country Club was one of his all-time favorites. Designed by Walter Travis, the 71 par course held an array of courses that varied in difficulty. Blind spots amid the wooded areas challenged a golfer in all ways, and four of the holes were rated most difficult on the PGA tours.

The rolling hills spread out in front of him in perfect manicured beauty. A few scattered golf carts were parked, but since it was a midweek morning, everyone was pretty much at work, stuck behind desks, and staring out the window, wishing for freedom.

When he took the job at Sector Space X, he insisted on Wednesday mornings off for this purpose. He wasn't a clock puncher, since depending on the project or where his head was, he could go for endless hours without a bathroom break or even getting up from his seat. It all balanced out in the end, and the company agreed with no problem. Wednesday mornings belonged to him.

And golf.

Nate didn't remember the first time he discovered his deep love and respect for the game. Connor was always into more physical sports, and it wasn't as if he knew anyone who golfed who could show him the game. He'd watched a few tournaments on television, and in college, he followed some guys to a par 3 to hit some balls and learn basic mechanics. Before long, he was hooked, and dedicated his spare time to reading up on the art of the swing and discovering how his knowledge of physics could be used to create the perfect swing. He spent hours with computer simulations using exacting formulas to match his body type to the ultimate efficient swing. He was a bit obsessed and enjoyed figuring out the unique dynamics of a person's motion in order to hit the sweet spot and natural stance to create an almost professional-level game.

It was a game of science, luck, and skill. It was elegant in all ways, from the beauty and grace of the ball soaring through the air to the gorgeous vivid scenery in the background. It honored discipline, practice, and precision. Each time he played, he found a new element to learn, tweak, or admire.

He couldn't wait to get Kennedy here.

Her image drifted in front of him. She knew science. Didn't seem bored and actually understood the basic philosophies. There was a depth behind her gorgeous face he wished he had permission to excavate.

It had taken the willpower of Peter the Apostle not to kiss her the other night. Her face reflected an open, happy, beautiful woman who twisted his insides and challenged his brain. For one sweet second, she had actually seemed interested in their conversation, and, more important, in him. Her lips had parted, her breath escaped in a rush, and her entire body softened. He smelled her excitement, that delicious musky, spicy scent that roared in his blood and made him crazed to drag her into his bedroom and explore every naked, wet, hot inch of her. Nate was afraid he might die if he didn't get another chance to slide his tongue between her lips and drink her essence. Instead, he held back, aware she wasn't interested in him for longer than a stolen kiss, and he needed his head in the game.

He told her things about himself last night he'd never confessed to anyone. Funny, each time he saw her they seemed to grow closer, like an invisible bond wrapping them in a delicate spider web. But he doubted he'd get another opportunity. She had run out like a politician scenting a photo op and never glanced back. He needed to focus. Because he believed that his brother was right about one thing.

Beautiful women like Kennedy Ashe would never be satisfied with him. Not long term.

Nate bit back a wimpy sigh and turned his attention to his game. He missed his normal group, but they had moved their game to Tuesday afternoons, and he had to quit. Still, he enjoyed the meditative silence of the air, the sun, and the smack of the ball. He set up at the tee box, took some practice swings, computed the angle of the hill, the tilt of ground, and analyzed the distance. He used the eight iron for his approach shot, and the slice of the iron whipped clean and true. The ball flew in a perfect trajectory and landed on the green a few inches from the hole. One perfect putt later and he sank the sucker.

Nate had refused a caddy today, so he gathered his

clubs and headed to the second tee. Lost in his thoughts, he suddenly realized a golf ball was winging through the air toward his head. The voice came a few seconds too late.

"Fuck! Three! I mean, fore. Ah, forget it, just get out of the way, man!"

Nate ducked just in time. A young man jogged over and stopped short. His face reflected a combination of disgust and confusion while he watched the ball roll drunkenly into one of the hazards and plop in the sand pit completely separate from the goal.

Nate shook his head. "Bad luck. Sorry."

The man gazed over the hill toward the sunken ball. "Hope I didn't mess up your game. Umm, is that a decent shot, though? It's kind of close to the hole."

Nate laughed and then realized the guy wasn't joking. "Oh, no that's a terrible shot. You went completely off the green to a different fairway. You're on the first hole, right? So you were aiming for over there." He pointed in the opposite direction.

The man's shoulders dropped. "Yeah, this is never gonna happen in this lifetime. Thanks a lot." He trudged away, but something about his frustration called to Nate. An interesting tattoo snaked up the man's neck and curled around his ear. The guy seemed like someone he imagined Kennedy would go for—cool and edgy in a way that could never be taught. Just owned.

Nate fought off the temporary depression. "Hey. Do you need some help? You can join me for a few holes, and I can give you some pointers."

"No."

"You're the direct type, huh?"

"Yep."

Wolfe shot him a grin. "Good. I've had enough bullshit to last the rest of my life."

"I bet. What hotel?"

"Purity."

"Ah, yes, you're opening in Manhattan. Nice place. No wonder you need the game; most hotel executives are huge golfers."

"I've always been more of the video game type. What do you do?"

"I work for a small private company that's trying to get people into space. I study propulsion mechanics and try to find a more economical, inexpensive way to get us to Mars."

"An aerospace engineer, huh? Cool."

Suddenly, Nate knew it was going to be a great day. "Yeah. Listen, I may be able to help. Let me study your natural stance and do some measurements. I'm working on an amateur program using physics to compute a sequence to increase your skill faster. I'd need to take some video, though."

Wolfe studied him again, and Nate waited him out. There was a darkness within Wolfe he sensed immediately, but his gut urged him to help. He needed to expand his horizons from the work crowd and his brother. Delving into a special project might be the thing he needed to get his mind off his bewitching, sexy as hell matchmaker.

"Sure I won't be taking up too much of your time?"

"I'm sure."

"Then let's do it. And thanks."

"Welcome."

They grinned at each other and got to work.

seven

KENNEDY SLID INTO the booth, plucked up her Skinny Girl margarita, and guzzled. The tequila smoothed away her worries of the day, including her calorie count—since the ice cream episode, she'd beefed up on her Greek yogurt and oven-roasted turkey breast, and hadn't indulged in carbs for a full forty-eight hours.

Maybe that was why she was so pissy.

"Another diet, babe?" Kate gave her a sympathetic look from across the battered table. Kennedy's inner circle knew that her push-pull with food never ended, though she managed to achieve a healthy balance most of the time. She watched herself carefully and was now able to yank herself back when she began getting nuts over daily caloric intake or a missed gym appointment. She thought of anorexia as alcoholism. She was always recovering and could never be completely cured. One twisted reflection in the mirror could be the catalyst to starve herself, but so far, she hadn't regressed in more than five years. Odd, she seemed much more relaxed about indulging around Nate. After the fries and ice cream, she hadn't gone home and beat herself up. She'd actually been . . . happier and more satisfied.

But then the old anxieties had come creeping back in, and she had promised to be stricter than ever with what she let into her body.

She refocused on Kate. "Always battling the enemy of carbs."

"Whatever you do, please don't give up chocolate. The last time you tried, Arilyn almost quit."

Arilyn laughed. The tinkling sound rang out like church bells. "I'm not afraid of Kennedy."

"If you keep wearing these outfits on a Friday night, you better be scared. How are you supposed to catch a hot man dressed in yoga pants?"

Arilyn looked a bit smug and a whole lot of satisfied. "Don't need to. We're back together."

Kate bit her lip. Worry bloomed from her expression. "That's great, but, well, did he decide to be monogamous with you?"

Arilyn shrugged and sipped her apple martini. "We didn't discuss it, exactly, but it's assumed."

Kennedy tapped her finger against her chin. "Darling, using the word *assumed* when it comes to sex brings one phrase to mind. It makes an ass out of you and me."

A rare frown crossed Arilyn's lovely features. Kennedy had been dying to make her over for years but was refused each time. Her background in yoga and meditation practice kept her firmly in the camp of organic cottons, environmental friendly make-up and hair products, and a tendency to downplay all her natural womanly assets. "There's only one ass at this table."

Kate laughed. "Listen, we're just worried. The last time you walked in on him with another of his students you went into a depression. We want you happy."

"I am happy. It's complicated. He decided to go deeply into his meditation and discovered he can't live without me. He won't stray anymore."

Kennedy fought the urge to find the asshole's yoga studio and demonstrate her kickboxing moves on his face. Instead, she tamped down her anger and focused on the alcohol. "How come we've never met him?"

Arilyn shifted. "We don't like to go public with our relationship. At least, not yet."

Kate met Kennedy's gaze, and they did the classic close girlfriend psychic thought volley. Both silently agreed he was going to hurt her again, and then they'd go and hurt him. Both agreed they needed to support Arilyn and play the denial game with enthusiasm. "We understand. It sounds like a great plan, and we're behind you all the way," Kate said.

"Me, too."

Arilyn calmed. "Thanks. So, tell us the update with Eliza Doolittle. Ming succeeded, and Benny rocked the cut. Didn't you say you were taking him to the gym?"

She plucked the cute umbrella out of her glass and twirled it around. "Yep. Can anyone say Zumba?"

Kate's eyes widened. "No. You didn't."

"I did."

Arilyn burst into giggles. "Oh, my God, that may

have been better than Slade's hot yoga session. You're brilliant."

She preened. "Thanks. He needed to get past some of the blocks regarding his body. He lives mostly in his mind and tortures himself about getting things right."

"Hmm, sure he's not a female you?" Arilyn asked.

"Funny. Nothing wrong with being a perfectionist. I'm going to keep him in the classes for a few weeks."

"So, you did skin, hair, workout. Clothes are next, right?" Kate asked.

"I have to move the role-play session up. He tends to come on too strong and scares everyone away. Will you guys help me out? Maybe we can meet at a bar and run some setup scenes for the first meet?"

Kate lit up. "I love doing those! Can I be the bitchy slut this time?"

Kennedy rolled her eyes. "Whatever makes you happy."

"Are you satisfied with his progress so far?"

She didn't meet Arilyn's suddenly piercing gaze. "Definitely. There's a lot underneath the surface that people never get to see. I think he'll be ready for his mixer in a week or two."

"You like him."

Kate's words sounded like an accusation. Kennedy tried to keep her voice casual. "He's a nice guy. What's not to like?"

"No, no, that's not what I mean. When you talk about him, you get a funny look on your face. Are you hot for the science geek?"

"No!" She slurped and got to the end of her drink, then prayed she wasn't blushing. Dear God, she never blushed, not even during phone sex. "Don't throw your witch energy on me. You need to sink your teeth into a new couple to hook up and leave me alone."

Arilyn gasped. "You do like him! Your cheeks are kind of red."

Kennedy picked up her head and snorted haughtily. "As. If. It's the alcohol and the room is warm. When are Genevieve and Jane coming?"

"And changing the subject!" Kate clapped gleefully. "What are you so freaked out about? I love the nerd type. He may be good for you."

Kennedy drew back. "And how, pray tell, can he possibly be good for me?"

This time her friends shared the psychic look. "You haven't liked someone in a really long time, Ken," Kate said gently. "You go through a different man every Friday and Saturday night and you still seem frustrated."

"The sex is fine."

"We're not talking about sex," Arilyn said. "We're talking about connection. What about Mark? He seemed to hit all your demands."

"He had a terrible habit of smelling his underwear and socks before putting them on."

"That's just called being a man. And what about Sam?"

She sensed a gang-up and stuck out her chin. "Sam had the ugliest feet in the world. When we got into bed together, if his troll toe touched me, I got the willies."

Kate dropped her face into her hands. "You have got to be kidding me. And Tim?"

"He was completely obsessed with the supernatural. Watched those awful TV series about ghosts, and his career goal was to be a paranormal investigator."

Arilyn nodded. "Well, I agree that one was weird. But what we're trying to point out is you seem to find something wrong with every guy. By the fourth date, you've listed over a dozen bullet points to back up your decision to stop seeing him."

Kennedy stuck out her lower lip. Damn counseling genes. She knew her best friends were right, but she didn't know what to do about it. There was always something lacking. And if a man tried to get too close, she reached a block inside of her that a nuclear explosion couldn't disintegrate. It was easier to concentrate on the physical—sensation, an orgasm, a few laughs. Anything deeper just didn't seem to work.

"What does this have to do with the scientist?" she asked.

Kate stared hard. "I'm not sure. But if something interests you about him, go for it. You have nothing to lose."

The image of that first hot, sweet kiss drifted in her vision. Oh, God, should she tell them? No, it would never happen again, and they'd obsess and drive her nuts. Not telling wasn't a lie. Just self-preservation from a grilling, torturous session to rival a prisoner of war. Kennedy drained the rest of her drink and shook her head. "He's a client, guys. I don't get involved with the clients. We decided that was rule number one, two, and three if we were going to make Kinnections a success."

Kate tossed her a dazzling smile. Her white blond hair shone like a halo. "I broke the rules and thank God I did."

"Slade is different. You sensed the touch with him and you knew you were meant to be. Nate needs a professional to guide him to the right mate. If I go scratching an itch on impulse, I can end up hurting him and messing up his chances at Kinnections."

"Ah, you *are* attracted to him."

She ignored Arilyn's smug comment and waved her hand in the air. "Look, I'll admit he intrigues me. But that's because he's a challenge. Emotions get crossed in most of these cases, like a counselor and a patient. Or a yoga teacher and his student."

Arilyn glared.

Kate spoke up. "Bottom line, we're here for you. And we'll have your back if you change your mind."

Kennedy's temper dissipated instantly and was replaced by the mushy goo of true friendship. "I love you guys. Thanks. And I promise to eat some bread tomorrow."

"Thank God."

They ordered another round and played a game of darts. When they returned to the table, Genevieve and Jane had just come in and wove through the crowd to reach them. Genevieve was Kate's close friend, but they had all ended up bonding over the past years with Kinnections and formed a tight-knit group. Engaged to a hunky doctor who was also her boss at Westchester Medical Center, Genevieve was a surgical intern. Kate worried about her steadily dropping weight and daily exhaustion, since she worked round the clock and was now planning a wedding. Petite and usually full of a bubbling, fierce energy, she seemed a bit flat tonight. Her brown hair was pulled back in a ponytail, and she wore a simple black shirt, pants, and flats. A strange premonition drifted over her like a cloud when she took in Genevieve's haunted blue eyes, tired smile, and gaunt waistline. Something was wrong. She held all the signs Kennedy knew well. Struggling with inner demons stole both the light and willpower from a person's soul. She made a note to try to get her alone for a private chat.

Jane was Slade's sister, and had met her fiancée through Kinnections. Kennedy was proud of the match and the serene happiness on the young woman's face. Kennedy had always known that Jane, once a true "Plain Jane" in more ways than one, was a beautiful woman, but needed to build up her confidence. The transformation had been both inside and out. With Arilyn's counseling, Kate's patience, and her own makeover skills, Jane had blossomed and found love.

Kennedy reminded herself of other happy-ever-afters when she lay awake at night, not able to sleep.

Her job helped others. The years of torture and growth and unhappiness were all made well worth it. And maybe, one day, she'd find her own brand of happiness in love.

The image of Nate's mouth sliding over hers flickered in her vision.

She pushed it aside.

"How's it going, ladies? Are we ready for the big engagement parties?" Ken asked.

Gen sighed. "I should've just hired a planner, but David says it's best to control all the details to guarantee perfection. The big news is I've made the decision to move out of my bungalow."

Ken noticed how she darted a nervous look at everyone as if afraid of backlash. Kate gave a long whine. "Nooooo! I'm gonna miss you as my neighbor. Who's going to feed you and supply you with caffeine?"

Gen smiled. "I'll miss you too, but David thinks it's the best move. Silly to keep schlepping my stuff back and forth, and his place is so much bigger and near the hospital. I'm thinking of renting it out, though. I don't want to give it up."

An image of Nate and Connor floated past her. The idea formed slowly, but in moments had grown to the size of Jack's beanstalk. Nate really needed his own place in order to cultivate an intimate, serious relationship. Somehow, she needed to convince either Nate or Connor to move out. Maybe she could offer up Gen's place? With a few updates and masculine furnishings, it could work.

"Umm, Gen, I may know someone who could rent it for a while."

"Great. I'll make a copy of the key and just let me know when they want to look at it."

"Done."

A few hours passed. She relaxed under the slight buzz of alcohol, good conversation, and some deep belly laughs. Honestly, girlfriends were the best remedy to any of life's challenges. Who needed men, after all? After the orgasm, it only went south fast.

The noise in the bar grew as a crowd of college students spilled in and began shouting over a beer funnel. Kate sighed. "I'm getting old. Way too loud in here. Call it a night?"

Gen hiccupped. "No, it's still early. How about we walk to my place? Ken, you can take a few pictures on your phone and show your friend."

"Sounds like a plan. Let's go, ladies. Road trip."

They slipped out of Mugs and hit the street. Even past eleven, the night was full of action. Lights twinkled from the shops, music spilled from the open door of different cafés, from hard rock to soothing classical, depending on the crowd. A full moon hung in the sky, orange and ripe, as if plucked straight from a children's picture book. Couples held hands and munched on pastries as they strolled through the town, and groups lounged on terraces, smoking cigarettes and drinking wine.

Ken linked her arm with Kate to keep them both from tripping on their high heels. Jane, Arilyn, and

Gen giggled and sang some pop song lyrics off-key. They finally reached Gen's cozy bungalow and streamed into the living room. The space was small, but the clean, simple lines gave it an impression of space. The eggshell walls set off bold splashes of rich ocean blue and dandelion yellow. A large braided rug covered the bare wood floors and led from the open space of the living room to the kitchen, which held a knotty pine table, small island, and breakfast counter. Ken snapped a few photos while Gen uncorked another bottle of wine. Not too girly, and the place held a lot of character, from the crooked steps that led up to an open-air loft/attic, claw-footed tub in the bathroom, and large Cape Cod windows with shutters. Now she just had to convince Nate it was time to break up the brotherhood duo.

Gen handed out glasses. "Hey, Kate, I have those books for you that I borrowed. I kept forgetting to give them back." She scooted over to the corner bookcase and grabbed a pile. "The one on stuttering was awesome, it really helped me with one of my patients."

"Oh, good, but you could've kept them. I've got so many books, they don't fit in my bookcases any longer," Kate said.

"David doesn't want me to bring too much over. Says most of what I have is junk."

"Okay, no problem." She scooped up the pile. "Ouch!" She yanked her fingers back and the books clattered to the floor. "Dammit, I got another shock from that thing."

"What thing?" Ken reached over and slid out a violet colored, fabric book. Small and square, it had the title *The Book of Spells* stitched on the front.

Kate glowered and rubbed her hand. "I swear the thing is enchanted. I thought you were giving it to Izzy."

Gen's face fell. "No. I thought we'd make a joke about it, maybe cast the silly spell together for fun, but we had another fight and she's not speaking to me. I hope she comes to the engagement party."

"I'm sorry, sweets. Your sister's going through a really hard time right now, but she has to find her own way. I'm sure she won't miss the party. It'll blow over," Kate said.

Kennedy cracked open the cover. A musty scent drifted upward. She flipped through the pages. "Holy crap, it's a real love spell. A chant to Earth Mother. Hysterical."

Arilyn snorted. "Spells are just imaginative ways of trying to control our future when we feel completely lost and misguided."

"I dare you to try it," Ken threw out.

Arilyn looked at her like she'd gone nuts. "What? I don't need a love spell, I'm perfectly fine in my current relationship. Gen, Jane, and Kate are engaged. You, my dear, are the one who needs to find Mr. Right."

Jane giggled. "Remember when you were young and you did the Ouija board thing? We always gave triple dog dares to try to conjure up dead celebrities."

She gave a mock shiver. "Those things creep me out. I'm scared of them."

Gen shrugged. "If I wasn't engaged I would give it a shot. Go ahead, Ken. I triple dog dare you."

Ken pushed the book to the side of the table. "I think true love has stolen your brain cells."

"Oh, come on. We don't do anything crazy anymore."

Kate chuckled. "Remember when we smoked that joint from my mom while we watched *9 to 5*?"

Arilyn hiccupped. "That was hysterical. Half of the night is one fuzzy, pleasant blur."

"Hey, you cut me out of that one," Gen said indignantly.

"You were working," Kate reminded. "Plus it's illegal. We can get away with stuff like that—we're not doctors."

"Oh. Well, then I get a do-over. Let's do something tonight."

Kate laughed. "Like what? Drugs are out, I'm done breaking the law for a while. We're already drinking. And it's not like we can streak naked through the streets of Verily."

"Hmm, that's not a bad one," Kennedy muttered.

"Not going to happen."

"Let's all do the spell together!" Gen shouted.

Kate pressed her fist to her lips. Closed her eyes. Then whispered, "I did it."

Ken stared. "Did what?"

"The spell. I completed the love spell."

"Before Slade?"

Kate nodded. "Yep. Not that I think it has anything to do with me and Slade ending up together, but it was a bit weird. So I'm not doing it again."

Jane laughed. "I'm not doing it either. I'm head over heels for Tim, and I don't want to screw it up."

Gen waved her hand in the air. "I'm happy too, but I'll do it. Arilyn? Ken? You in?"

"You want to do it here?" Ken asked. "Now?"

"Sure. Read it aloud and tell us what we need."

Arilyn nibbled on her lower lip. "I don't know about this. I really don't believe in the occult or spells or false deities."

"Come on, A, please? For me?"

Arilyn seemed to notice Gen's excitement over doing something silly and girly, and finally nodded. "Okay, I'm in."

"Yes! What do we need to do?"

Kennedy flipped through the pages. "We need two sheets of paper each to make a list of all the qualities we need and want in our soul-mate. We burn one, then go home and slip the other under the mattress." She paused, reading through the rest of the short book. "Then we chant something to Earth Mother." She recited the words.

"That doesn't sound bad," Arilyn remarked. "Like a blessing and gratitude to the earth. I can do that."

Gen scrambled off the floor and disappeared down the hall. She returned with a paper, pen, and a tapered candle. "Kate, can you grab a pot from the kitchen?"

Jane laughed. "You guys are crazy."

Gen distributed the paper and pens. "Now everyone make their lists."

Kennedy spoke up. "It says not to think too long. Just trust your inner gut and write from the heart."

She bent her head and wrote the number 1. What did she want in a soul-mate? What did she need? With the pleasant buzz of the margaritas softening her barriers, and the comfort of her friends around her, she didn't try to rationalize or ponder too hard. She wrote down the qualities of the man she'd always dreamed of in her secret soul. Qualities no man could really possess, of course. But she played fair and didn't try to get around the instructions. After all, that was the main rule in a girl's game. Treat the game with respect no matter how silly you may think it is.

After they filled out both sheets of paper, Kate lit the candle and placed it inside the steel pot. "Okay, Ken, read out the chant and we'll put our papers into the fire."

She recited the short phrases, and Arilyn and Gen followed. Then the papers caught flame and shriveled to black. Little pieces flew and drifted into the air as the fire burned. Everyone watched in silence until the last of the paper disappeared.

Ken stuck out her little finger. "Pinky promise we all take the second sheet of paper and place it under our mattresses when we get home."

"Pinky promise," Arilyn said solemnly.

"Pinky promise," Gen said.

Ken dropped her hand. They all stared at each

other, as if for one second they almost regretted the impulsive, juvenile actions of a love spell.

Almost.

Then Ken burst into laughter. Everyone followed, until tears streamed down her eyes and Gen swore she peed her pants.

A love spell.

As. If.

"YOU LOOK WEIRD, DUDE."

Nate stared at his brother. He was flanked by his two buddies from the job site, who were already wasted. Connor tipped back his third beer and studied him over the bottle. Nate reached for patience and responded. "Weird how?"

"You cut your hair. Chicks dig rocker hair. Now you look normal."

"Normal is good."

"I guess. And why do you have that stubble around your mouth? You coulda borrowed my razor."

Nate took a sip of his beer, wiped the table, and stared at the pretzels in the wooden bowl with trepidation before deciding to forgo them. He rarely succumbed to communal bowls of food. Too many people didn't wash their hands and as a result spread a crapload of germs. "It's a goatee. I'm growing it out on purpose."

His brother blanched. "You're not getting girly on me, are you, dude? Metrosexual or some stuff like that?"

"No. Just changing up my look before my mixer."

"Okay. Going to the gym is cool, though. You do weights?"

He avoided his brother's gaze. "Yep." *No. I danced around like a girl to reveal my inner goddess. So humiliating.*

"Good, gyms are great to hit up women. Any prospects yet?"

"Soon."

The waitress came back to the table. "Another round?"

Connor reached out and placed a hand on the curve of her denim-clad hip. "Absolutely, darlin', keep them coming. But make sure you come check on us often. I haven't seen such a beautiful face in a long time. You inspire me to be a better man."

Huh? That didn't even make sense. Wasn't that from *Jerry Maguire* or some chick flick? Nate waited for the scowl or her disgusted expression from such a lame line. Instead, she beamed and winked. "Part of my job, honey. Make sure you keep the tips coming, too."

Connor laughed and leaned back in his chair. "Saucy one. May have to ask her out."

Irritation hit. How the hell did his brother get away with this crap? Nate would've had a black eye and a pending harassment lawsuit by now. Kennedy would've killed him for such an approach. Was it just the bars? Maybe a different level of social interaction was expected at these establishments?

He decided to ask. "Hey, have you ever had a woman turn you down?"

His brother snorted. "'Course not. I keep telling you, Ned—ugh, Nate—just compliment their physical beauty and be direct. Women hate flowery shit, pussyfooting around, and a man who's afraid to make a move. Got it?"

No. "Yeah, got it."

Jerry clinked his bottle against Connor's. "Nice to see you here, Ned. Taking a break from rockets to slum with your brother?"

Connor punched his arm. "Call him Nate."

"Oh. K. Hey, I heard you put in the application for the supervisor position. What's that about?"

Connor shrugged. "I got the time in, know the jobs, and handle the men well. Why not?"

Jerry's brown eyes were shot with red. His laugh was a little slurred, and Nate couldn't say he cared for the guy, but he'd been Connor's friend and coworker for years. "Not for nothing, but Ed's going for the position. Might as well pull out now."

His brother stiffened. An expression of disappointment flickered over his face and was quickly replaced with something else. Something that made Nate suck in his breath.

Self-loathing.

"Oh, didn't know Ed wanted it. Maybe I should pull out."

Jerry slapped him on the back. "Yeah, he got that wrapped like a Christmas present, buddy. The foreman loves him, and he's got a college education in management. No need to waste your time."

"Why is it a waste of time?" Nate asked. "Connor has just as good a shot as Ed."

His brother studied his beer bottle. "Nah, Jerry's right. No need putting myself through the bullshit when it's already decided. Probably a lot of extra hours and responsibility. Who needs it?"

"Absolutely," Jerry agreed. "Did you snap up that pretty little thing already, Con? When are you going to learn to share and not hog all the women?"

"Part of my charm," Connor joked halfheartedly before lapsing into silence and nursing his beer. Nate sensed a shift of energy, a darkness that settled over him like a pissed-off spirit intent on a haunting. Funny, his brother always acted like he enjoyed his low-maintenance life. Refused to go for his degree at home, laughing as he gave his usual reasoning that there was only one brain in the family. When the hell had they become embroiled in stereotypes? It had been going on for so long that it was second nature—he even remembered his mother stating repeatedly that he had the brains and his brother the looks. Who was she to judge them? She'd left to pursue her own life and knew shit about them.

It seemed like all of Connor's confidence was directed only toward scoring with women. Maybe Nate could help turn it around. He spoke up. "Promise me you'll keep your application in for supervisor anyway. Forget about the competition."

His brother snorted. "Why bother? Don't worry about it."

"I'm serious. I've seen you on the site. You know how to relate well to the crew, you know scheduling, and you're smart."

His gaze swung around. A flicker of resentment shot at him. "No, I'm not. And I don't want to talk about it anymore."

"You think you can handle it, don't you?" Nate challenged, not willing to let up yet.

"Yeah. But Ed likes to wear those fancy suits and meet with the managers afterward. He's in the club. Got a degree. Talks smart like you. I'm not in his league, man."

Time for the big guns. "Con. Do me a solid."

His brother gasped. "No fucking way. You can't use a solid for that!"

"Yes, I can, there's no rules to it. Now you have to do it."

"That's like a pinky promise for girls! We did that years ago—you can't hold me to a solid."

Nate grinned. "I can and I just did. Do it or I'll call you a pussy for the rest of your life."

Connor glared. "This is the stupidest thing I've ever heard."

Nate drained his beer. "Whatever. You want to pretend you're not scared to go after a big-time job, go ahead. Pussy."

"Fuck! Fine, I'll keep in for it. But no more solids after this one. I call the game completely off."

Nate bit back a satisfied chuckle. Got him. They'd been addicted to the Cartoon Network show *Regular Show* for years, and knew every episode by heart. When one of the characters on the show tells the other one to *do him a solid*, it was the ultimate dare. If you didn't take the challenge, you were termed "pussy" for the rest of your natural life.

He still remembered when his brother got him to drive around the block stark naked to prove no one paid attention on the road. Yeah. He'd proven his brother wrong on that, especially when the police came to the door from a 911 call tracking his plate.

Bastard.

His brother was pissed, but Nate could live with it. He relaxed and drank his beer.

eight

"ARE WE READY, ladies?"

They sat on stools at the Purple Haze bar in Verily. The bar was a mix between the casualness of Mugs and the upscale restaurant Cosmos. Done in various shades of violet, from the fabric seats to the walls, it was decorated in trendy glass, mirrors, and lights to give it a fresh feel. Computer monitors were set up along with large television screens and attracted the technology set who wanted to drink and not stray too far from their gadgets. It was popular with the after-work crowd, but Tuesday nights were pretty dead and would give them the privacy they needed to give this exercise the right atmosphere.

Kennedy waited for her friends to respond. It was a daring approach that had never been done before, and she was afraid they'd object. Kate and Arilyn shared a look, then firmly nodded.

"I would normally never help employ such tactics, but after what you've told us, I'm in," Arilyn said.

Kate sighed. "When I heard about poor Bernadette being confronted about approaching thirty, I wanted to bop him over the head myself." She gave an evil grin. "But this is so much better."

Kennedy laughed. "Remember, we start small and follow his lead. I don't want to terrify the guy, just get him to a point where he stops and thinks before he speaks. He has a good heart. Nate just listened to the wrong advice about how to deal with women, and we need to straighten him out. No one ever took the time to show him the right way. But he has a wicked sense of humor, he's smart and successful, and now he looks the part."

At that moment, Nate strolled through the door, surveyed the crowd, and seeing Kennedy from across the room, locked on his target. Her heart beat a bit faster in spite of herself, and her tummy slid, flipped, and settled. The sexy scruff on his face would make a woman itch to touch it, trace the lines of those full lips, look deep into his eyes. If she could spot them behind those glasses. She made a mental note: next up, contact lenses and a decent wardrobe. He wore his usual staple outfit: lab coat, shiny cheap pants, orthopedic-type shoes—did he have a foot problem she didn't know about?—and sported a trail of tiny circles of coffee splatters down the front of his shirt. But he never broke the gaze as he crossed the room and stood in front of them. "Hey."

She fought a smile at his usual brevity. "Hey."

"Sorry I didn't get to change. Nice to see you again, Kate. Arilyn."

Kate spoke up first. "I hope you're enjoying your journey here at Kinnections. Kennedy is a master at transforming clients and building confidence."

"Yes. She also would've been quite helpful torturing prisoners of war to make them speak."

Kennedy puffed up with sheer pride at Nate's backhanded compliment.

"Are you experiencing any difficulty in your path to true love?" Arilyn asked. "I can always book a session with you to help overcome any barriers."

"No, thank you. After a cracked-up Japanese warrior ripped up my body, a cranky gay man attacked me with scissors, and I got my ass handed to me by a Zumba session, I think I'm good. What's on today's agenda?"

Kate laughed. Kennedy shook her head. "Don't be so dramatic, it all worked out fine. We're going to do role-play. It seems that one of your limitations is social conversation."

"So I've been told."

"We're going to run through some simple first meets with different outcomes so you get more used to handling various women and topics of conversation."

"And to think I gave up a prostate exam for this."

"Why don't we warm up with a round of speed questions?"

Kate clapped. "I love that game. Like *Jeopardy* but better."

Nate cocked his head and considered. She bet he assumed he'd be good at the speed round since he was probably the trivia king. She smothered a laugh. He'd realize quickly how different this was.

"What's involved?"

"We throw out scenarios and you give us a quick answer. It's to build up your reflex ability to approach situations in the proper way without overthinking. Let's get you set up with a drink first."

"Darth Maultini, please."

They stopped and stared. "A what?"

He shot them a suffering expression. "One ounce sweet vermouth, one ounce vodka, one ounce whiskey, two ounces pomegranate cherry, and two lemon wedges cut up and spread around the glass."

Kennedy's mouth dropped open. "You have got to be kidding me. How about a beer?"

Kate giggled. "No, I remember it. Got it covered. *Star Wars* junkie, huh?"

"A bit."

Kate ordered the drink while Kennedy fished out the contraption from her tote bag. "Now, we'll just slide this on you and get started."

"What the hell is that?"

Kennedy widened her eyes in the innocent doe look men died for. "A simple gadget that will be able to read your responses and catalog electrical sensors to correct behavior."

Nate took a step back as if she'd confronted him with a python. "It's a collar. A dog collar."

Arilyn spoke in her soothing, melodic voice that usually hypnotized her prey. "No, of course it's not a dog collar. Think of it as a band with a mini computer installed in order to sense bodily reactions and categorize behavior."

He pushed a hand through his hair and let out a half laugh. "Oh, you both are good. Brilliant, as a matter of fact. It's an electric dog collar. Put whatever spin you want on it. I'm not putting that thing on."

Kate slid his whacked-out martini drink across the bar. "The path to true love is never easy. You don't strike me as a quitter, Nate. And you may not have enjoyed what Kennedy threw at you, but take a few minutes and really think. Have the steps you completed worked? Do you feel better about yourself? Do you feel you grew as a person and are closer to finding your soul-mate?"

Kennedy shared a look with her friends. God, they were amazing together. Each of their assets and energy melded to cocoon their target to push them to goal. They waited. He stood perfectly still, studying them, thinking out every step, and then gauged the weapon she still held. Several minutes ticked by.

"Fine."

She didn't hesitate. Kennedy slid the slim leather collar around his neck, closed the clasp, and tugged his shirt up so most of it was covered. The controller was hidden in her tote for the moment. No reason to freak him out more or warn him of what was about to happen. The element of surprise was key, and if she explained too much, he'd walk out without a backward glance.

"Now what?" he asked.

"Relax, we'll start easy. I'll begin. Do I look fat in these pants?"

He blanched and choked on his drink. "Those types of questions? Are you kidding me? You're setting me up for failure."

Kate clucked her tongue. "Nate, that was the easiest one on the planet. Just say no. No, you don't look fat. No, your makeup's perfect. No, those shoes look great. No, it's my fault, not yours. Get it?"

He finished choking, wiped his mouth, and dragged in a breath. Kennedy almost felt sorry for him, but it was necessary in order to get him to the next level. Her finger stroked the button hidden in her tote. "Ready?"

"Yeah. I got this."

Kennedy threw out the questions in rapid succession. "Do I look fat in these pants?"

"No."

"Do you want me to pick up the tab this time?"

"No."

"Are you gay?"

"No."

"Are you just looking for a one-night stand?"

"No."

"Do you have any issues I need to be concerned about?"

"No."

"Do you find me attractive?"

"Yes."

She grinned and gave him a thumbs-up signal. He let out the breath he'd been holding, took another sip, and relaxed his shoulders. "Nice warm-up. Now let's beef it up. Kate, go ahead."

"I'm your hot waitress. I just came up to the table and took your order. Give me your best line."

"Make sure you come check on me often. I haven't seen such a beautiful face in a long time. You inspire me to be a better man."

Kennedy barely managed not to gag on that line.

So she pressed the button.

Nate jerked and shot off the bar stool. The electrical buzz hit his skin, and she imagined little tingles of energy rippling down his body, causing enough pain to force him to focus. His fingers drifted up to his neck, and he whipped around. His gaze narrowed.

"What was that?" he hissed. "That hurt!"

"Honestly, Nate, that was one of the worst lines I've ever heard."

"Quite cheesy," Kate agreed.

"You electrocuted me." He stated the words with sheer amazement.

She waved a hand in the air. "It's just a little behavior correction technique. A slight tingle to remind you when you go off track."

"You're all crazy. What type of agency is this?"

Arilyn clucked softly. "We're so sorry, Nate, but this really is for the best. Now, why don't we try again?"

He stared at each of them, trying to comprehend how three deadly females had just given him the equivalent of an electric shock, yet somehow managed to look completely innocent. "You don't want to give up when it's just gotten interesting, do you?" Kennedy asked.

He touched the collar and narrowed his gaze. "My brother just used that line last night and the woman loved it. Are you sure you know what you're doing?"

Kate gave an irritated sigh. "She's the exception. Women hate that stuff. Is your brother Brad Pitt? Or maybe she knows him casually and it was a joke?"

Nate rubbed his head. "Not Pitt. He got her to laugh."

"Forget what Connor does and says. You need a different approach or you'll get slaughtered."

"Fine. Let's do this again."

They shared a glance. Kennedy nodded. Kate picked the reins back up.

"Picture your first date. She leans in after the meal and asks what's next on the menu. What do you say back?"

He blinked. "Dessert."

She hit the button.

He twitched and cursed viciously under his breath. "What?"

"That sounded like you wanted to take her to bed. Not cool."

"I meant just dessert, for God's sake, not sex."

"Sounded a bit creepy to me. Your response should have been, whatever you like. She was really asking about the next step with you, not the menu."

"That's stupid! Why would she use a food connotation?"

Kennedy shrugged. "Women are deep."

Arilyn jumped in. "Clear your mind and picture an unyielding canvas of white."

Pure male irritation radiated from him, but he sat back down and glared at Kate. "Again."

Kate shifted on the bar stool. "Two women are talking to you together. You're attracted to one friend and not the other. What do you do?"

"Address the woman I like and ask for her number."

She hit the button.

He slapped at his neck. "What the hell did I do wrong now?"

Arilyn gave him a sad look. "Never, ever ask for a woman's number in front of her friend. It must be done privately. You set yourself up for extreme embarrassment if the one you asked out doesn't like you but the other one does, and then the one you like feels bad for her friend and the other one hates you, so it's a lose-lose situation."

"I'm going home."

Nate began to unbuckle the collar. Kennedy dove over and grabbed his hands. "I know it's confusing, but we just wanted to give you some general scenarios. The real role-play is much more important."

"What type of role-play?"

"Kate will be the first one up. She'll pretend to be a stranger at the bar, and you approach her. Conversation will go from there, and we'll be able to analyze how you interact."

He gave a disgusted sigh but stopped trying to tug off the collar. "Is she gonna judge me on my first pick-up line? I suck at that."

"No, just say hello, she won't be hostile. This exercise is about the flow of good conversation, not approach. If there's one thing I teach as the cardinal rule for first meets, it's this. Say hello, give your name, and ask how she is. Simple. Not rocket science."

"Ha, ha."

"Arilyn and I will watch from the end of the bar."

"Great. I feel like I'm auditioning for *America's Got Talent*. But instead of the X, I get electrocuted."

"Good luck."

They moved a few seats down. Kennedy gave him credit. Most men couldn't handle the pressure of role-play, and though Nate's face reflected misery, he drew himself to full height and dove in.

"Hey . . . My name's Nate, how are you?"

Kate swiveled around on her stool and gave him a sexy smile. She'd transformed into the one-night competitor. This woman wanted hot sex, one night to forget her troubles, and had no intention of settling into a long-term relationship. Kate practically purred, her gaze caressing and analyzing his entire body from under heavy lidded eyes. She was a walking, talking cliché that most men could never resist.

Including Nate.

"Hey, darlin'," she drawled. "My name's Wanda. And my crappy day just got a whole lot better."

"Mine, too." He sat next to her, his confidence shooting back up in the face of Kate's obvious flirtation. "Do you come here often?"

Kennedy winced but let it go. Terrible line, but not *Titanic* bad.

"Yes, every night. And why haven't I seen you around?" Kate tossed her hair, and reached out to trail a finger down his arm. She leaned in and Kennedy knew he got a nice shot of cleavage.

He cleared his throat. "Just moved into town. So, Wanda, what do you do?"

Hmm, he liked to focus on career. "I'm a waitress."

Kennedy held her breath.

"That's hard work. No wonder you had a bad day."

She let out her breath. Nice recovery. No judgment or abrupt ending—she guessed Connor had never broken up with anyone in the food industry.

"Oh, yeah. Hours on my feet with these heels." Kate flexed her leg and Nate's gaze snagged on sexy three-inch heels. "I really need to relax. Lie down. Maybe get out of here. What do you think?"

Kate's face screamed sex. Nate widened his eyes as if he had hit the jackpot. Kennedy waited and hoped for a particular response.

She didn't get it.

"Well, I would say we should get to know one another a bit better. See if we're suited. But why not? Let's go. My place is close."

Ah, yes. The little head always won out over the big one.

Buzz.

"Son of a bitch! She came on to me!"

Kennedy gave him an encouraging smile. "You were doing really great until that point. You just forgot the goal. You want to meet your wife, not hook up for one night of nonsense sex."

"There's nothing wrong with no-commitment sex if both parties agree. Connor raised me on that philosophy."

"You need to keep the main goal in sight. A short sexual affair or a one-nighter will throw your game off, and no one wants to date a male slut. You want a nice girl, right?"

"For God's sake, I'm not a male slut. Is this your normal behavior training class? This must be illegal." He looked about ready to storm out again, but Kate touched his arm and murmured something in his ear. A few beats passed, and finally, he gave a curt nod. He shot Kennedy one last glare, sat back down, and refocused on Kate.

"That was a close call," Arilyn whispered.

"Yeah, but I think we got him now. He's going to look at this as a challenge and refuse to lose."

"So, what do you say, big boy? Wanna get out of here?"

Kennedy tried not to laugh at Kate's slutty voice, and knew her friend was enjoying the hell out of her character. She usually played the sweet girl next door.

"Actually, you seem like a fascinating woman. I'd like to get to know you better first. Tell me about yourself."

Kennedy grinned. Nice.

Kate did a little pout. "I guess we can talk for a few

more minutes. Well, I'm a single mom, I work at Mugs, and I'm trying to put myself through school."

"What are you studying?"

"Massage therapy." She batted her eyelashes. "Want to be one of my practice clients?"

He didn't bite this time. "I just read a study quoting an increased space in the market for massage therapists. There's quite a demand lately. Experts are citing more people need careers with jobs at graduation, so that was a smart move."

Kennedy puffed up with pride. Arilyn gave her a thumbs-up sign.

"It's nice to have a man finally understand that. I want to be able to properly support my daughter."

"How old is she?"

"Twelve. Super smart and beautiful. Hope she does better than her mom."

Kate put a bitter twist into the words to see what reaction ensued.

Nate turned serious. "Seems to me you're teaching her to stand up, be independent, and follow your passion. I'd be proud to have a mom like you."

Emotion clogged Kennedy's throat. Kate looked surprised, then a bit misty-eyed. She squeezed Nate's hand. "Thank you. I really like you. Let's go to my place so I can show you how much."

"Okay."

Kennedy closed her eyes. And pushed the button.

"Ow! What'd I do now?"

Kennedy shook her head in disappointment. "No

sex, Nate. You spent a few minutes with her. Is that enough to tell you she's worth a long-term dating relationship? Sex is serious business and not something to be handled lightly."

He rubbed his neck and muttered something foul under his breath. "I liked her, okay! And there's nothing wrong with wanting to have sex."

Arilyn smiled with sympathy. "We understand. But at Kinnections, we try to guide clients to think of sex as a big turning point. We encourage steady dating and a monogamous relationship before sexual activity."

Nate glowered at both of them. "Then you should've told me that so I know the damn rules." He drained the rest of his drink. "Come on. Let's do this."

"Umm, I'm done with my part," Kate said. "Arilyn, you're next."

Nate stared her down as she stepped up to the bar stool like he was a pitcher ready to strike out Babe Ruth. Kennedy wondered if this was a bad idea. He liked competition and enjoyed the win. He now viewed the buzzer as something to beat or die, and Arilyn was standing right in his way. Kate took Arilyn's place next to Kennedy and shot her a worried look.

Arilyn turned her back and waited. She was about to introduce her client to the next female prototype: eager to commit, fall in love tonight, and live happily ever after. Nate leaned in.

"Hey. My name's Nate. How are you?"

Arilyn shifted and gave him a huge smile. "Hi, Nate. I'm Wanda. It's nice to meet you. What brings you out on a weeknight? Hard day at work? Do you live in the area? What do you do?"

She threw the questions out with deft ease, meant to keep a man's mind in a tailspin. Nate fielded the questions and took his time answering. "I felt like unwinding with a drink tonight. I'm an aerospace engineer, and I just moved to Verily."

Arilyn pumped up her usual calm aura to supersize. "Wow, that's pretty awesome. I own a bakery in town, and work all the time, and said to myself tonight, 'Self, you need to get out more and have some fun.' So I took myself down to Purple Haze, and now here you are! Kismet, right? Do you know what kismet is?"

He never faltered, his entire attention focused on not failing this task. "Yes, kismet is a wonderful thing. I agree about the work issue. I'm currently doing a lot of research for a firm looking to put the private sector into space, and it's hard to remind myself to get out and relax."

Kate looked impressed, but Arilyn wasn't done with him.

"Are you married? Have kids? I'm really looking to settle down and have kids, and I'm so impressed with your career! I mean, so many men nowadays just want to find themselves and make no money and be drains on society. Look, I usually don't dive right in, but I like you. Want to have dinner with me? I want to meet a serious partner who's done partying and wants to get married quickly. I just sense you feel the same way, Nate. Kismet, right? So, what do you think?"

Sweat beaded his forehead. Kennedy leaned forward. This was the man's wet dream come true—a woman to get serious and be ready to talk marriage right from the gate. She'd coached Arilyn to offer him his dream woman and see how he liked it. His brow crunched as he seemed to try desperately to figure out the correct approach not to get zapped. Her hand paused on the button.

"I'd love to have dinner." His voice came out strained. "And yes, I'm looking for a serious relationship."

She dropped the controller on her lap.

"Wonderful! This is such a relief. I sensed an immediate connection between us and just feel that you, as a businessman, will completely understand me."

"Why do you feel better understood by businessmen?" he asked.

"Well, when we have the babies, I intend on going straight back to work and hiring a nanny. My bakery chain is everything, and I don't feel I need to give up anything. I intend to have it all, Nate, and hopefully with you." Arilyn chirped out the last of her words with a confident smile and waited for complete agreement.

The words spewed out of him. "I don't believe a woman should rush right back to work after giving birth, and I don't believe in nannies. You'll have to give up your job and stay home with them, of course. That's the only proper way to raise children."

Kate gasped. Arilyn stared.

And Kennedy pressed the button.

"Son of a bitch!" He jumped and slapped at his nape. He curled his hands into tight fists and gritted his teeth. "What'd I say now? I nailed that scenario!"

Kennedy sighed. "Why on earth would you believe women have to give up their jobs to become mothers? Haven't you heard of balance?"

"Connor explained that if women keep themselves in the work force, they end up having affairs and breaking up the family. The children are the ones to suffer. I sure as hell am not going to have that type of life for my kids. Not after seeing what my own mother pulled."

Sadness leaked into her heart. Her friends were quiet as they pondered his words. Arilyn was the one to speak finally in a quiet, supportive voice. "I completely understand why you would think that. But not all women have affairs or run off. This is the point of the search. You want to find women who have similar ideals, but if you close yourself down to possibilities, you may miss out on the right one. Love can change people, make them compromise."

He vibrated with unspoken tension. "Why would I want to waste my time chasing the wrong woman?"

"Because the wrong one can end up being your true love," Kate answered. "It happened with me. When I met my fiancé, Slade, I categorized him as the completely wrong type for me. We were opposites and held different core philosophies. But we fell in love. Changed. Grew. And if I had stuck with the ideal man I had in my head, I would've missed out on the greatest thing in my life."

Raw yearning reared up and swallowed Kennedy whole. She breathed through the sudden emotion and need to experience what Kate had: true love. Real love. Full of mess and hard work and worth every moment. She averted her gaze and concentrated on the buzzer, trying to pull herself back together. What was wrong with her? She'd never experienced such a primitive longing to throw herself into a relationship no matter the odds. The long line of men behind her were like ghosts, haunting her future and reminding her over and over she'd never be fulfilled.

"I understand."

Arilyn slid off the stool and gave him a hug. "That was a big moment, Nate. Thank you for sharing with us."

She imagined that a slight red tinged his cheeks. "Sure. Are we done?"

"No," Kate said. "Kennedy goes next."

She lifted her head.

His gaze locked on hers. Those green eyes burned with a banked fire that promised everything . . . if she was brave enough to take it. The odd thought skittered through her mind, but it was too bizarre to analyze, so she walked slowly over and took her place on the stool.

"Dare I ask who has the buzzer?"

"Kate. She's fair."

"And what should I expect from you?"

A smile touched her lips. He'd ditched the awful cologne. His natural scent swarmed over her and wrapped her in spice, soap, and lemon. "Everything you hate."

He smiled back. Dropped his voice. "Bring it."

Goose bumps broke out on her flesh. She squeezed her thighs against the sudden wet ache throbbing in her core, as excitement and challenge woke up her nerve endings. Her body hummed and prepped for the mental battle about to begin, responding as if he had just ripped off her clothes, spread her on the bar, and pleasured her mercilessly with his tongue and hands and teeth.

"Keep looking at me like that and you'll get more than you bargained for."

She shivered at his words. "Bring it."

He growled something under his breath.

"Okay, guys, you can begin."

Kate's voice drifted in and broke up the bubble. Kennedy turned her back on him and waited till she heard his voice.

"Hey. My name's Nate. How are you?"

"Hi, Nate. My name's Wanda. What's up?"

He slouched comfortably against the bar. "Just relaxing after a hard day's work. How about you?"

"Same."

"What do you do?"

"I'm a makeover consultant for a matchmaking agency."

He never missed a beat. "Bet you meet a lot of interesting people. Matchmaking agencies are growing bigger. You're savvy to get into such an industry."

Her smile dazzled. "Thank you so much. I love my work. It's my entire life. I can't imagine ever giving it up for anything."

Nate positioned his body so his legs straddled her stool. It was a power move that forced her to get close and personal. Fascinated, she waited as he gave an easy grin and closed the distance between them. She could see the perfect curve of his lip. "Anything?" he murmured. "Even love?"

She waited for him to get buzzed for that one, but nothing happened. "The person who truly loves me would never ask me to give it up."

"Touché. What type of hobbies do you enjoy, Wanda?"

"Anything physical. Rock climbing, kayaking, hiking. I hate stationary type of sports."

"Like what?"

"Like golf. Golf sucks."

The muscle by his eye ticked, then stopped. "Would you be willing to try golf? Maybe you'd like it."

"I doubt it. I dislike boring men."

"What type of man do you consider boring?"

She smiled sweetly. "You know, nerd types. Engineers, accountants, careers involving science or math. Ick. I like the passionate, artistic, creative types. The brooding actor or passionate writer or inspired yoga teacher. What do you do, Nate?"

His gaze shred past her barriers and ripped them off. "I'm an aerospace engineer. I love golf. I can't write, do art, and I suck at Zumba. But I think you're an incredible woman and would love to get to know more about you. Have dinner with me."

Dizziness swooped through her. She clutched the edge of the bar to steady herself, but he was already there, grabbing her arm in a strong, stable grip. Kennedy pursed her lips and stood her ground. "We're complete opposites. I don't think it will work between us. But thanks for the conversation."

A low chuckle rumbled from his chest. "Tell you what. You answer one question for me. If you get it right, I'll prove we're meant to try dinner at least. You get it wrong, I'll politely step away and thank you for your time."

Again, she waited for the buzzer that never came. Damn you, Kate. Intrigued, she studied him under her lashes. "What question?"

"You have to agree to the deal first. Get it right, I buy you dinner. Deal?"

"What if I just lie and say I don't know it?"

He moved to whisper the answer in near her ear. "You won't. I trust you."

A shudder wracked her body at his intimate tone. His breath rushed warm and sweet and stirred the hair at her temple. "Okay. Ask your question."

"I'm a physicist who works on researching advanced propulsion in rockets. I base many of my theories and core findings on Newton's Third Law of Motion."

She feigned boredom. "So?"

"What is the main assumption in Newton's law?"

The air left her lungs in a soft whoosh. Shock overtook her and claimed her words. Her mouth unhinged and Kennedy realized she must look ridiculous. She snapped her mouth closed. "You can't ask me that question."

"Why not?" he drawled.

"Because, because it's impossible. A makeover consultant doesn't know science and physics and all that stuff. Ask me something else."

"But that's the question we agreed on," he pointed out. "If you don't know the answer, I understand. Remember, I trust you to tell me the truth."

She glared, hating him for putting her in this delicate position. For God's sake, how could he sense something no one else ever knew about her? That underneath all her girly clothes and flirty actions and sarcastic wit, she was a closet nerd? Sure, they had tossed around a few ideas about velocity during their ice cream outing, but this seemed different. She'd been distracted before, lulled into a false sense of security by the sugar rush—but right now she was stone cold sober. And his gaze challenged her, as if he was openly forcing her to admit she knew things she shouldn't. Things she denied. Her past reared up to haunt her. All those years stuck in her room, alone, had turned her into a book freak. The clear lines of math and science had soothed her need for answers and fed her brain, but she'd forced herself to become someone else, and made sure that knowledge of Manolos and the latest hot handbag took the place of aerospace dynamic theory and Newton's Laws of Motion.

She'd lie. He'd never know. Hell, it was a ridiculous scenario anyway, and Kate should have been hitting that damn button already. She set her jaw. Opened her mouth. And spoke.

"In every interaction, there is a pair of forces acting on the two interacting objects. The size of the forces on the first object equals the size of the force on the second object. The direction of the force on the first object is opposite to the direction of the force on the second object. Forces come in pairs. Therefore, Newton's law assumes for every action, there is an equal and opposite reaction."

Triumph gleamed in his eyes. Kennedy stared at him, horrified but somehow helpless to avert her gaze. He brought the whole charade home by lifting her hand to his lips, and pressing a hot kiss in the center of her palm. "Thank you, Wanda. And now it will be my pleasure to take you to dinner."

"I—I—I—"

"That was incredible!" Kate shrieked. She rushed over and practically jumped up and down. "I can't believe it. You listened to us and followed through exactly. You were nonjudgmental, focused, funny, and intelligent. Kennedy, wasn't that a triumph?"

She forced a weak smile. "Yeah. Really great stuff."

Arilyn floated over. "What a pleasure to watch. I can't wait till Ken sets up your mixer. I think you're going to be surprised at the number of quality matches you'll have. Thanks for having an open mind. And we're really sorry about the buzzer."

Nate smiled. "No problem. I guess I did need a bit of a hard-core approach."

Kate laughed and put her hands on both of their shoulders. "I think—oh!"

With a sharp yelp, her friend crashed onto the floor in a heap of limbs. Nate threw his stool back and knelt down. "Are you okay?"

Kate's blue eyes widened with horror. Oh, no. She must have tripped on those wicked heels Kennedy had forced her to buy. She joined him on the floor, and they all crowded around Kate. "I'm sorry, Kate, I should've never made you buy those heels. They're walking death contraptions. Here, let me help you up."

"No! Ugh, I m-m-mean, no thank y-y-you. I got this." She crawled on her hands and knees and jumped up. "Um, s-s-sorry, guys, I forgot I have an important appointment and I gotta go. Arilyn, will you walk me out?"

Arilyn shot her a confused look. "Sure. Are you sure you're okay? You look like someone shocked you. Did the buzzer backfire or something?"

"I'm f-f-fine." Her laugh came out high and a bit crazy. "Stay here and finish up. I'll see you tomorrow. Nice to role-play with you, Nate."

She bolted out of the restaurant. Arilyn gave a half wave and followed her out.

"Weird," Kennedy said. "Must be all those wedding plans. Makes a woman a little crazy."

"I bet."

They stared at each other. The faint sounds of glasses clinking and people chattering drifted to her ears. Waves of heat radiated around them and tried to pull her in. "You did good."

"You owe me dinner."

Her heart stopped, then pounded so loud it echoed in her ears. "No, Wanda owed you dinner. It was role-play."

"You knew Newton's Third Law of Motion."

Annoyance flickered through her. "Who cares? Every student learns that in high school. Big deal, I remembered."

"You lie about yourself, Kennedy. Pretend to be someone you're not because you think it's easier. You think it'll protect you."

Annoyance broadened into pure temper. "Ah, so you're an expert on me now, huh? Just because you're my client doesn't mean you have any right to know about me on a personal level. Back off. My job is to find you love and I intend to do it."

"What if you already did?"

His question blew through her defenses and shattered rock and brick and stone. Kennedy couldn't breathe, couldn't talk, and for the first time in her life, felt on the verge of a panic attack. She shook her head and denied his words. "Don't. You'll only end up hurting yourself. Do you understand?"

Frustration simmered in his eyes, on his face. He seemed to choose his words carefully, as if he had reached a turning point and made a rational decision to take a leap. "What if I believe in the risk? What if I think she's worth it?"

The panic slowly drained away and was replaced by a bitter realization and sadness she didn't want to deal with. Hell, she had no idea *how* to deal with it. In some bizarre way, Nate had worked his way past her walls and reached a part of her she'd never realized she had. But she knew it was an illusion. She'd made a promise to find him happiness, and it wasn't with her. Nate deserved a like-minded woman to settle down with, have babies with, and grow old with. Someone with no screwed-up issues. She shone on the surface, was broken on the inside, and could never give Nate the depth he needed. Her punishment in this life was the constant craving to move on, searching for something that wasn't even out there, a peace and stability with the one man she never seemed to find. No, she wasn't good for him, and she needed to protect him from a temporary weakness of attraction and sex.

Her heart hardened. She made sure she spoke in a cold, firm voice. "She's not, Nate. And she never will be. Not with you."

He jerked back only once. Stiffened his shoulders. And nodded. "Got it." He disguised the hurt, but she knew her comment hit home and pierced deep. "What's next?"

"Saturday. Mall. Meet you at ten?"

She wished his gaze didn't burn, disrobe, and try to expose her for the fake she was. Kennedy made sure she kept the bright smile pasted to her face. A heavy silence pulsed between them with unspoken words. "Fine." Then he left without another word.

Kennedy squeezed her arms around her chest for warmth and reminded herself she had done the right thing for both of them.

nine

"I HATE MALLS."

Kennedy glanced over. Nate was definitely grouchy. Why were men never pumped to get new clothes and a sizzling look? Maybe it was some type of gene the male population lacked. She felt truly sorry for them all. "Cheer up. We have a game plan, and I'm not dragging you in and out of a million stores. We need to hit the eye place first."

She walked with purpose into the vision center and spoke to the woman at the front desk. "Dr. Murphy is just running a little late. Can you take a seat?"

"Sure." She led Nate to the waiting area, but he didn't sit. Just paced back and forth. "Geez, a bit over the caffeine limit today?"

"I don't like eye doctors."

She laughed, then realized he was dead serious. A panicked gleam lit his eyes, barely visible from behind his thick frames. "She's not going to hurt you. I just want to make sure she fits the contact lenses correctly."

"No contacts."

She studied him. The stubble sculpted his jaw and lined his upper lip, giving him an edge. His brows were now perfectly separated, and the slight wave in his hair set off the hint of blond, warming his skin. But her pièce de résistance would be the glasses, and she needed to address his concerns. "Why not?"

His jaw tightened. "I don't like them."

She remained patient. "Why?"

He leaned in and hissed out the words. "I don't like anything in my eye, okay? I am not sticking my finger at my eyeball. Forget it. Let's just get out of here."

She bit back her smile. "I hear you. Everyone has something—mine happens to be the GYN. I see stir-rups and shudder."

"TMI, Ken."

She laughed. "Sorry. Look, just go through the exam and we'll talk. I don't want to make you do something you hate, but the types they have nowa-days are really different. Will you promise to try? If you hate it, we'll get you new frames and forget it."

He let out an aggravated breath. "Fine. But I won't like it."

"Nate Dunkle?"

He shot her a glare and followed the doctor into her office. The exam was short, and they were set up at the counter to try some contacts. A pretty woman in a white coat lined up some supplies. Her eyes were a star-tling blue green that contrasted dramatically with her black hair. She introduced herself as Tracey and went into her spiel about the way to wear contacts, the kind the doctor recommended, and how to maneuver them.

"What are the statistics on eye damage from con-tact lenses?" Nate asked.

"Umm, I'm not sure, but as long as you follow the instructions for care, it's pretty low."

"How low?"

Kennedy slid her hand over the counter and squeezed his hand. Hard. "Nate, most of the population wears them. Give it a try."

Tracey seemed to sense his fear and smiled brightly. "You'll look amazing. Your current frames are a bit outdated."

"How many instances have occurred with the lenses scratching a person's cornea and causing blindness?"

Tracey blinked. "Umm, I'm sure I can find out for you if I Google it."

Kennedy squeezed again. "Just try it. Now."

He muttered something under his breath and took the lens. Tracey guided him through the procedure, until both were safely in his eyes. He blinked madly and stared into the mirror. "How do they feel? They look amazing," Tracey said.

It took a while for him to answer. "Not bad. Actually, I can't even feel them."

The assistant lit up. "See, I told you. Why don't you wear these for the day, and if they work, we'll order a three-month supply."

He kept staring in the mirror as if fascinated by the technology. "Damn, everything's so clear. I can see better than with glasses."

Tracey nodded with enthusiasm. "The frames actually limit your line of vision. I'm so happy you like them. You look amazing."

Kennedy stifled her giggle. The woman seemed to know only that one word—*amazing*. But what the hell. She seemed enchanted by Nate. Another good opportunity to see if he'd learned a few lessons. "Doesn't he?" she cooed. "Wait till the females get a look at you."

Tracey looked confused. "You're not married?"

"No, Nate's free and single."

Tracey sharpened her gaze. Took in his hair, face, and new eyes. Kennedy noticed she winced at his outfit but was able to overlook it for now. "How wonderful. Well, Nate, I'd be glad to give you my number and you can call me anytime with your questions."

He was so intrigued with his reflection, he didn't answer. Kennedy nudged him again. Harder. "Oh! Yes, sounds good. I guess they make color contacts, too. I like the ones you're wearing."

Tracey shook her head. "Oh, I'm not wearing contacts; this is my real eye color."

"You have beautiful eyes," Kennedy offered.

"No, they're contacts. I can see the lines around her pupil. Her real eye color is brown."

Tracey stopped smiling. "You must be mistaken." Uh. Oh.

"No, I'm not. Just like your hair, it's obviously not black since I can see the roots coming in. How come you changed it? I like brown hair with brown eyes."

Tracey froze. Her voice dripped icicles. "I'll write up your bill, Mr. Dunkle. If you have a problem, you can call the customer care center." She stalked away, hair swishing, and Kennedy dropped her face into her hands and groaned.

"What? What'd I say?"

Kennedy wondered if another dog collar session with higher electrical shock capacity would make a difference. "You broke the cardinal rule again. Again. I thought you read *Cosmo*!"

"I do. I never said a word about her body. Or her weight, or age. I gave her a compliment."

She lowered her voice to a hiss. "Some back-handed compliment. You mentioned her *roots*. And called her a liar. Yeah, that'll get you to the first date."

His mind clicked for a few moments. Finally, he groaned. "Crap, I did. Sorry, I was distracted by being able to see so clearly. It's intriguing how sharp the world looks."

"Forget it. Let's get out of here and get you some new clothes."

She averted the stores with loud rap music and teen clothes, and started in J.Crew. She wove in and out of the Saturday crowds with the ease of an expert. He stumbled behind her, trying to keep up, muttering "Excuse me" to a bunch of people before reaching their destination. The buzz of adrenaline lit up her blood, and she needed to breathe deeply to remain calm. God, she loved shopping. Everything about it revved her up. The limitless possibilities of sales, new looks, confidence, and hope. And shoes. Oh, my, the shoes . . .

"Ken?"

"Yeah?"

"I'm scared. You have a weird look on your face."

She rolled her eyes. "Wait here." She hit the register and came back with measuring tape. "I need to confirm your sizes. Stick your arms out to the side and hold still."

He regarded her as if she had asked him to strip naked and dance on the corner of Times Square. "I'll tell you my sizes."

Kennedy wielded the tape as a weapon. "I already know you wear the wrong size. Your pants are too big for you."

"I beg your pardon."

She tamped down another laugh. He was so damn funny in his own way. "Not around the crotch. The waist." The words shot out of her mouth, and automatically her gaze lowered. She stopped laughing.

Suddenly, an image of what he would look like naked clouded her vision. Back off, girlfriend. Fantasizing about her rocket scientist was off limits. "Arms out."

This time, he obeyed. And the whole time, his gaze burned into her. Ate her up. And licked her clean. Her fingers trembled slightly as she wrapped the tape around his waist. His distinct scent hit her nostrils, and she fought the urge to bury her face into his chest and breathe in deep. His muscles jumped under her touch, and stiffened. Kennedy tried to breathe and stay calm. What was going on? She'd never been attracted to a client this intensely—let alone this type of man—in her life. "Thirty." Her voice came out husky. She eased her way up.

How had she ever thought he wasn't toned? It must have been the ill-fitting clothes. His actual chest was quite broad and had a delicious hardness underneath the cotton fabric that she itched to explore. What type of lover would he be? All focused and serious? By the book? Or so intent on her pleasure nothing else would matter?

A shudder wracked her spine. "Forty," she squeaked out.

He stared at her, unblinking, a flare of pure male lust gleaming from his greenish eyes. "Must be all that Zumba working for me."

Ken bore down and slid the tape up and around his neck. Swallowing hard, she managed to touch the two ends together. Then looked up.

His lips were a woman's dream. Full, sculpted, with that sexy stubble wrapping them around like a Christmas gift all for her. His features boasted new definition, now that the bulky frames were gone. Sharp cheekbones and a strong jaw gave him a hint of the badass type she'd always been weak for. His shoulders and biceps suddenly seemed massive and meaty, with enough power to lift her and hold her against the wall while he pounded inside her and . . .

Oh, God, she had to move on or she was going to lose it.

"We're done." She dropped the tape and scurried back. But his gaze refused to release her, and she waited for him to say something, anything to break the ratcheting sexual tension zinging her like Kate's touch.

"I don't think so." A smile touched his lips. "Not yet."

This was no timid, nerdy rocket scientist. This was all testosterone and *hear me roar* male ready to claim a woman. Last week, he'd surrendered and walked away, leaving her alone, frustrated, and sad but knowing she made the right decision. They could never be a couple. Yet here he was, confidence restored, giving her that yummy look like she was a lollipop he was dying to get his mouth on. He wasn't as meek as she originally thought.

She chose to ignore his words and hope things would return to normal. "Be right back."

She took a few deep breaths at the register and calmed her racing heart. Time to refocus her intentions and think about his future wife. Who was not her. Kennedy returned with a battle plan, in her mind and heart. No more episodes. They couldn't possibly lead to anything good.

"Let me give you the ground rules. I'll hand off the clothes, and when we have enough, we'll go to the dressing room. No questions, whines, or protests. You try everything on, and if you hate it, we'll discuss."

"What about—"

"No questions. Let's begin."

She dove for the first rack. Her fingers flew over the hangers, pulling, testing, assessing. She talked to herself under her breath, completely in the zone, and shoved items into Nate's hands in an endless motion.

"That shirt's expensive!" Nate tried to show her the price tag, but she ignored it, refusing to break rhythm. "I could get this at Target for half the price."

"Do you make six figures?"

"Yes."

"Then you can buy this shirt."

"But—"

"No talking."

Waves of frustration beat from him and attacked her, which she resolutely ignored. They moved from casual to dressy, until colors and patterns and textures surrounded her in a cushy glow that gave her a high reminiscent of smoking the joint with Kate and Arilyn. Finally, she could barely see his face peeking over the mound of clothes. "Let's take a break."

"You're certifiable. Think of the starving children in Africa. The factory workers in China. The massive layoffs in our own country."

She quirked a brow. "The economy is in desperate need of Americans spending money on products and services. I'm just trying to fulfill my patriotic duty here. Follow me to the dressing room." Kennedy set him up in the front corner and took a seat on the bench right out front. "I want to see everything. Go in exact order, since the pants I picked out work with the shirts. I hung them exactly as they should be tried on."

"These jeans are worth more than my car!"

"Then you need to upgrade your vehicle. You're being dramatic—the Tesla is much more than those jeans. Close the door, Nate."

He shot her a look and closed the door. Kennedy stifled a laugh. It took him a while before he finally shuffled out. Pissed off, he stood in front of the mirror with a sulky expression that rivaled her signature pout. Her gaze took in the total transformation she had been waiting for.

He was hot.

The dark denim cupped his ass like an adoring lover. He was slim hipped, and though not overwhelmingly tall, his stance was powerful. He didn't slouch or duck his head. He stood in front of the mirror like he owned it. That mysterious male sexuality vibe was hard to teach, and the man actually had the quality all along. It was just covered up by bad clothes and glasses.

The black button-down shirt was fitted, with embroidery down the front and large cuffs. His chest and shoulders filled out the lines nicely, begging a woman to flick open a button or two to see what lay beneath.

Oh, yeah.

Nate Ellison Raymond Dunkle had arrived.

"I've never worn stuff like this before. Feels a little weird. Do I look like an idiot?"

"No. You look amazing." He glared at her in the mirror for using Tracey's word. "Are you comfortable in this type of outfit?"

"I guess." He pulled at the cuffs and turned to the side. "Aren't the jeans too tight?"

She grinned. "No."

He rolled his eyes. "Hmm, Connor said I had a wimpy ass and to hide it in bigger clothes."

"Connor was wrong."

He swung around at her softly spoken words. She cleared her throat and changed the subject. "Speaking of your brother, I did want to discuss a possibility with you." Her approach had to be flawless or he'd get defensive. "I know you've been living together for a while, and I think it's great. I always wished I had a sister. But I also know how a roommate can affect a new romantic relationship. You want to find your wife. She wants to know you're serious about a long-term commitment. If she gets the idea you like to hang in a bachelor pad with your older brother, she may get spooked."

Nate nodded. "What do you suggest I do?"

"My friend Genevieve has a lovely bungalow in Verily. Rent's pretty cheap. She just moved in with her fiancé but doesn't want to sell it at this point. She said she'd be willing to allow Connor to move in."

Ken held her breath. He kept still, his brain obviously shifting through her scenario. She imagined him probing the weaknesses, the assets and liabilities, and the proper solution. He shook his head. "No, wouldn't work. Connor would hate Verily. He's in construction, and the job site is close to our apartment. He goes to the bar down the street every Friday and Saturday night. He's gotten into a routine, and he's happy. That's why I'm having a hard time kicking him out."

Ah, so he did want Connor to leave. That helped her overall strategy. "Understood. What if you moved to Verily?"

His gaze shot to hers. "Near you?"

She nodded. "Most of the mixers I set up for clients are in the area. It's not that much further for you to commute. And you'll have the privacy you need to begin a long-term relationship."

He studied her face for a while. Kennedy tried not to shift on the bench. Damn, his attention was like a laser pointer, leaving her nowhere to hide. "Okay."

"Huh?"

He grinned. "I'm in. Thank you for the offer."

"You're welcome." Their connection lit, caught fire, and sizzled. Why was his directness becoming so damn sexy? "Now try on the next outfit."

They rang up the purchases and hit Brooks Brothers. The stylist measured him and confirmed his sizes, then set him up with a variety of suits. He grumbled nonstop. "I don't need suits, Ken. I wear a lab coat at the office, and I tend to drop things during meals."

"Every man needs two designer suits in his closet."

"I'm not touching pink. Connor will never let me hear the end of it."

"I can live with that." She nodded at the salesman, who looked disappointed but picked out a bright red tie to match the charcoal classic three-button.

"I like the double-breasted. They wear those in the mob movies."

She rolled her eyes and waved it away. The salesman loudly agreed and put it back on the rack. "No double-breasted. It will swallow you up. You'll do better with the European cut."

"Is this my body or not?"

"I know how to dress it better."

The salesman laughed. "How long have you guys been married?"

She froze. Looked up. His gaze took, held, and silenced her. "Not long enough," he answered.

The salesman smiled. "That's nice. Trust your wife. Let's try the navy blue."

Speech still eluded her as Nate ducked into the dressing room. A few moments later, he exited and stood on the pedestal in front of the three full-length mirrors. "What do you think?"

Her girly parts flamed to life and begged for relief.

Nate Dunkle was gorgeous.

The dark blue pinstripe was a lean cut and accented the strength and grace of his body. The bright red tie gave him a flash of style, and the crisp white shirt was unmarred and showed off the toastiness to his now normal skin tone. He was pure deliciousness wrapped up for one lucky woman she was about to introduce him to.

"Perfect. You look . . . perfect."

The salesman fussed with the fabric and beamed in the mirror. Nate stared at his reflection and caught her gaze in the mirror.

"We'll take it," he said.

He stepped off and walked back to the dressing

room, closing the door behind him. She let out a shaky breath and clenched her hands into tight fists. The transformation was complete. He was ready to meet the woman of his dreams.

She ignored the strange bolt of pain that pierced her heart and chalked it up to indigestion. Nate was right. Too many salads.

She forced him into the shoe store, where she bought three pairs for him, and one for her. He lifted the bags and groaned. "I'm starving. And exhausted. My arms hurt from all the packages. Can we eat now?"

Kennedy let out a laugh. "You have no stamina, golf boy. Women do this for hours without a break or a sip of water."

"I surrender. How about pizza?"

"How about the deli? I can get something healthy."

"Done." They ordered, found a table in the food court, and began to eat. Nate spread out a bunch of napkins first and lined the white Formica tabletop before resting his elbows on the edge. A group of teens lingered in the corner, tattoos, heavy makeup, and various piercings pegging them as the rebels. Or maybe that was the cool group now. Thank God, she was out of school. "Did you live at the mall when you were in high school?" Nate asked, taking a bite of his roast beef sandwich.

She shrugged and picked at her perfectly rolled oven-roasted turkey breast. She was so sick of lean meat. She eyed Nate's club roll with longing. Maybe a pickle would help liven up her taste buds. "Didn't most kids?"

"Nah. I went once on a Friday night and tried to fit in. Got beat up in the parking lot. Then they swiped my video game I'd saved months for."

Kennedy looked up. He told the tale with no emotion, as if reciting a narrative from a book, but something deep inside her lunged up from the darkness and clawed for the light. "Were you bullied in school?"

"Yep." He bit into a potato chip. "Can't blame them. I'd skipped a grade, so I was younger and much smaller than the majority. The teachers loved me and always set me up as an example to the class. And I was a walking social disaster. If it hadn't been for Connor's protection, something bad could have happened. Kids are vicious."

Hey, fat girl. You be nice to us, and we'll be nice to you. Got it?

The pickle fell from her fingers. She wiped her clammy hands on her designer jeans. "Yeah."

He pointed to her half-eaten turkey. "How can you enjoy that without a roll? Here, take the rest of mine. And some chips." He pushed them over to her. They sat in her line of sight, taunting, reminding her again and again if she didn't stay skinny, people wouldn't love her. Reminding her of all the times she looked in the mirror and hated who stared back at her. Trapped in a body she despised and a mind that screamed for help.

The anger flooded past the dam and snapped her chin up. "Stop pushing your crappy food on me," she hissed. "Just because you can eat anything doesn't mean the rest of us can."

His brows lowered in a frown. "I don't understand. You looked like you wanted them. It won't hurt you to have a few bad things, Ken. Your body is perfect."

"I'm not perfect!" she ripped out. "You want to know what I was doing while kids hung out at the mall? I stayed home with a bunch of pizzas, soda, chips, and anything else I could fit in my mouth. A drive-through to me meant two Big Macs, super-size fries, and a shake. And I still wanted more. I couldn't shop at the mall because I needed a special fat person's store since regular sizes never fit. I was tripped, tortured, abused, and reminded every fucking day that I was ugly. That I was fat." Her hands shook with rage, but the words spewed out of her mouth like vomit, dark and ugly. "I conquered that problem pretty fast. Decided to stop eating. I starved off forty pounds and then I had lots of friends. Boys wanted me. Everything was great. Until I realized I had dropped so much weight my ribs showed, and my period stopped, and I was disappearing just like I always wished." Completely spent from her emotional tirade, she blinked furiously to keep her eyes dry. "It took me a long time to climb out of the pit. I went to therapy, learned how to eat and work out, for balance. Now, I can look in a mirror again. Remind myself I'm a successful, healthy woman. But I haven't forgotten. Sometimes food drags me back into hell. And I sure as hell am not perfect."

The full realization of what she had just done hit

her like a karate kick to the head. My God, what had she told him? She had just spilled the venom in her soul to her client in the fast-food court. How could he continue working with her? How could he ever respect her for such an admission? Now he knew she was a complete fake—a mirage in the world of the flawless and fabulous. Humiliation choked her, but she raised her head and looked him dead in the eye.

Pride.

Those deep moss green eyes were filled with a fierceness that froze her in place. He reached across the table and snagged her hand. Warm, strong fingers interlaced with hers in a sign of friendship. Support. And something else. Something deep and beautiful and so very fragile that she sucked in her breath, afraid it would disappear like a curl of smoke.

"I'm sorry. I didn't know. I see you light up when you let yourself go a bit and think you deserve to be happy. But I get it." He leaned in. "I *know* because I've been there. You fought, survived, and flourished. You gave the world a big fuck-you and didn't let them break who you were. That's perfection, Kennedy. Sheer perfection."

She blinked, unable to pull her gaze from his. The touch of his skin on hers made her crave more. His thumb rubbed the sensitive pulse point on her wrist, massaging, pressing. Her nails dug gently into his palm, and a low sound came from her throat, a slight whimper of need and want she'd never experienced before. It took all her willpower not to get up, cross over to him, and slide into his lap. Drag his mouth to hers and finally take what she wanted, his taste and essence on her tongue. Filling her body.

A loud clatter of a tray dropping to the floor broke the spell.

She jerked back and pulled her fingers from his. Kennedy spent the next few minutes organizing her trash and recapping her water bottle. She dumped the garbage. He never moved, just sat and stared at her, as if not knowing what to say. An awkward silence dropped between them.

"I think we can call this a successful trip," she said lightly. "Ready to go?"

"Not yet." His eyes gleamed with purpose. "Let's dump the bags in the car first."

"Then what?"

He smiled slowly. "Then it's my turn to collect on my favor."

NATE GUIDED HER INTO the computer simulator and prayed for focus. As much as he hated malls, this one boasted a huge indoor playground that included a roller coaster, video games, bowling alley, and an updated golf simulator. He rarely used them anymore, but he didn't want to drag Kennedy onto a course without teaching her the basics first and getting an idea of her swing.

Usually golf calmed his mind when he was feeling overstimulated, and he desperately needed a distraction. So did Kennedy. The humiliation on her face after her confession shredded his control, until he ached to hold her in his arms and make her feel safe. Her strength and sheer force of will took his breath away, but her truth and vulnerability destroyed him.

He was crazy about her.

A loud sigh drifted toward his ears. She wiggled her ass and shifted on her heeled black sandals. Her toenails were scarlet red, and strings of rhinestones were encased across her foot. The famous toe ring shone brightly and dared him to do something naughty. "Do we really have to do this now? It's too crowded."

He pushed her gently to the front of the line. "I need to know your natural swing ability so I can help you develop when we get on the course. It'll give you great feedback."

"Sounds like work, not fun. Why are you intent on torturing me with something I hate?"

He grinned at her playfully. "Payback's a bitch."

They went into the room. She took in the large screen on the far wall, the row of clubs hung to the side, and the computer set up in front. "Oh, yay. A dark, airless room so I can swing a ball at a fake movie screen. Sign me up."

He ignored her and picked a beginner's course from the screen. "What have you told me throughout our sessions? Have an open mind. Trust you. Be willing to stretch boundaries."

She snorted. "Fine. What does this thing do anyway?"

"When golfers want to analyze and fine-tune their swing, they can get feedback from the computer. It calculates speed, angle, distance, spin, trajectory, et cetera. There are radar and light sensors around the ball and screen."

"Hmm, more advanced than a Wii, huh?"

"Yes." He tried a few clubs, picked one, and handed it to her. "We'll use this. Get a feel for it first and take a practice swing."

She grasped the club in her hands, lifted it back, and swung through. "There. Can I do it for real now?"

"No. I need to show you the proper stance and hold. Come here."

She stepped over, and he positioned himself behind her. Dragging her tight against him, he brought his arms around her waist and wrapped his fingers over hers. Her body stiffened. "What are you doing?"

"Trying to show you the correct way to tee off." He bit back a groan when she did another wiggle. The lush curve of her rear pressed against his dick. Her scent swarmed him, a touch of tangerine and sandalwood that made his mouth water. The silk of her hair brushed his cheek. Nate yanked his mind off his body and ran through mathematical sequences until he was able to refocus. "Hands placed over each other. Index fingers pointing down. Choke up on your grip."

He adjusted, then drew her arms back behind her head. "This feels awkward," Kate remarked.

"It should at first. This is about where you want to

stop. Now, shift your hips back. Your power is going to come from the hips and legs." Her denim-clad thighs slid past his and ripped a groan from his lips.

"What's the matter?"

"Nothing. Now you need a complete follow-through. Keep your eyes on the ball and swing." She did. "You didn't keep your eye on the ball."

"Yes, I did!"

"No, you thought you did. That gets beginners all the time. What's the best thing you've ever seen in your life?"

"What?"

He let out an impatient breath. "An image. A photo. What was the most intriguing image you set eyes on, where you felt like you couldn't look away?"

Her cheeks turned pink. "My cousin showed me a copy of *Playgirl*. I had never seen a naked man before."

Nate stabbed a finger toward the floor. "That ball is your first naked man. Got it?"

She giggled. "Don't you mean balls?"

"Concentrate."

"Sorry."

"Now, do it again." He made her practice a few times until he was satisfied she got her basic grip, stance, and gaze on the ball. "Good. Let's try it now with the simulator. Move up to the swing pad and get ready."

"That grassy thing there?"

"Yes. Relax, breathe, and concentrate on the ball."

She mumbled something under her breath but obeyed. She wriggled her hips, adjusted her grip, and gazed at the ball. He wondered what man she was fantasizing about naked. The idea annoyed the crap out of him, so he pushed the thought aside.

She swung.

The ball hit the screen with good trajectory. She peered at the screen while the ball launched toward the fairway, hooking a bit left, but sailing nicely to land for perfect setup to the green. She frowned. "Is that good? How come it's so far away from the hole?"

"That's excellent for a first swing. Okay, you hook left so we need to straighten that out. Speed is a bit low. Trajectory decent. Now you're going to set up the shot to get onto the green." He took her through the steps, readjusting her stance and swing, then stepped back.

Gaze glued to the imaginary naked man, she nibbled at her lower lip, then drew back. And swung.

The ball landed on the green a few inches from the hole. "Oh, yay! That's good, right? Now I just have to push it in the hole."

"Putt. Huh, you corrected the hook, even though there was a dog leg on this course."

"Dog what?"

"Dog leg is a hole that's not straight. I haven't seen a beginner able to accomplish that. Can you putt?"

She stuck out her chin. "Of course. I like miniature golf. It's fun to try and get through the windmills and water fountains."

He rolled his eyes and grabbed a putter from the shelf. "Here, try this one."

She set herself up and sunk it in one perfect putt. "Yay, did I win?"

"There's no winning here. It's a game of how many strokes it takes to get your ball in the hole. Your statistics are impressive. Let's do the next one."

They completed the nine-hole course. Nate computed her numbers and watched them increase in quality with every hole. He went to push up his glasses on the bridge of his nose, then remembered he was wearing contacts. Odd. It was almost as if she had a natural swing. Which was impossible, of course. Maybe a bit of beginner's luck? But the computer didn't lie.

"Nate? Can we go now?"

"In a minute." The club face dimensions were a gift most golfers prayed for and never got. Her grip was still awful. But what would she be like when she increased her strength and practiced more? Would she get even better, or worse? He reached for his pencil to do some quick calculations, but the pocket protector was gone.

"Nate, I'm done with golf. I want to go."

He came out of his fog. "Sure. Listen, any chance you can take off Wednesday morning? Meet me at the golf course? I really want to get you on a real green."

She narrowed her gaze with suspicion. "How many more sessions do I have to complete before our favor is officially over?"

"Three times on the course. I can drag you out on a weekend morning if that works better."

"Wednesday's fine. I can rearrange my schedule."

"Excellent."

"Do you have decent golf clothes?" she asked. "We forgot to pick anything up today."

"Actually, my golf wardrobe is highly rated and all designer."

She perked up. "Cool. I always wanted to wear this tennis dress that's been hanging in my closet."

He followed her out and tried not to groan. Great. Watching her short skirt flip up when she bent over and took a swing would likely kill him. Kennedy was with him to find his soul-mate. Crushing on her wouldn't help either of them. They shared a similar past and understood one another on a different level. And he wanted to sleep with her.

Bad.

That didn't mean they'd make a good couple or that she was interested in something more. Yes, he swore a few times she had also sensed the connection and wanted to kiss him back. But it quickly disappeared, and Kennedy wasn't the type to follow impulse if it affected business. He needed to concentrate on the original plan to find himself a suitable woman. One who wanted to settle down, share his life, and love him as he was—geekiness and all. One who would stay and not be tempted by the next hot guy who came along.

"You okay?" she asked.

He forced a smile. "Yes. Actually, I'm *amazing*."

Her laughter soothed his soul as they walked out.

"YOU'RE MOVING OUT?"

Nate winced and kept his head down, taping down the box and clearly marking it in black marker. "I told you yesterday. I managed to get a small rental in Verily, near Kinnections. I think we both need some private space."

"I don't mind you bringing women home, man." Connor paced through the cluttered room. "What do you expect me to do? I can't afford this rent on my own."

"No worries, I'll take care of it. It's not fair I sprung this on you last minute."

"I can pay my way."

The resentment in his brother's tone made Nate look up. "I know you can. This isn't about you. I just don't want my future wife to think I'm a partyer who likes hanging with his brother and getting drunk."

"Yeah, I did teach you well. Where are your glasses? You're blind without them."

"I'm wearing contacts."

His brother gasped. "You put something in your eye? Holy shit, you're going hard core on this makeover thing. Does it bother your eyeball?"

Nate tried not to squirm at the thought. Damn older siblings. "No. And don't talk about it, or I'll get weirded out. I don't feel a thing."

"Fine. Listen, Ned—"

"Nate."

"Sorry. I'm worried about you. I think you're focusing too hard on this one-woman thing and it's gonna blow up in your face. Why don't you play it cool for a while? Sleep around a bit. I bet you can get some serious play with this new look you got going for you."

He studied his brother. Usually Connor reflected an easygoing, uncomplicated guy who wanted nothing more than to get laid. But today, underneath the words, something darker loomed. He simply looked unhappy. Nate gentled his voice. "Aren't you tired of just getting laid? Don't you want more from your life? More of . . . anything?"

His brother jerked back. "Who'd want more than a good piece of ass?"

"Not all women are like Mom."

Connor stopped pacing. His cheeks grew ruddy. "Don't ever talk about Mom. You don't know what happened."

"She left us. Doesn't mean they all will."

The anger deflated but left behind only a shadow of the brother he knew. What was going on? Flat hazel eyes gazed back at him without expression. "Yeah. They will."

"Forget it." Nate grabbed the last box and unrolled the tape. He knew from experience that Connor was well versed on the family-and-kids speech. He cited their own parents' failings, the divorce statistics, and the innate biological drive of the male species to stray. Depressing. His brother was right on most counts.

Love and marriage made no logical sense if approached analytically; the failure rate way outran the successes. Yet, here he was, a scientist who devoted his life to analytics, aching to take the leap, while Connor refused to get hurt again. "The truck's coming this week. I left you enough groceries. You should have plenty of time to get paid from the new job."

"Don't need your charity, bro."

"Not giving you any." He laid the last box on top of the pile and wiped his brow. "You put me through school and gave me everything I needed. Let me handle the rent on this place for a while. Hell, when you get supervisor, I'm making you take me out for a steak dinner."

Connor's lips turned up. "Prime rib?"

"New York strip at Delmonico's. Nothing less."

His brother grunted. "Whatever. Wanna hang out tonight? We can go to the bar and meet Jerry, knock back a few, then catch *True Blood*."

"Can't. I'm meeting Kennedy for a session at the gym."

"Again? What's up with all the working out? You sure you're not screwing her?"

He tamped down his anger at Connor's crude words. "I'm sure. She's just helping me find my best self. I'll be meeting a bunch of women at a mixer next week, and she wants to be sure I'm prepared."

"Prepared? I did that for you, man. My advice is stellar."

"Maybe for you," he muttered. The memory of getting shocked at the bar over and over still made him squirm. Talk about hard-core therapy. "I'm looking for more than a one-night stand. I want something real. Is that too much to ask?"

Connor turned his back. "Do whatever you want. It's your funeral."

The door slammed behind him.

Nate groaned. Ah, hell. He didn't want to hurt Connor's feelings or insult him. He just needed to be his own person and stop being his brother's clone. Guilt ate at his gut, but soon he heard the outer door close and knew he'd left. Probably out to the local bar to drown his sorrows and talk smack about his ungrateful little brother.

Nate checked his watch. He needed to meet Kennedy for Zumba in a bit. He'd make it up to Connor later. Maybe take him out for dinner and spend some quality time with him. He tossed on sweat pants and a T-shirt and shoved his feet into sneakers. Then looked in the mirror.

Funny, he looked . . . normal. Even halfway attractive. His eyes seemed more interesting without the large frames, and the goatee that he'd despised and wanted to shave off had grown in nicely. He'd gotten in the habit of lifting some weights after Zumba while Kennedy drilled him, and the muscles he sported already seemed a bit tighter and more defined.

He was officially deemed socially acceptable. His big mixer was set up for Friday night. All three women had declared him ready to hit the next level.

Now, if he could only learn not to shove his foot in his mouth like Fred Flintstone, life would be perfect.

He grabbed his jacket and headed out the door. Shame on him for wishing Kennedy Ashe would be his very own Wilma, ready to accept and love him even with all his noticeable flaws.

This wasn't primitive times. And that cartoon got canceled a damn long time ago.

Nate ignored the ache in his heart and told himself he was looking forward to the mixer.

ten

NATE WATCHED GREEDILY as Kennedy climbed out of her car, the short tennis dress flipping up in the spring breeze. He figured she'd text him an excuse rather than show up on a midweek morning on the golf course. Her hips swung with an innate sauciness that was part of her core, and she stopped in front of him. Her scarlet nails contrasted sexily against the white dress.

"I didn't think you'd come."

She arched a golden brow. "I don't welsh on my promises. I'm ready to play some golf."

He almost laughed at the disdain in her voice as she said the word. His spirits lifted and suddenly, he was excited for the few hours ahead. He was such a chump.

"I'm helping someone else out with his swing, but he's running late. He may catch up with us later. Let's hit the course."

He shifted his clubs, guided her into the golf cart, and led her to the first tee. The wooded pines and fir trees tangled amid acres of bright green under a cloudless sky. The air held a hint of chill, but the sun poured down bright and cheerful. Her hushed voice floated in the wind. "It's so beautiful. And quiet."

"Midweek is the best time. We can just relax and play around a bit. Less serious stuff."

"Do you ever think of playing professionally?"

He shook his head and set the clubs down. "Nah, not interested. I enjoy helping others, though, and I'm constantly looking to shave a stroke or two off my game. It's a mental challenge, but it's also soothing. Out here, I can clear my head."

She dragged in a breath and smiled. "Yeah, I see what you mean. I'm always focused on my next task, even when I'm alone, I forget what it's like to just be."

"Must be tough trying to bring love to the world."

She crinkled her nose. "You making fun of me?"

"No. I think you're held to a higher power than me and my rockets. I help people get to space. You help people find love."

She drew back in surprise. Those gorgeous whiskey eyes softened. "Thanks."

"Welcome. You remember the grip we talked about?"

"Like this?"

He spent a few minutes going over the basics and rules of the game. "Use this club for your approach shot. Do you know the target?"

"Oh, can I put the ball in that pretty beach thing there?"

"No, that's a hazard. Sand trap. If it looks pretty, avoid it." He pointed right. "Over there, see the flag?"

"That's a million miles away!"

"You don't get there in the first shot. Aim that way,

and we do it in stages. Each one is a stroke. Right now I want to concentrate on your natural swing. We learned a lot from the simulator, but this will be different. Remember to keep your eye on the ball."

"Hello, naked Channing Tatum."

"Thanks for the visual. I just threw up in my mouth."

Her giggle charmed rather than annoyed him. She drew the club back, rotated nicely, and slammed the club forward, completing a nice full arc.

The ball flew in a perfect spin and landed on the edge of the fairway.

Very close to the green.

How the hell had she done that?

"Oh, man, I suck! I told you I'd suck."

"Ken, that was a great shot. Most men I teach can't do that for at least a few weeks. Have you practiced?"

She snorted. "With what? Listen, we need to talk about something serious. I thought you said your golf clothes were designer. When are you going to start listening to me regarding your wardrobe?"

Nate ignored her, studied the landing, and did a few calculations in his head. How could she have completed a good square club face as a novice? Her natural swing was off the charts. This time, he found the pencil in his pocket, grabbed his scorecard, and scribbled down some calculations. Again, she held a slight left hook tendency, but that was an easy tweak.

"Earth to Nate."

"Yeah?"

"The orange pants. That is a crime against nature. You're scaring the birds."

He looked up with a frown. "Are you kidding me? These shorts are from Rickie Fowler's line. They cost a fortune."

"Who's Ricky?"

"One of the best golfers in the world."

Kennedy rolled her eyes. "For God's sakes, why is he designing clothes if he golfs? Golfers have the world's worst fashion sense. You can't wear those again."

"Fine."

"Your turn, right?"

"Yeah." He quieted his mind and his breath, and hit his approach shot. Damn, he'd end up getting a bogey if he didn't clean it up in the next swing. He barely missed the hazard and fell into the rough close to Kennedy's ball.

"Yay, you did good. Cool, we're together."

"Let's go."

They trudged to the next hole. This time, he studied the way she set up her body. Her pullback was amazing, a gorgeous, graceful arc that connected cleanly with the ball. Rarely did females follow through with enough power to hit the ball far, let alone keep their eyes so securely on the target. Her shot cut through the air and landed right next to the hole.

No. Fucking. Way.

His eyes bugged out. She stuck out her lower lip in a pout to rival a movie star's. "Aww, I missed."

He jerked around. "Missed? You can putt the ball right in. You got a par three."

"That's good?"

"It's almost impossible for a beginner. Or so I thought."

She brightened and did a little dance. Her skirt swung and showed off tanned, muscular thighs and a cute rear. The little white socks and sneakers gave her a juvenile look. Her full breasts strained against the dress and bounced to the rhythm. He cursed under his breath and bit his tongue on purpose. The sudden pain grounded him.

He was missing something. What did she have that most first-time golfers didn't? How could she line herself up so perfectly without strain and manage to pitch the ball so far? "Your turn!" she chirped.

"Fine." This time, the ball rolled in a drunken arc too far from the green and slid into the sand trap.

"Oh, I'm sorry. That's bad, right?"

Aggravation stirred inside him. "Yes, that's bad. You go. Use the putter."

"Cool, I like the little stick better." She wiggled her ass and with a delicate tap, sank the ball. "Yay, I did it!"

"Goody for you."

"How are you going to get out of that sand thing?"

"Watch." Usually he was a whiz at the sand traps, but this time he took two swings to get himself out. When he finally sank his ball, he was wondering if he was being pranked on some hidden camera show.

The nightmare continued. Nate watched as she

commanded each hole, her swing never wavering and giving her perfect pars while he struggled with his own game. She grew perkier, and he grew more annoyed as he started sporting a massive erection and a headache.

By the time they were halfway through, he was done.

"Maybe we should break. I don't want to tire you the first time we're on a real course," he said.

"Good idea. Hey, this wasn't as bad as I thought. I'll do it again."

"Hooray," Nate said humorlessly.

They climbed into the cart and took off. Nate wondered if he could sneak back in an hour and finish his game. It must be the sexual energy that had messed him up. He quickly texted Wolfe that they'd need to reschedule for that week and decided to go to work early.

"Nate?"

"Yeah?"

"Did you always want to be an aerospace engineer?"

Her off-topic question pulled him back to the present. "No. I wanted to be a superhero. I always felt I could make Batman's cave a hell of a lot better, and the Batmobile needed some tweaking."

That earned him another of her husky laughs. "Bet you were always smart."

"Yeah. I got bored too quickly in school, so they pushed me ahead a year. And of course, once they

introduced higher mathematical concepts, I understood exactly what they meant. I never struggled, and
in my spare time I studied formulas. So I changed
from becoming the next Batman to helping get a man
into space. When the NASA program disassembled,
I sided with the camp of the private sector that wanted
to open up space travel to everyone. Rich billionaires
began creating their own companies for the purpose,
and I came back to New York."

"Was Connor here?"

"Yeah, my family grew up near Westchester so it
was a chance for us to get back in the same state. I
missed my brother. He's the only family I have left."

She nodded. "I always wished I had a sibling.
That's why I'm so close with Kate and Arilyn. We met
in college and bonded and they became my family."

"What about your mom and dad?"

Darkness stole over her face, momentarily captur-
ing the jubilance that had come from her earlier success at the game. "We don't talk much. It's better that
way." He nodded, not digging any further. The gentle
whirr of the cart's wheels broke the silence. "I know
you study propulsion, but what exactly are you trying
to find? Are you hired to build a certain rocket?"

"No. We're looking for more efficient ways to create spacecraft. I'm working on new formulas to challenge our current ideas. Something called the thrust
equation."

"The thrust equation depends on the mass flow
through the engine and the exit velocity, right?"

He narrowed his gaze. She acted like she'd just told him she liked the color red. "Exchanging *Vogue* for *Science Today*?" he asked casually. He was afraid to scare her off after the other night, but dear God, she was trying to kill him.

"I looked up your company on the net to get some info on your job."

His heart shifted. There wasn't one person in his entire life who cared enough even to figure out what he did all day. His throat closed up. "Why?"

"I wanted to get an idea of who you were. To match you with the right woman, of course. Career is an important part of your life and expectations for your future wife."

He pushed down the strange mix of emotions that tore through him. "I'm just the nerdy guy behind the notepad."

"Nate?"

He pulled into the main area and parked. "Yeah?"

"Nerds are underrated."

Their connection slammed through him and punched out his breath. Damn her. Every time he tried to get his footing, she knocked him back on his ass. Her face softened, and she was staring at him as if she wanted him, but didn't want to want him, and his head swam and his dick ached. Suddenly, he didn't care about right, wrong, or reason. He leaned in, got a whiff of her heady scent, and cupped her cheeks.

"You can't say that and expect me not to kiss you, Ken."

His lips covered hers, and she gave that little hitched moan he bet she uttered during an orgasm. She opened for him and he slipped his tongue deep, drinking in her essence, thrusting in and out like he longed to do between her thighs. The sun beat down, the birds sang, golf balls flew, people chattered, and nothing else mattered except the touch and taste and smell of her.

She kissed him back. Stroked his tongue with hers. Gave it all back to him.

Too soon, she drew back and stared. Her lower lip was slightly swollen and gleamed with wetness. "Don't do that."

He wanted to laugh at her admonition, but he was too painfully turned on. "Sorry. But I don't regret it."

"I'm throwing you a mixer, dammit. To hopefully meet your wife. Let's pretend this never happened, because I promise you, Nate, it will never happen again. Got it?"

Those amber eyes sparked with temper and a passion he craved to tap into, but he did the right thing and nodded. "Got it."

She slid out of the cart in a flash of white fabric and bare skin. "See you Friday. At the mixer."

He didn't answer. Just watched her walk away and wondered if he'd ever meet someone who would match her.

THAT FRIDAY EVENING, NATE walked into Cosmos like he was about to face a firing squad.

The small group of women hung in the corner, drinking wine and chatting like they were friends and not about to compete for his attention. Not that he felt like a prize. In fact, his stomach lurched at the thought of having to conduct not only safe but sparkling conversation with strangers and then pick one to date. He must've been crazy to agree to this. His gaze swung to the object of his thoughts, dreams, and lately his fantasy world. She was dressed in a yellow tweed suit that looked custom fit with a super-short skirt accented by her matching yellow sandals. Her gold ankle bracelet winked at him, and her gorgeous hair streamed down in streaks of blond and brown. She moved around the room like a firefly, bright and quick and impossible to ignore.

Since the golf outing, Nate had focused on the upcoming event and targeted his energy into his real future. With a woman he'd marry, have children with, and love till death do they part. His head was now wrapped tight around one rule: Kennedy Ashe was only his matchmaker.

If only he could wrap his dick around the rule, too.

Nate walked up to her. "Hey."

She smiled. "How are you doing?"

"Just peachy."

She laughed. The deep, husky tone stroked him everywhere and set off an explosion of heat. "Don't freak out on me. These women were handpicked. They're easy to get along with and really looking forward to meeting with you. I'll introduce you to everyone first, and then escort each of them to a private table so you can have some alone time. You look great."

"Thanks." The charcoal pants and silk shirt had an easy elegance he liked. And the shoes were pretty damn awesome. He'd never thought of Italian leather as the bomb, but now he didn't know if he'd ever go back. "So do you."

She opened her mouth to respond, but a large guy swooped in on her and pulled her into a tight hug. His hands slid comfortably around to her backside. A violent impulse sputtered within him like a bad car engine refusing to turn over, and he barely held back from knocking the asshole's grip away from the full curve of her ass.

"Hey, babe. What time you done? Wanna hook up for a drink afterward?"

She tossed him a flirty look and shook her head. "Sorry, can't tonight."

"All work and no play makes for an unsatisfied woman, Ken."

"Speak for yourself, Ron."

He gave a big bear laugh that annoyed Nate. "I'll be in the kitchen if you get a break. Come visit." He winked. "I promise not to get dough all over your nice clothes this time."

"Promises, promises," she sang. The dude walked away with a stupid come-hither look on his face and pushed his way back into the crowd. His sheer height and weight cut an easy path through the throng of people, but his rudeness and ego were evident. Definitely a prior high school bully. She pulled her gaze away from his retreat and refocused. "Okay, are you ready to meet everyone?"

"Who's that?" he demanded.

She blinked. "Ron? Oh, he just works in the kitchen. We do a lot of mixers here."

Nate held on to his temper. "I don't like the way he just talked to you."

Astonishment widened her golden eyes. "He's harmless. Treats all women like that. Sound familiar?"

The arrow met its mark and pierced cleanly through. Nate shifted on his feet. All those awful comments he never thought of flickered through his mind. How many times had he treated women like objects under the misguided advice of his brother? But Connor wasn't to blame. Nate had never paused long enough to think about how someone would want to be treated. Maybe he was just as selfish.

"You don't deserve for any man to devalue you, Kennedy. Even me."

Her expression softened, and suddenly, it was if they were alone in a warm, floaty bubble. "Then it's a good thing I have my zapper."

They smiled at each other, and he forgot about the group of women awaiting him, one of whom might be his future wife. He wondered if she had forgotten, too.

She seemed to catch his thoughts and shook her head. "I already ordered you a Darth Maultini. The women you'll meet tonight are Mary, Sue, Vera, and

Sally. They're all professionals with college degrees and good senses of humor. Two of them love golf. One has a physics background. Don't worry about assets or liabilities right now. Just talk, have some fun, and see if you feel any type of connection. Remember the rules?"

"No commenting on age or body parts, asking about the future, or judging before a longer conversation."

"Good. Ready?"

He gazed at the woman he wanted and lied.

"Yes. Let's go."

He took a deep breath and plunged into the crowd.

KENNEDY SAT ON THE edge of the room, monitoring but giving Nate the privacy and support he needed. So far, so good. They all seemed to be enjoying themselves, and he was already involved with his third private date. She sensed that Mary was the best match and hoped Nate felt the same. Funny, she'd never had such a difficult time setting up a mixer. Every time she narrowed down the matches, something bothered her about a certain woman. She was probably so intent on success since she'd spent the last several weeks with intensified training. This would be good for both of them. They were probably getting a bit too attached, which caused weird feelings to surface. Sexual feelings, for instance.

A shiver raced over her skin. When Ron had left, she caught the primitive flare of masculine temper in

Nate's intense green eyes. Almost like he was jealous and didn't like Ron touching her. But what disturbed her most was her own reaction. She'd liked it. The thought of him trying to teach her a lesson, and putting that fierce focus all on her pleasure lit her up like one of those rocket ships he worked on. And the image of her rational rocket scientist losing his temper completely turned her on.

Maybe it was time to focus on her own love life. Or lack of it. A round with Ron would take the edge off, but she needed a real date with possibilities. When was the last time she experienced that tiny flare of anticipation over a man? There was nothing as exciting as the first bite of sexual attraction, the dive into an initial kiss, the energy of falling into bed and hoping for something . . . more.

She sipped her Pinot Noir and watched Nate. He handled himself well. The moment he strolled into the restaurant, the women perked up, gazes roving hungrily over him. He was her perfect Eliza, transformed, transcended, and ready to find love. He moved with a predatory grace, his gaze focused on each woman he spoke with as if she were his universe and he had no need to go anywhere else.

He handled the one-on-ones even better. Open body language, and he was obviously speaking in more than one-word answers. Sue moved her chair a bit closer, and played with her hair, twisting a curl around her finger in the obvious flirtatious manner of a woman wanting to catch a man. He seemed a bit taken with her, too. His attention never strayed. She laughed and touched his upper arm. He seemed to like it.

Kennedy clucked her tongue against the roof of her mouth and pondered the match. Sue loved golf, and her father was a scientist, so it was a strong background of shared interests. Still, Sue had a prim and proper way about her and could be a bit of a snob. She wondered if one slip of Nate's tongue would throw her off. Or if she would judge his brother's questionable behavior. Mary had a tiny slice of badass within her that would balance him more correctly. Maybe she should whisper her own opinion in Nate's ear. No one would know.

Kennedy froze. What was she thinking? That was the cardinal rule of matchmaking—give them the possibilities and let them make the choice. Suddenly the creepy voice from the *Saw* movies flooded her head. *Make Your Choice*. She should've never watched that damn midnight marathon.

Nate rose, smiling, and walked Sue back to the group. The women seemed to make a little joke, where everyone laughed, and then finally Mary was escorted to the private table. Kennedy scrolled through her text messages, sipped her wine, and waited for the magic to happen between them. She always had great instincts, and she'd studied Nate more than she'd studied any other client. Mary was the one.

When he finished his private conversations, Kennedy strolled over to the group. She chatted a bit with the women, made sure they all knew how impressed Nate was with each of them, and escorted them out the door. No reason for anyone to linger while waiting for his decision. *Awkward*. Kennedy refreshed her drink and sat down with Nate in a cozy corner.

"How did it go?" she asked.

"Good." His brow furrowed. "Really good. I don't think I messed up once. And I liked them. They were all pretty much my type."

"I'm so happy. Did you have one particular woman you bonded with? I want you to begin your one-on-one dating."

"Yes. Sue."

She paused. "What about Mary?"

"Mary is nice, too. But I'd like to date Sue."

She swallowed back her protests. "Wonderful. I'm glad you sensed a connection. I can set up a date for you this weekend. You're in charge of the venue. Don't bring her to a business function or your personal home. Make sure it's private enough so you can get to know one another and don't pick something weird, like bowling."

"Are you afraid I'll take her to midnight golfing?"

"Maybe."

He grinned. Her gaze was pulled to the lush curve of his lower lip. She strangled the impulse to touch the facial hair around his mouth. She remembered the delicious roughness against her cheek when he kissed her. Remembered the thrust of his tongue, the pressure of his lips, and the taste of raw male hunger.

He wrinkled his forehead in mock contemplation. "Sue is a huge golfer so she may not mind that, actually."

"Nate."

"Kidding. I can handle a date. What about the others?"

"I'll make sure they know you'd be open to dating one of them if it doesn't work with Sue, and confirm how impressed you were with them. I'll also redouble my efforts to find them their matches."

"This is a touchy type of business. How do you manage not to hurt their feelings?"

Ken shrugged. "I'm good at my job. I've been rejected so many times it became my mantra and my albatross. I make sure all my clients are confident and know I believe in them. Everything we do at Kinnections is structured to try to get people to deal with rejection in a healthy way without letting it destroy them."

Nate smirked at her. "What would you know about rejection? I can't imagine a man alive who could reject you."

A bite of pain seized her. She ignored it. "You didn't know me ten years ago."

A gentle finger lifted up her chin. Startled, she gazed into the endless depths of his eyes. "Don't need to. Bet you were just as beautiful then. You just didn't know it."

She ached to step closer and let him hold her. When was the last time a man had comforted her other than for sexual gratification? Instead, she balled her hands into fists and forced a smile. "I'll contact Sue in the morning and you can set up your date."

"Okay. I better head out. I promised I'd grab a beer with Connor and I'm already late." Nate paused. "Thanks for everything. Sue seems like an incredible woman."

She watched his retreating back and kept the bright smile pasted on her face, the perfect picture of a matchmaker poised on the brink of success. And wondered why her heart didn't seem in it.

eleven

KENNEDY SAT IN her office and brooded.

Her screen saver flashed in front of her with the cheerful purple and silver logo of Kinnections. A large stack of folders lay to her right, with endless names and possibilities to match. Usually she dove in with gusto, the journey to polish and perfect each client to his or her full potential an endless joy. Instead, she examined her nails and wondered where Nate was taking Sue tonight.

This was their fourth date in only two weeks.

The first was an intimate dinner. Sue raved about Nate. How polite he was. How charming. How funny. How smart.

The second time was golf. Kennedy had called him up and raged when she'd heard the news, but he swore Sue requested to go and it was a Sunday afternoon, so therefore it didn't count as a *real* date. Just one of those half-assed outings men threw together to test the waters. She let it go because Sue was excited and had initiated the meet-up.

The third was lunch. He'd taken her by the water, where they'd fed the ducks and feasted on seafood. She'd complimented him on his originality and ability to step up the intimacy without pushing too fast.

But date four was a big one. Usually, it turned the tide toward a real relationship or a breakup.

Where would he go tonight? Were they moving toward a physical connection? She was happy for them, really, but she refused to have Nate get his heart broken by moving too fast. The last time he'd shown up for Zumba, she noticed his goatee was perfectly trimmed and shaped. He admitted he went to see Benny on his own, which should have made her ecstatic, but only pissed her off. She felt out of the loop. Tossed aside. Discarded like a used tissue, crumpled up and stuffed in the garbage without so much as a good-bye. He no longer bothered her about joining him Wednesdays for golf or asked her for advice. She guessed Sue was the one who knew everything about him now. And that was a good thing. A great thing.

Really.

She reached into her desk drawer and pulled out a mini liquor bottle stolen from a past hotel. Rum. Nice choice. She uncapped, tilted it back, and took a long swig.

Kate walked in.

Her friend took in the scene before her, kicked the door shut, and dropped in the chair. Then stuck out her hand. "I want the Bailey's."

"I don't know if I have any of them left."

"Look harder."

Her fingers closed around it and she tossed it over. Kate sipped it more delicately. "What's the matter with you?" Ken asked, noticing the harangued look on her friend's face.

"Dumb-ass client. Wedding stress. Worried about Gen. Robert's got another bladder infection, but he's okay, Slade's staying home with him today. His purple bunny squeaker shredded, and Slade had to run to a ton of pet stores to find the same exact one. The poor thing can't sleep without it."

Slade had fallen in love with Kate's paraplegic rescue dog, Robert, and they had become a true family. "Robert or Slade?"

"Both. No one sleeps if the other is unhappy."

"Got it." Kennedy sighed. "You know I'll help with the wedding. I'll plan the whole damn thing for you, babe, so no worries."

"I know, it's just little annoying stuff, and Gen's been acting weird."

"Yeah, I wanted to talk to her but haven't gotten a chance. Something's up."

"She's blaming it on work and the engagement party, but maybe she took on too much? Moving in with David and changing her whole life so fast? She used to stop by for coffee, but now I never see her. I feel disconnected."

"We need to pin her down for some alone time. A quiet place. Maybe she'll open up."

"Maybe." Kate took another swig and leaned back in her chair. Her blue eyes gleamed with a strange intensity. "How are you?"

"In a bad mood."

"Have you eaten?"

"Yogurt and fruit. But I plan to have a wrap at lunch with sweet potato fries. That will make me happy."

"How's Nate?"

Kennedy hesitated. "Good. He's dating Sue."

"I see. You must be thrilled. Over the moon. Is he happy?"

Annoyance simmered at Kate's question. "He just met her, so we don't know what will happen. I'm just not sure she's right for him."

"Huh."

Kennedy leaned over the desk. "What does that tone mean?"

"Nothing. Why don't you think she's right for him?"

"I think she's too rigid and he won't feel comfortable being himself. We may have worked on his physical appearance and social skills, but he has a unique personality that shouldn't change just because she doesn't like it."

Kate pursed her lips. "Huh."

"Why do you keep saying that?"

"You seem protective of him. Do you have feelings for Nate?"

Kennedy spluttered on the next sip and fell into a coughing fit. She swiped at her tearing eyes. "Are you crazy? Of course, I don't have feelings for Nate. He's my client. I just did a lot of work with him and I don't want him to backslide."

"How many times have we discussed this? Our clients will get hurt because love is a painful journey. We can only prepare and lead them in the right direction. He may need to get his heart broken before he finds his soul-mate."

"Not on my watch," she muttered.

"I stopped by his new place. He seemed happy and settled in."

Greed for information stole through her. "Was he surprised to see you?"

"I told him I lived right down the street and let him know I was there if he needed anything."

"Did he change up the apartment?"

Kate pondered the question. "No, he left the decor the same, but he's got a lot of books. Golf stuff. Computers. And of course he upgraded the television and sound system because he's male."

"Typical. You didn't see anything feminine, did you? Any hint that he brought Sue home with him? Because that's against the rules I gave him."

Kate looked at her oddly. "When was the last time you had a date, Ken?"

She shrugged. "A week. Maybe a few. I think a month now."

"Do you know why?"

Kennedy glared. "Are you taking Arilyn's place today? Geez, why are you on my case? I've been busy."

Kate stretched out her legs and crossed her ankles. "Bullshit. I can't remember the last time you didn't have a date on the weekend. You get nuts if you don't have a man chomping at your ass, but it seems you've been putting all your energy into Rocket Scientist Man."

"Aerospace engineer."

Kate lifted a brow. "Do you want him for yourself?"

"No! No, absolutely not. I've just been going through a funk, but I'm over it now. I think you're right, it's been too long without a man. I need to focus on my love life now, and get things revved up."

A small, secret smile tugged at her friend's lips. As if she knew something delicious but was keeping it to herself. "I'm sure you will."

Kennedy crossed her arms in front of her chest. "What's up? You know something and you better tell me."

Kate finished her Bailey's and stood. "I don't know what you're talking about. I'll invite Gen over for coffee this week. You should come, too." Her hand paused on the knob and she looked back. "Do what makes you happy. You deserve it."

Kennedy stared at the closed door. What the hell was that about? She was happy. She did anything and everything that made her happy. She knew she deserved happiness; that was the first rule of therapy. Believe that you deserve good things and they will happen.

She believed.

Ken grabbed her iPhone and scrolled through her

contacts. Time to reconnect with the land of the sexual living again and get even happier. She paused on the name and thought about it. Possible. Derek was hot, and she'd met him at the big expo when representing Kinnections. He was a power suit, loved the good life, and seemed interested. They'd conversed, flirted, and exchanged numbers, but she had never followed through. Got too busy.

Not anymore.

She hit the Compose message button and texted him. God, she loved the technical era. No more awkward phone calls and trying to figure out voice inflections. Just a simple "Wanna get together?" and a quick exchange of information.

His answer didn't take long. In a matter of fifteen minutes, she set herself up with a date that night.

It was official.

She was back.

NATE ESCORTED SUE INTO the bungalow and wondered why his brain screamed the move was a mistake. Dinner was nice. Sure, he spilled some Pinot Noir on his brand-new J.Crew shirt, but she'd wanted to get a bottle and he hated to tell her he preferred microbrews or a cracked-up martini. She eased through the menu like an expert, ordering wine pairings with each course, which was really classy. Conversation flowed organically. Her father's scientific background set her up nicely to understand Nate's job, and though she didn't seem very interested, at least she understood the nuances. She also loved golf. She was good at the sport, though a little stiff and too stuck on the rules without appreciating the touches of grace and beauty that made it a truly great game. Her swing was technically perfect but didn't have the natural ability and exuberance that Kennedy's had exhibited.

Not that he was thinking of Kennedy.

Sue was available. She'd made it clear she was seeking out a long-term relationship and was interested in marriage, children, and settling down. She appreciated his career and agreed one parent should quit his or her job to raise children. Of course, he'd changed his mind on that topic since starting with Kinnections. After all, Kennedy would probably be an incredible mother and would never give up her career. Another ridiculous opinion from Connor that had just stuck in his psyche. He reminded himself to stop thinking about Kennedy and focus on Sue. She was a Republican, believed in charitable works, and was truly an intellectual.

Her gaze swept across the tiny space filled with charm, and a frown settled on her brow. "Charming," she said brightly, walking from room to room. "This is temporary though, correct? You just moved out of your brother's house, so this is what you would call your transitional living quarters. Correct?"

Her habit of using the word *correct* like a question annoyed him a bit. Much better than slang or cursing though. He headed toward the kitchen to brew some coffee. "Yes, I decided to give us some space. I'm happy here for now."

"When you finally do buy, are you thinking Manhattan? Verily is a sweet place, but the best schools and culture are in the city."

"Maybe." He always believed he'd settle in the city, but lately he'd gotten used to the small river town. Better to leave his options open, especially since Sue had powerful leadership qualities and liked to forge ahead with a plan. He noticed that whether it be golf, dinner, or a phone call, she liked scheduling. Which was great, because so did he.

She gave a wry laugh and took a seat on the ocean blue sofa. "I'm sorry, I tend to race ahead of myself. I swear I'm not one of these women who froze their eggs and already have us picking out china."

He relaxed, pushed the button on the coffeemaker, and grinned. "It's okay. I'm a little regulated myself. One recognizes the other." He settled beside her and left a respectable distance between them. He'd kissed her a few times, but they were more like polite, can-I-go-any-further-without-getting-slapped type of inquiries. The embrace was not full of crazed passion, but it was extremely pleasant. With her curly brown hair, petite frame, and serious dark eyes, she was pleasing to the eye, well groomed, and considered a true catch for someone of his stature.

Nate wondered why he kept mentally cataloging her assets like an online dating site.

"Thanks again for dinner," she said softly. "I had a wonderful time. It's been a while since I've been comfortable with a man. I feel like you really understand and respect me."

"I do. It was nice."

"I know it's a bit soon, but I wanted to ask if you'd accompany me to a charity ball next weekend. My father does a lot of research work, like you, and it's taking place at the Museum of Natural History. Are you interested?"

The idea of formal clothes, stilted conversation, and an endless evening of dried-up crab cakes drifted past his vision. But this was what he wanted, right? Real stuff. Parties and social events with a date was part of the package. "Sure. Sounds fun."

She lit up and scooted an inch closer. "It will be now." She touched his arm. "I'm very glad we met."

"Me, too."

She tilted her head up. Her lips were very nice, full and defined, with just a touch of lipstick. Even her scent was subtle, a hint of lavender drifting from her skin. "Do you want some coffee?" he asked.

A smile touched her lips. "Not now, Nate. Kiss me."

Oh. Duh. He'd missed that one completely. Kennedy would've zapped him good. He pushed his thoughts away and complied. His lips fit comfortably over hers. This time, she opened her mouth and invited more. All the books he had studied, erotic novels he'd dutifully read, and *Cosmo* magazine surveys and articles he'd pored over came down to this. Time to pull out the big guns.

He took the offer and slid his tongue in her mouth. Her hands rested on his shoulders and she kissed him back. She was an excellent kisser, the strokes of her tongue matching his, the pressure of her lips not too hard and not too soft, and her fingers somehow managed to massage his skin lightly without digging in. He kissed her for a while, then slowly eased back.

She smiled up at him. "Let's go to the bedroom."

What?

He stared at her. Wasn't this too soon? Four dates wasn't enough for sex, right? Wait a minute, who cared? An attractive, intelligent, single woman who liked him wanted to have sex. Damn, it had been way too long since he heard those words. This was awesome.

"Do you think it's appropriate to sleep together on the fourth date?"

She blinked. Her smile disappeared. "What do you mean?"

"Well, when I signed the contract with Kinnections, they told me no sex until the relationship is completely solidified and we decided to be exclusive."

Sue gave a half laugh and patted his shoulder. "I think that's exactly what we're moving toward. And I won't tell Kinnections if you won't." She winked.

"I'm not sure I'm ready to commit completely on the fourth date. Won't you be limiting your options?"

Irritation flashed in her brown eyes. "No. But it

seems like you're telling me you'd rather wait to see if someone better comes along."

Oops. Definitely a double zap. "No, I'm sorry, I didn't mean it that way. I'd hate for us to breach our contracts."

"I don't care about the contract, Nate. What's the real problem here? Are you not attracted to me?"

Sweat prickled on his forehead. He fought the urge to wipe it off. "I'm extremely attracted to you. You're beautiful."

She sighed. "Good. I don't think we need to talk about this anymore, do you?"

"No."

"Let's go to the bedroom."

Shit. What was wrong with him? Sure, he'd experienced a bit of a tingle at the kiss, but mostly his dick was flat as a pancake, and this type of pressure definitely wasn't helping things down there. Maybe the fifth date would be more of the pop he needed. Maybe—

She screamed.

He jumped off the couch, ready to beg her forgiveness, and noticed her pointing to the front window. "There's someone out there!"

Nate peered out the window. His brother's face pressed against the glass, displaying a huge grin.

Thank God.

He opened the door and pulled him across the threshold. "Connor! Man, what a surprise! Welcome, welcome, come on in."

His brother looked awestruck at the enthusiastic greeting. Sue stiffened on the couch and forced a polite smile as she stood. Connor smiled sheepishly. "Sorry, didn't know you were on a date. Figured I'd pick you up for a beer since Jerry bailed on me. Hope your mojo isn't messed up." He turned toward Sue with a friendly leer that most women actually found appealing. "Nice to meet you. I'm Nate's older brother, Connor."

She offered her hand, which Connor took and pumped heartily. "Nice to meet you. What a pleasant surprise."

Her face said it was anything but pleasant, but she was a lady to the core. Nate wondered why he was so frickin' relieved that his brother had just interrupted his one opportunity to get laid. Maybe he did need to talk to Arilyn. "Hey, nice place. A little girly but doable. So, darlin', how did you two meet? At that crazy matchmaking place?"

"Er, correct."

"May have to sign myself up if it means I'll meet a hottie like you." Connor strolled through the rooms, grabbed a Sam Adams from the refrigerator, and popped it open. Nate noticed his date studied the construction boots, worn jeans, and T-shirt. His brother's muscles were evident, and his shaggy blond hair gave him a bit of a rocker look that never had him lacking for dates, but Sue crinkled her nose just a bit like she smelled something bad.

And in that moment, Nate didn't like her anymore.

"Did Nate tell you he works on rockets? That he came from NASA? This is one together dude."

"Yes, he is. And what do you do, Connor?"

"I'm in construction. Know that new court building in Westchester County? I headed up the crew."

"Very nice. It's lovely to see two brothers so . . . close."

Connor laughed and squeezed his shoulder. "Taught him everything he knows, darlin'. If you know what I mean." He gave a good-natured wink.

Sue dropped her mouth in horror.

Nate smothered a groan and said good-bye to the possibility of any close encounter of the sexual kind. "Sue, why don't I walk you out?"

The direct approach wasn't a good idea. The room dropped a few degrees under her chilly stare. "Of course. I don't want to interrupt your family time. I'll speak with you tomorrow?"

"Yes, I'll call you."

"Fine. Nice to meet you, Connor."

"You too, babe."

Her shoulders stiffened as she walked out. He closed the door behind him and faced his brother. Connor took another slug at his beer, wiped his mouth, and grinned. "You get any?"

Nate couldn't help it. He laughed. His brother was a walking, talking chauvinistic cliché and would never change. What the hell. Blood was blood, and anyone who judged that quickly was someone he didn't want to sleep with. Connor's heart was pure gold.

"Nah, I got none."

Connor paused. "Sorry, man. Did I screw it up for you?"

Nate shook his head. "Nope. Let's go to Mugs. I think you'll like it."

They grinned at each other and left.

twelve

KENNEDY CROSSED HER legs and watched her date's gaze snag on the short hemline of her skirt. Good. Her body was back in working order and all systems were ready to go. Tonight, she may decide to have sex.

A reward for skipping carbs all week.

She'd dressed carefully, knowing a fine line lay between elegantly sexy versus cheap and available. The black skirt may be short and snug, but the fire-engine red Donna Karan blouse she paired with it had bell sleeves and a demure neckline. The red heels were all "come and get me if you dare." The peekaboo game was a classic, and she always won.

Always.

Derek slid her another drink across the bar. A real estate mogul, he'd already taken a few phone calls and clearly knew how to work a room. He wore his hair cropped close to the scalp, sported a three-figure custom suit, and looked at her now with hungry blue eyes. His sharklike instinct and good looks kept her amused, and she was even hopeful a longer conversation would prove they had common ground to work with.

"So, how's your marriage quota doing?" He sipped

his martini and gave her an amused look. "Making money?"

She bared her teeth. Any potshots at the career she adored would never be tolerated. "How's the housing bubble treating you, babe?"

He laughed. "I like a challenge." His eyes gleamed. "Don't you?"

"Always. That's why I buck the odds every day. Finding love in this era and going head to head with divorce statistics reminds me to be brave."

"An interesting theory. Still not sure why you wanted to settle in Verily. You're missing out on the excitement and big bucks of Manhattan."

She swung her foot in rhythm to the blare of rock music. "I like the small-town atmosphere. And we do better with our niche here."

"Make sure you call me when you're ready to up-grade your residence. Your gorgeousness deserves a penthouse on the Upper East Side. Not a rundown cottage on the Hudson."

She tried to concentrate on his compliment rather than on the slight put-down about her choices. It didn't work. "You barely got through the door. Who are you to judge?"

Derek leaned in. His nostrils flared slightly. "I in-tend on seeing a lot more than the front porch. Un-less you'd like a tour of my new place? There's a hot tub you'd love."

"Presumptuous, are we?"

He took another sip. "No, just grown up. I haven't

met a woman who's intrigued me this much in a while. We'd make a great team."

Yes. They matched each other quite well. Derek seemed like a male version of her. Career oriented and direct, he obviously lived in the fast lane and loved beautiful things. He'd told her most of the night how much she pleased him—without making her feel objectified. His charm was potent.

He was very different from Nate.

As if her thoughts conjured him up, Nate walked into Mugs with a large man at his side. What was he doing? Didn't he have a date with Sue tonight? She watched him slide into a booth and imagined him ordering a Darth Maultini. Then needing to explain exactly how to create the cocktail. Ah, that was definitely his brother. Taller and larger, he wore casual clothes, had longish hair, but his sharp, angular features pegged him as family.

Derek's laugh jerked back her attention. "Any other woman I know would've jumped on my remark. You're gonna make me work for it, aren't you, babe?"

She tossed him a smile. "As Thomas Paine said, 'What we obtain too cheap, we esteem too lightly; it is dearness only that gives everything its value.'"

"I surrender. A rocking body and a brain. I'm yours."

She waited for the prickle of happiness she always experienced when she was able to enchant a man. The perfect foreplay banter usually got her body lit up and ready to go. Instead, her tummy remained steady and her nipples flat. One of her main issues was always the thrill of ensnaring male attention. She'd done the therapy and knew it came from her past of consistently chasing after approval from the opposite sex. When she lost the weight, it was as if she'd dropped into a candy store, and overindulging was an easy way to forget about her other problems. Beautiful men and physical pleasure. Did anything get better than that?

But tonight she just wasn't in the mood.

Her gaze flickered back to the booth. The drinks had arrived, and they sat with their heads bent together in conversation. Nate threw back his head and laughed. Connor grinned.

"Kennedy?"

She jumped. "Yeah?"

"I have to take this call, it'll be a few minutes. Forgive me?"

"Of course. I'll wait here."

He walked out of Mugs with the phone held to his ear, already barking instructions to his assistant or partner. Well, it was ridiculous not to go over and say hello. Introduce herself to Connor. It would only take a moment.

She grabbed her drink, slid off the stool, and marched to their table.

"Hey."

Nate looked up. Pleasure shone in his gaze as he took in her appearance, but it was more than a compliment. He seemed to look to the very inside of who she was, beyond the physical form she was so proud of. "Hey."

"I thought you had a date with Sue."

"We did. Are you here with the girls?" he asked.

"No, on a date."

His lips tightened. "Oh. That's nice. This is my brother, Connor. Connor, meet Kennedy from Kinnections. My matchmaker."

Connor reached out and shook her hand. "No kidding. I didn't know they made matchmakers like firefighters."

"Firefighters?" she asked.

"Darlin', you're so smoking hot you need a fire extinguisher for the job."

Nate winced.

Kennedy studied his brother and did the only thing she could under the circumstances.

She laughed. "I think that scores as one of the worst pick-up lines of all time. Please don't tell me you ever got lucky with that one."

Connor pumped up masculine pride. "Nah, but you're the first matchmaker I've ever met." He winked. "Had to bring out the big guns for you."

"Thank God. It's a pleasure to meet you, Connor. Nate speaks highly of you. Says you're in construction."

"Yeah, we just finished a job in Westchester. I may be heading out to Tarrytown next."

"Was it the government building?"

He lit up. "Yeah, that's the one we just completed."

"The architecture is gorgeous. But they have major flooding in that area. Do you do anything special with those types of buildings to protect from water flow?"

"Actually, we laid the groundwork with a few drainage systems, then built a special rigging beneath to withstand the pressure. It's a new technique they do now with the bigger jobs."

"Interesting, I always wondered about that. Did you hear about the project they're working on to save Venice?"

"Hell, yes. Called the Moses project. Working twenty-four hours a day and should be done in another five years. They're constructing a special wall that will release the pressure of the water when it comes in. Not too many people know about it. Hey, why don't you join us?"

"She's on a date."

Nate's voice came out flat and hard. She glanced toward the door and saw Derek pacing back and forth, the phone still pressed to his ear. "He's taking a call. I'll stay just for a few if I'm not interrupting."

"Nah, we're just bullshitting." He slid over to make room and she sat down. "How come you're not sleeping with Nate?"

Nate spit out his Darth Maultini. "What the hell?"

"Really, bro, you're a catch. I mean, I don't get it. You spend all this time at the gym making him work out, get him this new wardrobe, stick something in his eye so he looks good, and you're not doing him?"

Ah, the directness of the Dunkle brothers was quite refreshing. "We do go to the gym a lot. Has Nate told you how well he's doing in class?"

"Weight training," Nate interrupted. "It's weight-training class."

Kennedy ignored his glare and tried not to giggle. "Yes, of course, weight-training class. He's quite the star."

"Just like I taught him."

"Yes, but since he's a client, I'm afraid we can't 'do' each other."

Connor nodded. "Makes sense. So, I had a great idea. Instead of running a matchmaking agency to set up people for marriage, why don't you start a one-night-stand agency? It'll make it a hell of a lot easier to hook up for an evening."

Nate groaned and reached for his drink. "That's asinine."

"Actually, Connor is brilliant. It will make a ton of money. I just need to change the description to a brothel. Or a high-class escort agency. Then I'll get my name splashed in the newspapers, score a Lifetime movie of the week, and have to use my piles of money to bail myself out of jail. Thanks for the idea."

Connor shook his head when Nate laughed. "You're a real pistol, darlin'. Maybe I should let you hook me up after all."

"Only if you're open to love."

"A mirage. A perfect night of pleasure is realistic."

"Actually, that's the real mirage," she said. "The dark hides a lot. No one has to tell secrets, get messy, or deal with morning breath. Daylight is the hard part. The realistic part."

Nate stiffened. His gaze swung to hers, and suddenly, her breath shortened and her heart pounded and time stopped. God, his eyes were pure fire and burn, pinning her beneath his stare and forcing her to acknowledge there was something between them. Her words hung in the air, heavy and ripe with promise. What was she doing? What had she said?

Connor cleared his throat, as if he knew that he had interrupted something big. "Pretty deep. So, how about you ditch your date and we take a quick trip to Paradise City?"

"Where's that?"

He dropped his voice. "My place, darlin'. What do you say?"

Nate rubbed his forehead as if in deep pain. Kennedy laughed with delight. It got better and better. "Awful, just awful. As much as I adore Axl Rose, I'll pass." Derek strode through the door, his gaze scanning the room. "Gotta go. He's back." She slid out of the booth. "Nice to meet you, Connor. Nate, I'll talk to you tomorrow."

"Sure. Bye."

She walked away and wondered why she felt more

alive after a two-minute conversation with Nate than she had the whole evening with the man she might sleep with.

FUCK.

Nate finished his drink and tried to listen to his brother's long narrative about Jerry's cheating ex. He should've never come to Mugs. How the hell was he supposed to know she'd be out on a date? Not just any date, either. But with someone who matched her perfectly. He wore his clothes like a male model, towered over her in height, and had his hands on her thigh like he had a right to be there.

Prickface.

He brooded, drank, and imagined punching Mr. Pretty Boy in the face. The violent tendencies came from a dark, deep place inside he never knew existed. They chatted at the bar, clearly engaged in a flirty, verbal sparring that twisted his gut. He bet her date never stumbled over his words, or said idiotic things, or dropped food on his outfit. Bet he never got buzzed by a dog collar either.

Depression pressed down on him. He should've slept with Sue. Who cares if she was a bit judgmental of his brother? Most women raced for the door once he opened his mouth. She would've gotten used to his behavior, and eventually come to love him, and then Nate would've had an orgasm, and been happy instead of sexually frustrated and in the depths of misery.

Fuck.

The guy tugged her off the stool, grabbed her hands, and led her toward the back. Great. Probably sneaking in a good make-out session before moving the grand finale to his house. Or hers. The image of the kiss they shared in the rain floated in his vision. He'd thought it was hot and passionate and beautiful. But of course, it meant nothing to her. She was already dragging out the flavor of the week back there to imprint a new memory. He was a schmuck. Chasing after someone of Kennedy's caliber only set him up for failure.

He was done. He'd call her in the morning and get a new date set up. Mary was his second choice and seemed like a good fit. This time, he'd be more open and less opinionated. This time, he'd have some damned sex.

He sat for a while until Connor finally wound down on the new chapter of how beautiful women sucked and would eventually rip your heart to shreds. "You okay, bro? You look weird."

Maybe it was that third drink. Sometimes he was a bit of a lightweight. "Gotta hit the bathroom. Then I think I'm ready to wrap up."

He pushed his way through the crowds, took care of his business, and began to head back to his brother. Then paused. Was she still out there? Was he that much of a pussy that he needed to see her kiss someone else with his own eyes? Yes. Maybe the image would finally sear into his dick and his brain and he'd finally stop fantasizing about her.

Muttering under his breath, he went to the back door and stepped out. The small porch was black and silent. Gone. Probably home with him right now, taking off her clothes and diving into bed. Bastard.

"Don't."

The tiny whisper floated on the breeze. Nate paused and cocked his head. The low murmur of voices came from the side of the building, hidden beneath a few large bushes. A laugh. Crap, he so didn't want to interrupt some edgy role-play. He'd never recover.

"Don't play the virginal tease. Unless you like that. We've been leading up to this all night."

"Get your fucking hands off me."

A body slam. "Fine, we can do rough. Undo the blouse. Show me your tits."

A moan.

"I know you want it." A rip. "Nice tits, baby. Very hot."

"No."

The whisper was full of agony, not pleasure.

Nate moved.

In seconds, he ripped the guy off her. He stumbled back and shook his head. "What the hell, man? You're interrupting a private moment."

Nate studied Kennedy. She leaned back against the wall, her hands holding up her torn blouse. Her lips looked well kissed. She was breathing hard, as if aroused. And then he saw her eyes.

Vacant.

She stared back at him as if she were somewhere else, somewhere she didn't want to be, and was trapped in a hell of her own making. Jesus, what had happened? He tamped down hard on the swirling rage and temper dying to fly out, and concentrated on her. "You okay, Ken?" He spoke gently. It took a few seconds, but her gaze finally cleared. She blinked, as if surfacing from a deep sleep.

"Huh?"

He walked over and touched her cheek. His hand shook as he surveyed her defensive position. "Did this guy hurt you?"

Prickface's voice piped up in sheer disgust. "For God's sake, we're fooling around out here, Lancelot. You ruined a good moment."

Nate didn't break his gaze, just kept stroking her cheek. "Want me to beat the shit out of him? Call the cops? Talk to me, Ken."

Her voice came out husky. "No. I just want to go. I want to . . . go."

"With him?"

"No!" Her body burst into tiny convulsions that tore his heart to shreds.

"Shhh, it's okay. I got you." He put his arm around her back and led her forward.

"Oh, I don't think so." Prickface stood before them, a tiny smirk on his lips. He was a good few inches taller than Nate, with broader shoulders. "I'll take her home. I didn't do anything wrong, and you're not treating me like some scum date rapist. Don't embarrass me, Kennedy. Tell this guy we were just fooling around."

Humiliation flickered in her eyes, but it was the second emotion on her face—fear—that helped him make the decision that he would fight this asshat if he had to. "Forget it, things got a bit out of control. Nate, can you take me home?"

"Aww, babe, don't be like that. We'll talk. Let's not ruin a good night."

She flinched as he took a step forward. Nate stepped in between them and put out his hand. "This is how it's gonna be. Walk away and don't contact her again. I'll get her home. Got it?"

Prickface sneered. "Don't think so. I take care of my own dates and my business."

Nate tried for calm, he really did, but the fury exploded from the cold ball of lead in his gut and burst through his veins. "Last chance. Then I'm going to beat the shit out of you."

Prickface laughed. "You and what army?" He rolled up his custom designer sleeves and came at Nate slowly. "You know what? This is gonna be fun. I haven't taught someone a lesson in a long time."

"I agree. It's time I teach you when a woman says no, she means it."

"Nate!" Her cry of alarm soothed his soul. "Please, let's just go. I don't want you to get hurt."

"Stay here, Ken. I'll be right back."

"But—"

Prickface came at him with a pathetic lunge and a

sloppy right hook. Nate dodged left and connected. Score. Asshole blinked through a puffy eye, cursed, and got reinvigorated. "You're gonna pay for that one."

With a bored sigh, Nate judged his next move to be an uppercut followed by a kick to the knees. So nineties. He compensated with a sidestep and a few lightning jabs to the chin. Bone cracked. Score.

Prickface fell this time but got up. With a vicious curse, he went for the full-out body slam. Nate swept his front ankle and gave him the full left.

Knockout.

He left him bleeding in a pile by the bushes. Kennedy watched his approach with wide eyes. He took off his jacket, slid it over her shoulders, and buttoned it over her torn blouse. "Let's go. I got you."

"Not inside. Not like this."

He nodded. "I know. I'm taking you out the side, we'll walk."

She didn't answer. He tucked her in close to him for warmth, and they made their way through the streets of Verily toward his house. This time, she ducked her head instead of soaking up the sights and sounds of a busy evening, and he hurried his pace. She didn't question him when he settled her on the sofa in the living room, or when he put on a pot to boil water for tea. He quickly texted his brother to let him know he ditched him and walked home, promising to check in tomorrow. She sat docilely, staring at the wall. He left her alone with her thoughts.

But the anger burned.

He calmed his mind and his temper by pouring the water in a bright yellow mug Genevieve had left behind and dunking a honey-vanilla chamomile teabag. When a nice, rich color had been achieved, he used a teaspoon to fish out the bag. He didn't bother with milk, honey, or lemon, already sensing that she'd drink tea like coffee—straight up. He wiped off the droplets on the side of the mug, grabbed a coaster, and brought it into the living room.

"Drink this."

She automatically reached out for the cup. "I don't like tea."

"I know. But this will soothe your nerves."

She sipped the steamy liquid. He waited. She looked up and nodded. "It's good."

"Would you like a cookie to go with it? I have Stella D'oros in the pantry."

"No, thank you." She sipped more of the tea. "How did your date go?"

Nate sat down on the couch next to her, almost exactly as he'd positioned himself a few hours ago with Sue. Now, everything was different. "Not good. She didn't like Connor. I don't think I can see her again."

She studied her cup for a while. "I was afraid she'd be too stiff. I'm sorry. Maybe you'd like to date Mary?"

"Maybe."

"I liked your brother. He needs some training on what to say and what not to say, but he's real. And he took care of you. He sticks with the people he loves. I like that."

Dear God, help him. He was crazy about her. Just stick a fork in him and call it a day. Nate swallowed around the thick constriction in his throat. "Yeah. He's pretty cool once you get to know him. Guess your date didn't go too well either, huh?"

She snorted out a half laugh. "Guess not. You really beat his ass."

"Guess so."

"I had no idea you could fight like that. You went all Bruce Lee and *Fight Club* on me."

He fought a smile. "Nah, I didn't make those weird noises. It's easy. Body stature and strength are only a portion of success. It's mind-set, agility, and planning. Connor taught me the basics of how to defend myself. I came home with a broken arm one day from getting jumped, and after he drove me to the hospital, he took me straight to the gym. Showed me how to kick and use my natural abilities to fight. After that, I studied everything on martial arts and boxing and fine-tuned the process."

"You always seem to surprise me, Nate Dunkle."

"As do you, Kennedy Ashe."

She looked up, startled. Must have spotted something scary in his eyes, because she bent over and busied herself with finishing her tea and setting it down carefully on the coaster. "I better go. Thanks for helping me out."

"What happened?"

She froze. Curled her fingers into fists before deliberately relaxing them. Her voice wobbled only slightly before she pulled it back, but he caught it. "Just a kiss that got out of hand. I'm embarrassed you had to see it. Let's forget about the whole episode."

"You said no quite clearly. Why would you be embarrassed?"

The first sign of temper flared. She lifted her chin as if trying to gain strength and get her badass back. "Because normally I would've taken care of it myself. I've mastered my own moves over the years. Something freaked me out and I—I—panicked. I hate that you got involved."

"He almost hurt you. If I see him again, I'll kill him."

Her mouth fell open. Those lips were soft and moist, reminding him of a ripe honeydew melon before that first bite. She seemed taken aback by the violence in his words, but it was another part of himself he kept hidden. Years of bullying and being dumped for the next best thing had caused a buildup of scar tissue. Nate learned how to compartmentalize, using logic and reason to keep in the light. But anyone who laid a hand on his woman would pay.

His woman? What was happening to him?

He dragged in a breath. His body was on high alert from the adrenaline, which usually translated into sexual arousal. Textbook. Not that it took much to get there with Kennedy in the room. It was a hotbed of emotions, and his dick was just responding to the overstimulation of the whole damn evening.

"Don't say that. He said something to me. Stupid, I know, but it released a memory I wanted to forget."

He figured she wouldn't tell him, and that was okay. But he didn't want her alone tonight. Not when the monsters in the closet came out. "Stay here tonight. With me."

"Oh, I can't—"

"Not *with* me, of course. I know you're not interested. I'll crash on the couch. Take a few hours, sleep it off, and we can forget about it in the morning. Okay?"

She hesitated, but the flare of relief in her amber eyes settled the deal for him. No way was he sending her to an empty house. He may not be able to wrap his arms around her, slide between her thighs, and promise to slay her dragons. But he could damn well make sure she was safe.

"Are you sure?"

He didn't answer. Nate went into the hall closet, took down a blanket and spare pillow, and dropped them on the sofa. "Yes. Go to bed, Ken. There are T-shirts in my top drawer. I'll be out here if you need me."

She stared at him for a long time. Her lashes were extra long, dark, and thick; she lowered her gaze to the floor, as if she was still considering trying to keep her pride and return home. Finally, she rose and headed toward the bedroom. Her meekness broke his heart, but he bet her tiger roar would be back at the first light of day.

The door gently shut behind her.

Nate sank to the couch and dropped his face into

his hands. He'd never sleep tonight. Choppy emotions coursed through him like a water-rafting ride gone bad. Rarely did he get the opportunity to take care of someone. This was a time he could be her friend and supporter, and he wasn't about to screw it up by thinking about sex or wanting something to happen between them that was impossible. The next day, she'd be back to dating prickfaces again, but for a little while, she belonged to him. Sleeping in his bedroom, her head on his pillow, her scent soaking into the sheets.

It was enough.

He got himself together. Cleaned up the tea, turned off the lights, and lay down on the sofa to keep watch.

It was going to be a long night.

KENNEDY LAY ON TOP of the comfortable cotton sheets and stared at the ceiling. The lights blared full strength, and she knew Nate was right outside the door, but the words kept drifting in her brain.

Show me your tits.

Her body shook, but her mind raged against her weakness. Just words spoken by an idiot male pumped up by hormones. Ridiculous to backslide into the past. The worst was the way she shut down, helpless to fight or process the scene. What would've happened if Nate hadn't interrupted? Goose bumps broke out on her arms, and she pulled up the comforter to her chin in an effort to get warm. She rarely made mistakes with men, and yet she'd committed a doozy with Derek. Women didn't get a second chance.

Hadn't she learned that lesson years ago?

Sometimes the sounds haunted her most—fingers ripped, voices laughed. The crippling humiliation of helplessness while her body was exploited, as if it didn't even belong to her. She remembered afterward looking down at all her math and science books scattered on the concrete. Picking them up one by one and wishing she wasn't smart, wishing she were beautiful, so beautiful and thin that she held the power.

A whimper caught in her throat. The lights didn't help. She needed to banish the memory, forget the ghosts, and there was only one way to do it.

Kennedy climbed out of the bed and opened the door.

"Nate?"

"I'm here." He sat up, lifted the blanket, and beckoned her over. She dove for comfort, shivering with her bare legs exposed from the T-shirt. Blessed warmth wrapped around her as he tucked her into his chest, slid his arms open, and held her close.

The sweetness of his touch drove out the numbness, and she relaxed against him, her muscles melted into the hard planes of his chest, the strength of his biceps, the powerful thighs underneath her. He murmured soothing words into her ears and rested his chin on top of her head. In this darkness, she felt safe. In this darkness, with him, she opened the past and shared.

"There was a boy in school. He used to wait for me in the hallway and say things. Sexual things. He'd call me fat and say I needed to know about sex or I'd never get a boyfriend, that smart, fat girls would always end up alone. I was afraid of him, but no one ever helped. They thought it was funny. A lot of times, other boys would join him and laugh when I tried to get away."

His body tightened, but he kept stroking her hair, and she spoke against his chest, in the dark.

"He'd—he'd make me show him my breasts. Told me if I didn't do it, he'd send his friends to find me and they wouldn't be so nice. I was scared. I never knew when he'd show up or where. He'd just be standing there with this grin, and these sick eyes, and say 'Show me your tits' over and over. At first, I refused, but he threatened me. Said he'd send over his crew to play. So I finally did, Nate, I did, because I didn't know what else to do, and then he'd go away for a while."

She gulped for breath and hung on tight.

"One day, he followed me after school and pushed me into an alley. I thought it was the usual, but there were two other boys there. They surrounded me. Pulled at my shirt, kept telling me to show them my tits. I cried, but they didn't care, and they ripped open my shirt and bra and touched me. Laughed at my fat belly. Said fat girls needed to be good at blow jobs because that's how they got men to like them. They pushed me down and touched me in places, but I fought, and then someone saw them and came into the alley and chased them away."

Her heart pounded and sweat drenched her skin, though she shivered and buried deeper into his chest for warmth. "I hated them for making me scared. For taking away my body and my self and my sanity. I told my mother and went to the police. I reported it to the school. And after that, I stopped eating. I decided if I were thin and beautiful, I'd have power. I got sick, and they won after all. But not anymore. I got strong, and healthy, and owned my body again, on my terms."

"They didn't win," Nate growled. "Never again. My sweet, brave girl." He pressed kisses to her temple, holding her so tight she knew nothing could ever get to her if he was around. How long had it been since a man held her to comfort her? To give her strength? Never. She used men for companionship, for sex, for distraction. Not once had she told another person the truth about her past except for Kate, Arilyn, and her therapist. They'd kept her sane, but now she'd broken her cardinal rule and Nate was in the inner circle.

"I close my eyes and see it again and again. I need to get them out of my mind. I won't let them win tonight. Help me."

"What, sweetheart? What?"

"Make love to me."

The silence pulsed like it was alive, the demand hanging over them in a big bubble, awaiting his answer. She knew she was going to hell, knew what she asked was selfish and horrible and wrong, but already her body was alive, demanding she slake the primitive hunger roaring through her soul to be claimed by this man. One night. Just one night with her rocket scientist and she'd let him go again.

"Are you sure?" He forced her head up, digging his fingers into her scalp with a delicious pressure. "I'm not a saint, Ken. I've wanted you for a damn long time, but you don't have to promise me sex to get what you want. I'll hold you and kiss you and keep you safe, and you can go home in the morning. Don't offer me something out of guilt."

This time, she got angry. "How dare you accuse me of offering pity sex!" she hissed. "If I had a damn collar around your neck, I'd buzz you twice! I want you, Nate Dunkle. I want to replace those horrible memories with something good and right and sweet. And I know I'm screwed up, and I'm your matchmaker, and this is the worst thing I can ask you to do, but I don't care. So a simple yes or no at this point would be a good thing."

"Yes."

He crashed his mouth over hers.

She never saw him coming. He simply took over, possessed her mouth, and buried his hands in her hair to keep her still. His tongue stroked her lips until she opened wide and gave him what he wanted. He sunk in deep, and she moaned under the gorgeous skill of his teeth and lips and tongue. Using the perfect suction, he sipped and commanded and gave, until her head spun and she grew wet between her legs. His taste and scent swamped her senses, and she hung on for the ride, already under his spell and seeing no need to fight it. He kissed her endlessly, taking his time, learning every secret of her mouth. She arched up for more and clung to his shoulders, but he never hurried, as if she were a science experiment he intended to study and learn no matter how many hours it took.

Finally, he lifted his head. Her lids were heavy when she opened her eyes. Her entire body throbbed with need, from the tight ache of her nipples to the drenched core between her thighs.

"I want to fuck you, Ken. Slow and hard, in so many ways there's not a part of your body I haven't used and pleasured. Don't think this is going to be a quick round with sweet kisses and politeness. I've waited too long. Understood?"

Dear God, who would've thought her rocket scientist knew how to talk dirty? Heat sizzled in her veins and her mouth grew dry. "Yes."

"Good." Without another word, he lifted her from the couch and walked into his bedroom, laying her down on the bed. He stripped her quickly of his T-shirt, and his gaze devoured the flesh left bare by her black bra and thong as he stood beside the bed like a conquering warrior about to partake in his spoils. His stillness only heightened her arousal, the way he took in every inch, probing, his moss green eyes filled with intentions of what he was going to do to her. She shuddered with pure anticipation. She was used to being the aggressor, taking what she wanted, and guiding her lovers in the way she enjoyed. This time, she realized he was in charge.

And she loved it.

"You deserve multiple orgasms every day, sweetheart. The female body is designed for pleasure in a way the male can never attain." As he spoke, he ran his palm down her belly, across her quivering thighs, to her calves. He paused to pluck at the silver chain still clasped around her ankle, linking his fingers in a loose circle and bending her leg by the knee. "So many erogenous zones men ignore in the quest for the almighty orgasm. It should be a crime to miss out on such foreplay. Each step leads to a more intense explosion and release."

He hadn't even touched her, and she was already panting for breath. Her nipples stabbed against the lace of her demicup and demanded to be sucked. He was like a witch doctor for sex.

She allowed her legs to bend open, hoping for some early action, but he brought both hands to her foot and took a firm hold. "Take a woman's foot. There are certain pressure points that stimulate sexual arousal." Using his thumbs, he pressed, rubbed, and rotated over the sensitive soles, keeping the pressure just firm enough not to slip into being ticklish. Bending his head, he nibbled on her toes, his tongue coming out to lash the tender skin until a moan spilled from her lips. So good. How had she never known a foot massage could make her so hot? She'd always thought them to be relaxing, like at a spa, but now tingles shot up her legs straight to her pussy. "Do you like that?" His voice was husky with demand. "I need you to tell me what you do and don't like."

"Yes. I like that."

"Good." He continued for a while, until her muscles gave out and she sunk deep into the mattress. He slowly released her foot, ripped off his T-shirt and boxers, and stood before her naked.

Oh, my.

"Umm, Nate?"

"Yeah?"

"You're very . . . well endowed."

He grinned. A totally masculine, seductive, "curl your toes and surrender now" kind of grin. "The more to pleasure you with, my dear."

"Or kill me."

"I'll make sure you're ready first." His eyes gleamed. "Three orgasms beforehand should do it."

"Wh-wh-what?"

"Shush. I'm busy." He pulled her legs apart and crawled on the bed between them. Kennedy sighed with pleasure, ready to be ravished, but he bent his head and began nibbling around her knee.

"Umm, a bit higher, please."

One sharp nip on the backside shut her right up. A hot flash sizzled across her skin. "Another zone sorely neglected. The back of the knee, and of course, the inner thigh. Let's see which spot you prefer, shall we?"

Kennedy gasped as his fingers played and stroked her inner flesh, while his mouth licked and scraped sharp teeth down the plump curve right before her ass. Her clit throbbed madly for pressure, and little sparks of fire bumped across her body, firmly connected to every motion of his tongue and fingers.

"Hmm, interesting, you seem to favor your right side. I'll have to remember that."

If he had access to his pocket protector, would he whip out his pencil and pad and make notes? And how was that the sexiest thing she'd ever experienced in her life?

"Nate, please, I need—"

"Moving on and up. The mons." He pressed his nose against her mound and breathed in deep. Her hips shot up and begged for more, and arousal leaked through the flimsy lace. She waxed regularly, and the feel of his stubble against her smooth, swollen center made her fist her hands in the sheets and almost beg for mercy. Almost. He wasn't even halfway done with her body and he'd turned her on more than full-out sex ever had. "You smell so fucking good. Spice and musk and honey all at once." He divested her of the soaking lace in one graceful swoop, and then lowered his head again. "I love you bare here, it gives me full access to every delicious part of your anatomy." He nuzzled and stroked but never got to the most sensitive, critical parts that screamed for attention. "Caressing you here gives your body the signal to demand more, which increases your fluid, ah, like that. You're so beautifully wet and swollen."

His educational litany on the female body drove

her crazy with lust. Seems temper and arousal elicited his use of curse words, another secret part of her lover she adored discovering. "Ah, God, can we get on with it?"

He made a clucking noise against her mons, which almost shuddered a mini half orgasm through her. Almost. "Of course, we'll get back to the most important parts." He dipped his tongue into her belly button and nibbled. His hands coasted behind and unsnapped her bra with one hand. Her breasts fell free from their restriction, and cool air rushed over her hard nipples. She twisted to get closer, aching to get his tongue on her and have him suck. He spread butterfly kisses over her cleavage and rubbed his stubble over her breasts. "The breasts are usually the first part a man goes to, but there's so much more than just the nipples. Take the areolas. Yours are gorgeously dark and dusty and puckered. If I scrape my teeth slowly around, like this, and avoid your nipple, how does that feel?"

She groaned, trapped between heaven and hell and a looming orgasm. "Hurts a little, but so good. More."

He obeyed, treating the other breast to full treatment. Studiously avoiding contact with his tongue, he used his teeth to pull and elongate her nipple while his other hand plumped and stroked. She drowned in the sensation of being the subject of his study and wondered if she'd die before he even slipped inside her. "So beautiful, and responsive. I want to spend hours sucking and licking your breasts until I make you come without anything else. But we don't have time for that now."

Kennedy whimpered. She tried to wriggle her legs to rub against his thigh for some relief, but he pinned her open without giving her what she wanted. "Ah, the nipples. I've dreamed of yours for so long, imagined their color and texture, but this puts my fantasies to shame." He plucked and ran one thumb over the aching tip. She jumped and his gaze narrowed in lust and satisfaction. "Perfect. Deep red like a ripe cherry. Will you taste tart or sweet? Some men use clamps to restrict the blood flow and make them more sensitive, but a few careful pinches and enough foreplay will do that without the jewelry. Let me demonstrate."

Oh, he did. His tongue swirled and licked, while he pinched with just enough pressure to keep her on the fine line of exquisite pain and pleasure. She was reduced to grunts and moans for more, until he bestowed mercy and moved a bit higher.

"The nape of the neck. Again, extremely underused. But a woman can feel that touch over every inch of her body, which shoots right to the clit. I bet you'll prefer the right side again." He used his teeth and tongue and found the spot. Just as he promised, little convulsions of pleasure shivered through her and settled on the pulsing bud of nerves in between her thighs.

"Please, oh, please, are we done? I need you so badly."

"I warned you, Ken. I'm not about to rush through when I have you naked and open and under me. Final zone. The lips. Open your mouth for me."

She did, and he took her in a deep, dark kiss, his tongue thrusting in and out as he deflowered her mouth of any innocence. Pressed into the mattress, her bones liquefied, Kennedy surrendered to anything and everything he wanted.

He slid down her body and used his thumbs to pull her apart. His gaze burned hot and hungry as he studied every inch of her splayed pussy, then blew gently on her open lips.

"Nate!"

"The first orgasm is usually from clitoral stimuli. Let's see how much we can build it before you explode." Then his mouth was finally on her, his tongue licking her labia and treating her to a full open body kiss. She cried out and wiggled madly for the pressure she craved, just a scrape and she would—

His teeth gently dragged over the nub and he sucked on it.

She climaxed hard and fast and violent. Spasms shook her and she screamed as the pleasure coursed through her and didn't stop. Waves of release leaked from her body and he never stopped the gorgeous sucking pressure of his lips, so as she floated down, he forced her right back up and over into another orgasm.

When she surfaced, he was staring up at her, drinking in her expression with those intense eyes that shred past barriers and dove deep. She was too far gone to hide, a delicious languor sneaking into her bones and making her pliant. His low laugh told her it wasn't over.

"You ruined me. You come as hard as you do everything in life—full force and no holds barred. I'll have to do that several times a day. Did you enjoy that?"

Her voice broke in a whisper. "Yes."

"Good. Now on to the g-spot."

She had no time to protest or beg off. He curled his fingers and plunged inside, pumping in and out until he hit something that burst into streams of fire.

"Oh!"

"Right there." He smiled with fierce satisfaction and settled into a maddening push-pull of his fingers thrusting in and out of her body. She tried to suck him in deeper, but he kept the steady pace, never losing rhythm, until her muscles tightened and she was drawn as tight as a bow. She panted for breath and unbelievably, another release. "Ah, you're close, so fucking sweet, come for me again, yes, like that, fuck yes."

She came again in a long wail.

Kennedy shut her eyes and moaned in surrender. "No more. Can't, no more."

Another low laugh. A rip. Then a massive, throbbing cock poised at her dripping center. "Now you're ready."

He filled her without hesitation, pushing inch by

precious inch until he was buried balls deep inside her. Her head thrashed back and forth at the feeling of being stuffed so tight, there was no room to breathe, no room to fight or hold anything back for herself. But he didn't care, she tried to buck him off, but he tugged her wrists over her head and held them tight with one hand. "Open your eyes and look at me, Ken."

She did.

His whole body pressed into every inch of hers. She was pinned beneath him, helpless under his strength, his cock, his burning gaze that demanded she give up everything, right now, right then.

"Tonight, you're mine."

He moved. Back and forth, restating his verbal claim with his physical possession and drive to eradicate every memory from her mind except how Nate fucked her, body and soul. As if he realized she needed to be held down, he never let up the grip of her wrists, and she bucked madly upward, demanding more. A groan ripped from his lips. He quickened the pace, his cock driving in and out while he ground against her clit until the tension broke and exploded.

He shouted her name and spilled his seed, his hips still pistoned madly, wringing the last drop of pleasure from both of them. Finally, he collapsed on top of her and let go of her wrists. Kennedy tried to remember how to breathe, and his heart pounded against her ear. His skin was warm and slightly damp, and the musky scent of man and sex rose to her nostrils.

He inched off her slowly, but never broke contact,

choosing to roll to his side, their legs still intermingled. Minutes ticked by. Their breathing slowly resumed. Kennedy wondered if she was dead, then realized she didn't care.

He dropped a kiss on her forehead. "Rest. We've just gotten started."

Dear God.

Nate Ellison Raymond Dunkle was a master.

KENNEDY CRUSHED HER FACE into the soft pillow and sighed. What a perfect dream. Lying on her stomach, she flexed her calf, and the tiny bite of pain in her muscles made her smile. Funny, it was almost like she had sex last night. A lot of sex. The ache between her thighs throbbed for something to fill it. It was still night, and she was so tired and happy, she didn't want to open her eyes and let reality intrude. An odd fulfillment coursed through her veins and there was no need to screw with it right now. She'd just go back to sleep and . . .

Oh, my.

A tongue ran up the back of her thighs and gentle, but firm hands pushed her legs apart. Her body perked up and slammed into demand mode, wanting more of that teasing, wet kiss. Those hands moved to her ass and rubbed her cheeks, pulling them apart and massaging deep, and the tongue kept stroking, closer to her wet, throbbing center that wept for relief. She bit her lip and moaned into the pillow. Oh, please don't let me wake up too soon, oh please, oh please . . .

Teeth bit deep into the curve of her ass.

The sharp pain zapped her to attention. She bucked, but the raw shot of pleasure stole her breath.

"How does that feel? Too much?"

The rumble of Nate's voice hit her ears. Raw images of what they had done together danced in her vision, and suddenly she was wide awake. "Hurts. But then it feels good. What are you doing?"

"Everything. I've neglected your rear and that's a crime. I knew I missed another erogenous zone."

Her belly dropped. This just wasn't . . . possible. "You didn't take a Viagra or anything, did you?"

He laughed low and the vibrations against her skin coaxed another shiver. "I have you. Don't need it. I studied tantric principles that teach control. A little BDSM. Various postures to ensure full stimulation."

He did something so erotic and naughty to her rear she whimpered. Usually, she hated men looking at her bottom. It was the one part of her anatomy she felt was too big no matter how much she worked out. "I'm more comfortable on my back."

"I'm not. Reach out and grab the headboard."

The command threw her off kilter, but she did it. "Nate, I don't think I can have another orgasm."

Another silky laugh. Those wicked fingers dipped into her channel, stretched, and played. "Liar. I love your ass. Firm, full, and sweet as sugar. I want to try something. Tell me if you don't like it."

"I—oh!"

As his fingers played between her legs, he slapped

her rear with the open palm of his other hand. The sound of flesh against flesh exploded in the room. She flinched, but tingles of warmth spread over her ass and into her clit. "Yes. No?"

She gritted her teeth together and told the truth. "Yes."

"Hell, there's just a blush of pink, I need more." He gave a few more firm slaps, then removed his fingers to rub her stinging cheeks. The mixed-up sensations of pain, pleasure, and arousal pumped through her and made her crazy. "So fucking beautiful. I was never into the dom thing, but damn if I wouldn't love to tie you up and pleasure you until you beg."

She moaned. "I'm begging now. Can't take it."

"Your back is so graceful. The smooth line of your spine, the dimples above your ass." He ran his tongue up and down, nibbling on her spine, continuing to rub, press, and arouse. Suddenly, he moved up and lay completely on top of her, his front pressed to her back, his erection at her dripping entrance. His hot breath rushed over her ear as he tugged her hair to the side. His tongue caressed the delicate shell of her ear, nipped her lobe, and his hands teased the plump sides of her breasts. She was trapped, helpless, waiting for him to make the next move, and she realized in that moment he held more power over her than any man before him. Her mind spun, her body cried out for relief, and still he pushed her limits, his throbbing cock slipping in a few precious inches and then stopping.

"I want to fuck you again."

"Yes!"

"How bad do you want it?"

A whine escaped her lips. "I'll do anything. Please."

"Even play more golf?"

"Bastard."

His dick slipped out of her and he bit her shoulder. A shudder wracked her body. "Yes! I'll play golf with you, I promise."

"Good girl. Let go of the headboard and get on your knees."

She positioned herself like he demanded, and she heard the rustle of a wrapper as he sheathed his penis with a condom. He pushed against her entrance with slow, deliberate movements until he was fully seated. He filled every inch, driving away her breath, and she wiggled her hips, desperate for him to move. His groan gave her a surge of satisfaction. "You're going to kill me."

"Good. Can we get on with it, please?"

"Brat. I read in *Cosmo* that if you line up doggy style, I'll have a better chance of hitting your g-spot every time."

She arched her back and tried to force him to do something. His length throbbed inside of her, making electrical circuits of fire shoot off at various nerve endings. "Sounds like a plan. Any time now."

His chuckle gave her a bad feeling. "Not yet. I need to properly stimulate you first."

"Trust me, I'm stimulated."

Remaining still, he rocked tiny inches back and forth, just to give her a taste, while his hands stroked down her back and reached underneath to play with her nipples. Little tugs tightened the nubs to hard points, and her breasts swelled underneath all the attention. Her hands trembled as she held herself up, helpless and aching for his next touch. Those talented fingers spent long minutes on her breasts, before moving to her back. He smoothed his palms down and nibbled on her spine, licking downward, pulling her ass cheeks apart to stab his tongue against her until she writhed and begged and pleaded.

Grasping her hips, he pulled out and slammed back into her.

The rippling delight spread out over her body and concentrated on her pounding clit. He swiveled his hips and did it again. Then again.

The fifth stroke hit the spot. She screamed as bliss shimmered and gripped every muscle.

"Ah, got it. Hold on, sweetheart."

She twisted the sheets in her fingers and gave up. Driving, hard thrusts met that magic place, forcing her higher and higher, the tension squeezing mercilessly until her throat clogged with tears and she knew she'd die from the ache. His fingers slipped between her legs, pinched her clit hard, and then let go.

"Ah!"

The orgasm took over and shattered her foundation. She rode out the release, but he kept going, until the second orgasm ripped through and she collapsed helplessly on the bed. He stroked and murmured soothing words as he rolled her boneless body over onto his chest and held her tight. She closed her eyes and wondered if her rocket scientist had ruined her for life.

thirteen

NATE KNEW THE moment reality broke through. He half opened his eyes to find Kennedy hopping around the bedroom, trying to get dressed. Tiptoeing softly, she kept darting worried glances at the bed, as if afraid he'd rear up and grab her. He enjoyed the view as she tried to wiggle into her ruined thong, then muttered a curse as she balled it up. She bit her lip as if making a decision, and then shimmied into her miniskirt without underwear.

Oh, yeah.

He wondered what she'd do about the shirt, but she tugged her discarded bra from under the pillow, slipped it on, and went to his closet. With another quick look at the bed, she tugged a white button-down shirt from the hanger and donned it, fastening every last button up to the neck. It hung past the short skirt but she didn't seem to care. She disappeared into the bathroom, and he heard the water running at a trickle while she probably tugged at her hair and brushed her teeth. He had a spare toothbrush in the cabinet, but he figured he'd let her find it and not ruin her escape plan.

At least, not yet.

Nate stared at the cheery light streaming through

the cracks in the shutters. Birds chirped merrily, happy to embrace spring, but morning brought the end of his fantasy. He mourned the loss of taking her one last time, watching her face when she came, her body shuddering under his, knowing he was the one who caused such fierce pleasure and feeling more powerful than a Greek god.

She'd want to forget. Pretend it was a blip on the radar and they could go back to the way things were. Nate knew it was already too late.

He was in love with her.

The shattering conclusion did not come accompanied by harps, choirs singing, or bubbling joy. Instead, he felt like shit. Depressed. Helpless.

Pissed off.

He sifted through all his options. Admit his feelings and beg her to give him a chance. She'd panic, cite a dozen excuses why they wouldn't work together, and maybe even stop being his matchmaker in an effort to run.

Scratch that one.

Pretend it was one great night of sex and he was already over it. Date Mary, date any woman who was interested, and focus on moving on. Connor would definitely advise this option. If he did that, Nate would come off a stud and keep his man card.

Scratch that one too.

Do nothing. Refuse to talk about it and see what happened. By not analyzing the entire episode, he'd give her enough rope to play the denial game, yet not enough to strangle any future interaction. In other words, leave all options open.

Best one yet.

The door creaked.

She tiptoed a few steps, saw he was up, and froze. A sick smile curved her lips. He craved to tumble her back on the bed, kiss her senseless, and give her the fortieth orgasm she begged him not to give her last night.

Instead, he said the first word that came to mind. "Hey."

Her smile turned genuine. She tugged at his shirt. "Hey."

He cleared his throat and threw off the covers. Ignoring his morning wood, he got up from the bed, dragged on his boxers, and turned. Her eyes widened at the sight of his erection, which only made it a hell of a lot worse. "Oh, my. Umm. I better get going. It's kind of late. Thanks for last night."

He raised his eyebrow.

She clapped a hand over her mouth. "I meant, thanks for letting me crash here. I meant—you know what I meant. Right?"

She was too adorable. There wasn't another woman alive who had so many layers. She was a sexy hot mess. "Right. But you can't sneak out just yet."

"I wasn't sneaking!"

"Baby, you're doing the entire walk of shame thing. Not that I'm complaining. But I took good care of you last night, and you owe me something. Something big."

Her gaze dropped to his straining dick. She swallowed, but the gleam of lust in her eyes almost killed him. "I thought you were satisfied."

He took a step forward. "Only one thing is going to satisfy me this morning."

"You're not being very gentlemanly." Her voice was breathless and had an edge of arousal. He took a deep breath and smelled her. "I think you got enough."

"You cut me short on something and you know what it is."

She trembled. Her tongue snaked out and licked her lower lip. "Maybe if you ask me nicely."

Another inch and he faced her. He lifted her chin. Her whiskey eyes blurred and he knew one push would put her down on her knees. She'd like it. He'd love it. They could delay the inevitable daylight for an hour more. Or two.

"Then I'm asking."

His thumb traced her pouty lower lip, picked up the moisture, and brought it to his own mouth to suck. She moaned. "Go ahead."

"I want you to come—"

"Yes."

"With me to have breakfast."

He stepped back. Confusion flickered over her face. "Huh?"

"Breakfast. I'm starving, and there's nothing good in the kitchen. Let me take a quick shower and we'll go."

"I have no clothes."

"We'll swing by your place so you can throw on a pair of jeans. Be out in a minute."

He shut the door behind him, then cranked the water to the coldest setting. The key was to throw her off balance. Maybe with enough time, she'd come to the conclusion she was just as crazy about him. He may not be in her league, but he damned well wasn't a pussy. Putting up a fight was nothing new to him, and he intended to give her a good one.

It was gonna be a hell of a morning.

AN HOUR LATER, THEY were squeezed into a booth at the Dish and Spoon diner. He asked for a Clorox wipe, cleaned the table on his own terms, and relaxed in the booth as if they hadn't just had sex a hundred times.

For reasons unknown, Kennedy had meekly followed his plan. Changed into a respectful pair of jeans and clean T-shirt, Coach sneakers, and threw her hair into a messy topknot. Her original plan was to get the hell out of Dodge, give them some space, and have the *talk*.

Guilt and satisfaction intermingled and fought for dominance. She was setting him up with women from Kinnections and had no right to screw with his head. How could he go on a date with a clear mind and heart when they'd just had a rollicking night of sex? Upon waking, she'd sworn to herself that it wouldn't happen again. She'd confess to Kate and Arilyn and turn over the rest of Nate's journey into their capable hands.

Instead, he'd confused her with that mouthwatering naked body and sexy speak. She didn't even fight him on the diner choice. Her breakfast consisted of fruit and Greek yogurt. The sight of his runny eggs, crisp bacon, and greasy hash browns made her sweat. She stuck with her original order and picked at a ripe strawberry, wondering why she suddenly felt cranky after experiencing a million orgasms.

"Do you know the fat content in that dish?" she pointed out. "That's more than your daily share of calories per day."

"I worked out. So did you." He forked up an egg with a piece of rye toast. The top gleamed wetly with butter. "A bout of standard, missionary sex burns about three hundred calories per hour. An orgasm adds about an additional one hundred calories. Calculating the various positions we used, number of orgasms, and hours divided, we're looking at about two thousand calories. One egg plus bacon is about one hundred thirty-six calories. Add the hash browns and toast, I'll still be way under my calorie count for what we burned off last night. Here, have half a strip of bacon. You need the protein."

Her head spun from his amazing facts and figures regarding sex. She sipped her black coffee and struggled. My God, was it possible to work off that much in one pleasurable evening? "But it's not even turkey bacon," she said. She tried hard not to whine.

A smile touched his lips. He broke off half, added a quarter of his egg, and a slice of rye bread. "You need some whole grains and straight protein, sweetheart. Just have a little."

She licked her lips and studied the food on her plate like sizing up the enemy. "Maybe just a bite." The moan escaped her the moment her teeth took hold of the crisp strip. Even the scent drove her crazy, and she closed her eyes to savor every bite. "So good."

He muttered a vicious curse, but she was too gone to care. "What's on your agenda for today?" he asked.

"Not much. Clean. Work."

"I need a golf partner."

She snorted. "I highly doubt it. Besides, you work on Saturdays, right?"

"I need a day off. So do you. And you promised me a favor last night, so I'm collecting."

Kennedy nibbled on the buttery crust. She realized she should be angry or irritated at him calling in a marker she promised during the height of sex, but the perfect combination of eggs, toast, and bacon had turned her brain to mush. "Fine. But then this entire thing is done with us. Understood?"

"The golf? Yes, I won't ask you to play golf with me again."

"And other stuff. All the other stuff."

"The sex? We can always talk about that later. Let's not ruin a good breakfast. Here, you have to try one hash brown."

"Oh, no, I—"

He forked it on her plate. "Just one. They're tiny."

"Maybe just one. So about last night. I think—"

"Something's been bothering me for a while. Wayne—my lab partner—believes in this new groundbreaking physics discovery of time crystals. Quite controversial. Guy from MIT, Wilczek broke the theory, and it's been dividing camps and causing quite a stir in the physics community. If they prove we can create time crystals, we're literally contradicting the entire basis of symmetry. Wayne thinks it will change the world. I think there are too many inherent problems from the origin. Though I'm not taking away the excitement of challenging mainstream theories and pushing physics to the next level."

Relief broke through her. He didn't want to talk about the sex or their relationship. Maybe he believed, like her, that it was a wonderful evening that shouldn't go any further. Maybe he'd already accepted they'd spend a few more hours together at the golf course, then part without another word of the encounter. Maybe he'd even begin to date Mary. That would be nice.

Damn, the hash brown was so good. Very tiny, though. Maybe a few more. "They're claiming it's possible at this point, not confirming," she offered. "It's not like we're talking time travel here. But to have a timekeeping system for space would be groundbreaking. The energy exists in the lowest possible state so there won't be any perpetual motion. I'd like to see more research before I jump in and make assumptions. I'm a bit surprised. I always thought of you as a more progressive brain."

She swiped a potato into the pool of ketchup, which was super low in calories, and smiled as the taste of salt and potato exploded in her mouth. She was so happy.

"I am progressive. I'm also a classicist."

She rolled her eyes. "Whatever."

"How long have you been studying physics, Ken?"

The hash brown dropped from her fingers. Shit. One peek at him showed his face as a complete study of concentration. He had the same look last night when he was between her thighs and bringing her to orgasm. Her body clenched in response, and she grew wet. How was he able to do that with just a look? "What are you talking about? I saw it on this science blog when I was searching for ShoeDazzle.com."

"Why are you lying?" he asked softly. "Why is it so bad to admit you're amazing at science and math?"

Her head snapped up. She was so not going there. She'd already told him too much. "Not to disappoint you, but I really don't know much in those fields. I remember stuff from school, I occasionally read a blog or two, but don't try to make me into something I'm not. I'll only disappoint you."

Green eyes burned into hers. She shivered under all that concentration, her mouth going dry as she tried to remain cool and detached. Those lush lips framed by his stubble gave him the rough morning-after look she found sexy as hell. The Calvin Klein denim jacket, button-down shirt, and snug jeans showed off his muscular body. Not that she needed reminding. Nope, she knew every inch of him, from his cut abs to the toned biceps able to hold her up while he pounded into her. He didn't look nerdy at all. In fact, he looked as steamy as a male model fresh off a catalog shoot.

She dragged in a breath. Focus. He wanted an explanation of her brains, and she wasn't gonna give it to him. She waited and prepared for a knockout battle. She'd walk out and end this right now.

Instead, his body slowly relaxed, and he nodded. "Okay. Are you done? I want to get to the course before the big groups come in."

"Maybe this isn't a good idea." She paused. "Maybe we should reschedule."

"No, you promised. Let's go." He grabbed the bill and went to the counter to pay, while she tried to rein in her sexual and physical appetite. A few hours of golf wouldn't hurt. It was a beautiful day, she'd get some light exercise, and they'd go their separate ways.

A FEW HOURS LATER, she admitted that Nate Dunkle was a sneaky son of a bitch.

Other than the crankiness he showed on the course after she got something called a birdie, he was the perfect companion. He showed her how to manipulate her grip and root her feet for more power. His fingers stroked, soothed, and caressed. He insisted on pressing his erection against her buttocks and wrapping his arms tight around her on the pretense of helping her with her swing. As they progressed past each hole, he muttered more and even began scribbling some ridiculous formulas on his notepad. Very confusing. Every time she thought she did really well, he seemed to get more frustrated. When his ball landed in that pretty lake, he'd almost lost his temper. Which was kind of interesting. And hot.

Instead of dropping her off afterward, he forced her to stop and rest at one of the outdoor cafés. He drank a microbrew, and she sipped a glass of wine as they people watched, bantered, and talked about a wide range of topics. He paused at a farmers' market, and made her close her eyes while he shopped for a variety of secret ingredients he refused to show her. Every time she tried to peek in one of the big brown bags, he rolled it tighter. Whatever. Maybe he was going to cook a special secret meal for Mary. That would be nice.

On their way home, he dragged her into an art exhibit, where they debated their favorite artists, and he came up with a ridiculous theory of how Monet used a famous mathematical equation to generate the randomness of his water lilies.

Yeah. Right.

It was early evening when he finally walked her to the door. Kennedy frantically searched for an easy, casual way to say good-bye and put their wild night of sex behind them. She decided on the straightforward approach.

"Well, thanks for a great day. I'm really tired, so I better get in." She smiled brightly, a connoisseur at the professional brush-off with men, but he ignored her and strolled right through the door.

"I like your place," he stated. His gaze took in the sparse, modern decor, clean lines, and overall expensive design.

"Thanks. Umm, Nate—"

"I know you're tired, but I need a favor. Remember how I said I don't cook much? I want to try. Building up a palate is the mainstay of a good culinary education." He set the bags on her countertop. "I need a taste-test dummy."

She closed the door behind her and faced him. "What?"

He waved a hand in the air. "Bad term. Not a literal dummy, of course. It's very simple. I blindfold you, and you let me know how each of the things I bought taste. I'd like to make a full-course dinner. Stretch my boundaries. What do you think?"

Her head was already spinning. "Umm, I think learning to cook is a wonderful idea. But it's late. And I don't know how me taste testing is going to help you."

"I'll get a woman's perspective on the menu I'd like to try. Won't take long. Please?"

She eyed the bags with suspicion. "Why do I have to be blindfolded?"

"I saw it on *Hell's Kitchen*. You have an open mind when you don't visually peg the ingredients. Allows your taste buds to take over as the primary sensory perception."

Her skin tingled with anticipation. This was a definite no brainer. Reject the plan, get him out of her apartment, and get to bed early. Alone.

"Fine. I'll do it."

He lit up. Removed his jacket and hung it neatly in the closet. Dressed in dark jeans that cupped his spectacular ass, he pushed up the sleeves on his casual aqua shirt as if prepping for something big. He washed his hands and dragged a chair over to the table.

"I can sit on the stool," she pointed out.

"No. A chair is sturdier. Trust me."

Sturdier for what? She shrugged. "What do I have to do?"

"Can you get me a scarf, please?"

"Kinky."

"I can be." She laughed, got him a colorful purple scarf, and sat down. "Now, I'm going to blindfold you and then I prep some of the food." He gently placed the scarf over her eyes and tied a loose knot. "Can you see anything?"

"Nope."

"Okay, just give me a minute." She heard cabinet doors open and close. The rustle of bags. The scent of freshness and a variety of herbs, all mixed up. The refrigerator door squeaked, then went silent. The shuffling around the kitchen slowly relaxed her, and she let her mind drift while she waited for the first taste.

She sensed him kneeling in front of her. The powerful aura of his male energy wrapped around her like an invisible vise. A rush of warm breath hit her lips. Her heart pounded in an uneven rhythm. "Are you ready for your first taste?"

The rich, sensual words rumbled over her ears. Her tummy dipped. "Yes."

"Open up."

Her lips parted. She expected the cool, smooth touch of a spoon, but he used his fingers. He placed something small and slippery on her tongue. The flavor of ocean, salt, and smoke tickled. The firm bite against her teeth exploded juice in her mouth. The raw earthiness swamped her in pleasure, and her body responded as if an electrical cord got plugged in and fried.

"Oyster." A smile touched her lips as she caught the last bite of citrus. "The balance is amazing."

He wiped a trickle of moisture from her bottom lip. "Good girl. It was an oyster. You like?"

She remembered the way he had plucked at her nipples, biting, licking, and then asked her the same question. Kennedy rallied for sanity. "Yes."

"Next one." She waited, her senses on high alert. "Open for me." Her thighs relaxed as if trying to respond to the command, and the morsel was pushed into her mouth. Creamy, thick cheese combined with a hint of garlic, olive oil, sweet basil, and crisp tomato. As if picked right off the vine, her taste buds wept with delight. "Cheese," she moaned. "Mozzarella cheese. Tomato. Oh, God, so good."

His hands began stroking her face, her shoulders, lulling her into a more relaxed trance. Her legs fell open and her pussy throbbed. The simplicity of the flavors flowed over her, in her, and she let her head fall back. He murmured something against her ear. "You're very good at this game, sweetheart." His hands cupped her breasts, massaging her through the cotton. "Do you want more?"

"Yes."

"I want to take off your shirt."

His outrageous demand was over the top. It deserved a slap, an electronic buzz, and a kick out the door. Instead, she was so turned on she couldn't speak for a minute. "Do it for me."

He growled. Worked her shirt over her head. Cool air rushed over her breasts and tightened her nipples. She wanted to cry, it felt so outrageously decadent. Sitting in her kitchen, blindfolded, topless, and having Nate feed her. His thumbs ran over the hard nubs, flicked them through the lace, and then his mouth was suddenly on her, hot and wet, sucking her nipple through the fabric and flicking his tongue back and forth. She cried out, and arched into him, her hands holding him tight to her. He pleasured the other breast, and then he was gone. A clatter of a utensil hitting the granite. The rustle of paper. Each second twisted the tension in her stomach another knot.

Breathing was a luxury now. She panted for air and scissored her legs, but he spoke quite calmly. "Ready for your next bite?"

She nodded.

"Open."

Ah.

Sushi. The texture was cool, and smooth, but the fish had a thickness to it that puzzled her. She bit down. The tanginess of teriyaki sauce dripped over it but didn't overwhelm the natural flavor of the fish, which broke open and became flaky.

"Salmon! It's salmon, I know it."

"Very nice." As she chewed and swallowed, he unhooked her bra. Her breasts spilled free into his waiting hands, and the combination of his touch with the delight of the food splintered her. "I think you deserve a bit of a reward before our next one." The button on her jeans snapped. His fingers coasted over her stomach and traced the line of denim around and around. "Lift your hips up sweetheart. You're losing the jeans."

She waited for her inner rational voice to scream like a banshee and tell him absolutely not. No way. No how. No.

"Yes."

He slid off the jeans, unhooking them from around her feet. She heard his sharp intake of breath. "You're so fucking beautiful." He stroked and caressed her calves and upward, gently parting her legs. "And so wet." His finger traced the line of her panties. She jerked, her body shuddering as if on the verge of climax. "We have two tastes left. Let's get you a little something to wash it down with."

She whimpered at the loss of his touch. A cabinet slammed. The sound of liquid poured into a glass echoed in her ears. "Take a tiny sip of this. Let me know what you think."

He cupped her chin and tipped the glass to her lips. The wine trickled down her throat, heavy and ripe, the scent of blackberries drifting to her nostrils and soaking her mouth. A complete sensual treat, she reveled in the intense tannins and boldness. "Red wine. Berries? Fig?"

"Blackberries. Nice. Have a little more."

She took another sip at the same time his palm cupped her sex.

Her hips shot up, the wine slid down her throat, and she almost fell apart right then. His thumb coaxed the hard nub of clit to come out and play, and his fingers danced and massaged over her core, until the fabric was wet and full of her scent. "Magnificent," he murmured, as if she was one of his scientific experiments. "Every time you try something you love, your body responds. You could probably orgasm from the right flavors alone."

A choked laugh spilled from her throat. She was crazy. He was crazy. Hell, they were crazy to be acting out a foodie sex scene, yet she couldn't stop, needed him to finish where he'd taken her. Why wasn't she feeling embarrassed or horribly vulnerable? She was naked, he was fully clothed, and yet she felt completely safe with him in a way she'd never experienced before. He'd take care of her, at the expense of himself. And right here, right now, she only craved more. "Stop teasing me," she moaned. "I need—"

"I know what you need, baby. Lift up."

Her panties came off.

She waited for his hands or his mouth, but there was only cold air and emptiness. "Nate?"

"One last taste." She may die. She squeezed her legs together for relief. "Legs apart. No cheating."

She obeyed, completely helpless under his spell. He caressed her cheeks, traced the line of her lips. "Open for me, Ken. Wider. More. Yes, just like that."

Her heart pounded like a pack of Thoroughbreds nearing the finish line. Every muscle locked with tension, awaiting the final spoonful.

His fingers pushed past her lips, her teeth, and lay the object on her tongue.

Chocolate.

Bittersweet, rich, and creamy, the chocolate coated her tongue, melted in her mouth, and took her over the edge.

"Oh, God!"

The blindfold was ripped off and his mouth took hers in a rough kiss, his tongue thrusting in and out of her mouth while his fingers delved between her legs and buried deep.

She came hard, bucking against the chair, a dozen sensations pulling her in different directions. He muttered something against her, hiked her up so her legs wrapped around his hips, and stumbled to the bedroom. In minutes, he tumbled her on the bed, shucked off his clothes, and fit himself with the condom.

She was still shaking from the aftereffects of the first orgasm, when he pushed her knees back and took her in one full, deep thrust.

Her body milked him, welcomed him deep, and clamped hard around his dick. He took her savagely, and she loved every moment, raking her nails down his back as she shattered for the second time. He called out her name with his lips merged to hers, jerking his hips against her as he came.

She tried to move, tried to speak, but it was too much and she was too far gone. A strange tightness in her chest smothered her. A sob caught in her throat.

Oh, no. Why did she feel like she was suddenly going to burst into tears?

He tucked her against his chest, and gently took the pins out of her hair. He smoothed the strands over her shoulders and pressed a kiss by her temple. He didn't say a word, just seemed to wait for some kind of response. As if he knew she was about to tell him something important.

She was so good at keeping secrets, even from herself, it took her a while to realize she ached to give him something on a deeper level. At this moment, in the dark, with a man who made her feel completely safe, she wanted to tell him the truth.

The words spilled from her mouth unchecked.

"I wasn't just fat. I was smart. Really smart. I loved

math and science and history. It was as if those were the things I could control, the things that made sense. I was in a bunch of geeky clubs. The day they attacked me, I remember seeing all those books spread out on the ground. And I realized the books, the subjects that I loved, had done nothing to protect me. They had actually made things a lot worse. Being smart really didn't get a woman anywhere; being beautiful and perfect was the key. I went home and ditched all my books, quit the clubs, started screwing up in school. I became obsessed with things that looked good. I switched my interests to fashion design, apparel, anything that made the world prettier. I became my own Frankenstein. My mother was thrilled—she hated having a smart, fat daughter, and once I began losing the weight, she kept encouraging me. Started to take me to charity events and seemed proud. My father was the one who put me in therapy when he realized I was killing myself. My mother said I looked fine."

She relaxed her viselike grip on his arm and finished. "I had a great therapist. One day, I realized I didn't want to die. I wanted a life, a real life, not the shadowy dark place I'd been living in, where food was the enemy and mirrors were to be avoided. I had lost myself, so I decided to put the pieces back together. My parents ended up divorcing, and my father remarried. We rarely speak. Mom moved away years ago with her new husband. I was alone, but I think it was better that way. Kate and Arilyn helped, and I found I really was great at design and running social functions. I concentrated on building those talents and tried to forget the past. But sometimes it sneaks up on me."

She fell silent and the emptiness hit. Suddenly, all the buildup of secrets and fear let loose and floated away. The only thing left to take its place was a deep sadness . . . for that vulnerable girl she once was, and what she'd given up because she didn't believe she was worth it.

Kennedy tried to roll away, needing the distance, but his arms held her tight. His warmth and scent wrapped around her and provided comfort. Slowly, she gave up the fight and took what he offered.

"It's probably time to realize the real truth, Ken. The truth that I saw the moment I laid eyes on you."

"What?"

"You're both. Smart and beautiful. On the inside and outside. You don't have to choose one over the other anymore. You can just be exactly who you were meant to be. And I think that's damn perfect."

She shut her eyes and buried her face in his chest. "I'm a mess."

"Shhh. Sleep, sweetheart. It'll all be better in the morning."

A smile curved her lips and then the darkness was coming and she gave herself up to it, letting sleep claim her.

fourteen

NATE WATCHED WOLFE pin his gaze on the ball, draw back, and swing through. The club face was nicely square, and he watched his approach shot fall close to the green. Quite respectable, especially for a novice.

Wolfe looked over, not trusting it was a good shot. Nate grinned. "Nice job. Your form has really improved and you're hitting the green. We haven't had to trudge through the water or sand in a long time."

Wolfe laughed as they began walking. "Hell, I'm getting it on the green *and* on the right course. It's a miracle."

"Nah, your swing is pure power. Must be that tattoo."

"You should see what a piercing can do. Especially in a painful place."

Nate winced. "Gonna pass on that one."

They played the next few holes in comfortable silence. Nate missed having guy friends. Wayne rarely spoke about anything other than work, and his brother was family, so he had to take his shit one way or the other. He'd never peg Wolfe as the type of guy who'd want to be friends with him. Nate figured he'd

ditch him after a few sessions, but he seemed genuinely interested in continuing the golf lessons and
even suggested meeting for a beer after work last
week.

"When's your golf meeting set up for?" Nate
asked. His club sliced the air and the ball sailed in a
full arc to drop a foot from the hole. *Yes. If only Ken
could see that one.*

"I maneuvered a Friday morning session into his
group. Let me tell you, it was tougher than infiltrat-
ing the CIA. This sport is hard-core."

"You'll be ready. How's Purity going?"

Wolfe took his shot. It hooked to the left but
straightened out enough to keep away from the hazard. "The big opening is in a few weeks, and I've recruited a solid list of celebrities. Decided to combine
it with a charity event to also give back to the community. New York is a breed unto its own, so I need
to run this one different than Milan, and my dad
agreed it's my call. First project I get to run from top
to bottom."

"Your dad sounds cool. Do you get to see each
other often?"

"He and Julietta, my stepmom, live in Milan. She's
the head of La Dolce Famiglia bakery and just had a
baby, but I'm sure she'll make it to the opening. She's
hard-core." The softening of his face told Nate she
was well loved. A stab of envy hit him in the gut. What
would it be like to have a parent actually care about
you and your life? At least Connor was by his side for

the long haul, and that was a hell of a lot more than most people got.

"I think I just had a brilliant idea."

"What?"

"Payment for golf lessons in sweets. I love my pastries."

Wolfe grinned. "Done. Two items are guaranteed to grab a woman's attention, and one is good food."

"What's the other?"

"A cute, furry animal."

Hmm. Nate wondered if he should invest in an adorable puppy and recruit Kennedy to help. The idea had merits. Ah, crap, he was nuts. Who thought about buying a pet just to keep the woman he loved? Since the night she had confessed her past, he'd been haunted by her strength and vulnerability. He also realized that she didn't see it.

He'd woken up Sunday morning in her bed, and she'd already escaped. Safely showered and dressed, she greeted him with a false brilliance that annoyed the crap out of him. He should've stripped her naked and dragged her back to bed, where she always listened, but his gut screamed to give her space. Without a word, he'd kissed her good-bye and walked out. He hoped a day to ruminate on their relationship might help bring her to the conclusion they were perfect together. But somehow, he doubted it.

She didn't call. Didn't show up for Zumba Monday evening either. And now it was midweek and still not a peep. He needed some sort of sign of what to do. His instinct drove him to be direct, but sometimes women needed subtlety. And he was playing for keeps.

He glanced at Wolfe's cool tattoo, confident air, and model looks. He always wore these badass leather wristbands that only added appeal. Damn man made it look easy. "Hey, Wolfe?"

"Yeah?"

"You ever been in love?"

He stiffened. Took his eyes off the ball and met his gaze. Those blue eyes suddenly looked haunted, but he answered the question. "No." Wolfe studied him. "You got nailed, huh?"

Nate pushed his hand through his perfectly cut hair. "Yeah. Literally and figuratively. It's the figuratively I'm having a hard time with."

His friend laughed. "Leave it to a scientist to tell it like it is. She into you?"

"I think. She's a certified commitment phobic. Afraid to stop and look too deep, as if she's already convinced it'll end badly. I don't know how to convince her I want long term. That I'll stick. That she's worth it. Ah, hell, any of this make sense?"

"Yes." Wolfe looked out over the horizon and remained quiet. Nate recognized in his silence another soul who needed to work things out, and suddenly he realized there was a hell of a lot more to Wolfe under that male model billionaire surface. "Sometimes people don't believe they deserve a happy ending. Most don't get it. Did you tell her how you feel?"

"No. I figured that would be the end of it. Damn woman would probably change her name and move out of state in an effort to get rid of me. I figured I'd play it cool. Not push. Let her have space."

"It's tricky, Nate. Could go either way. But I know one thing. You're gonna have to fight hard for her and you may lose. She still worth it?"

"Yes."

"Glad I'm not you."

"Thanks, Dr. Phil."

Another short laugh. "You're gonna have to tell her. She should know. If she runs, you just wait her out. Maybe you need to prove you don't scare easily."

He tried not to let a wimpy sigh escape. "Maybe."

"Listen, what are you doing Saturday?"

"Asking me out?"

"You wish."

Nate grinned. "Just golfing."

"A good friend of mine is having an engagement party. It's a pretty big event, and it'll be fun. Why don't you come with me?"

He drew back in surprise. He had a feeling it was a big deal to be invited into the inner circle of his new friend. "Will he mind?"

"It's a she, and no, the more the merrier. Listen, it will be good for you to meet some new people. If things don't work with this woman, it's good to realize you have options. Gen's family is incredible, and it will take your mind off this stuff for a bit."

"Wouldn't you rather bring a date?"

"Nah, I just got out of a weekend relationship thing—I'm exhausted. A buddy is what I need right now. You in?"

"Yeah. Thanks."

"No problem."

They finished the game and headed out. Nate slid into his car, buckled up, and heard the ping of his phone. Like a lovesick teen, he quickly checked the text.

> Hi Nate, it's Mary from the mixer. Kennedy told me to contact you about scheduling a date. Said you were really excited to get together. I'm free this Friday and Saturday night so let me know. Looking forward to it—enjoyed speaking with you at the mixer. Have a great day!

He dropped his head on the steering wheel. Well, Kennedy had finally made the first move, and it was a doozy. Scheduling him a date with another woman after they slept together was definitely a sign.

Just not the one he wanted.

His next move was critical. Time to scan the newest issue of *Cosmopolitan* and pray.

KENNEDY LOOKED UP AT the sprawling mansion set out on endless acres of property and turned to

Kate. "Wow. Alexa went all out for this event, huh? Can she be my adopted sister?"

Kate laughed and grabbed her fiancé Slade's hand. He juggled the gaily wrapped bridal gift—two small pink bags with Barbie splashed on them—and still managed to look masculine. "You can be mine, Ken," he said.

She blew a kiss at the man who had stolen her best friend's heart and began walking up the elaborate stone pathway. "Her mom's house was too small, and David only has an apartment. They went back and forth on different venues, but Gen really wanted something with a homey feel," Kate said.

"Yep, all six thousand square feet of cozy. It's gorgeous."

"Nick designed it himself. I keep forgetting you haven't been here. The whole crew is coming, so things should get lively. Holy crap, is that a peacock!"

A gorgeous blue and violet creature strolled elegantly past them and toward the back of the manicured lawn. White umbrellas were scattered amid rows of pristine white and yellow roses. A seven-piece orchestra played classical music on a platform flanked by marble sculptures. A harpist sat in a long white gown with flowers in her hair and strummed as if plucked right from a fairy tale.

"Oh, boy. I'm never gonna let Gen live this down. Is that a champagne fountain? Let's go."

Slade laughed. "That's my girl, always the most excited over the liquor."

"I bet it's the good stuff," Kennedy piped up. "I'm right behind you."

They weaved amid the crowds with their target in sight. Slade did a quick turnaround at the last minute. "Were those crab cakes? Babe, they got crab cakes."

"Yes, darling, pace yourself. The buffet consists of New York strip and lobster tails."

"I love engagement parties. Catch you later."

Kate giggled and watched him zero in on the elegantly dressed waiter. "The man knows good food. Uh-oh. Are you ready?"

"For champagne? Yes."

"For chaos. One, two, three, and—"

"Kate! Kate's here, Kate's here!"

Two screaming little girls came tearing across the lawn at high speed. The older one wore white patent leather shoes and a long pink dress, and her inky dark hair was coiled in ringlets. The younger one trailed behind, ribbons half cocked and twisted at odd angles on her head, dress torn and muddy, and barefoot. Kate knelt down and caught both of them and they tumbled back laughing.

"Hi, girls! Do you remember my friend, Kennedy?"

The girls looked up and gave her big grins. Ken remembered Alexa's daughters well. The older one, Lily, was quite the sophisticate, and the younger one was all free spirit. Maria pointed. "Like Barbie's Ken! But you're a girl."

Lily huffed. "Maria, her full name is Kennedy. I

think it's a beautiful name." The little girl's gaze roved over Kennedy's citrine sheath dress, shiny jewelry, and four-inch matching sandals. "And I love your outfit!"

"Thanks, honey. I love yours too."

"Where's your aunt and mom, girls?"

"On the deck. Kate, I'm gonna be a flower girl for Aunt Gen! And I get to hold a basket and drop flowers all over the church!" Maria burst out.

"Just on the aisle," Lily corrected.

"Did you bring us presents, Kate?"

"Maria, that's rude!" Lily admonished.

Kate tugged on a wayward lock stuck around a ribbon. "I did. If you can find Slade, and give him a big hug and kiss, I bet he'll give them to you."

"Yay!" Maria tore off across the lawn.

Lily sighed. "Thank you, Kate."

"You're welcome, my sweets. Now go get him and we'll find your mom." Lily took off.

"Mom's right here."

Kennedy took in the dark-haired, curvy woman before her and smiled. Alexa was Gen's older sister and one of the sweetest, kindest people she'd ever met. Whenever she tagged along with Kate and Gen, she was treated like family. They all hugged.

"Where's Slade?" Alexa asked.

"Running after the crab cakes. I cannot believe this place; it's incredible. You did an amazing job."

Alexa settled her hands on her hips. "It was fun to plan. Since my nuptials were a big hoax, I'm putting all my backed-up wedding enthusiasm into Gen's. Do you like the peacocks? They're from an animal conservation farm and very well cared for. The swans were too nervous to be around large crowds, but these do quite well."

Ken wondered if she had heard wrong. Kate looked just as surprised.

"Love them. Umm, wedding hoax?" Ken asked.

Gen's sister waved her hand in the air in dismissal. "Not important. It ended up becoming real. I need to find the guest of honor. We spent only a minute together before she disappeared."

Kennedy spoke up. "I'm sure she's meeting so many people, also from David's side. Engagement parties are a lot of work."

"Yeah, you're probably right. Mom and Dad are fawning all over David's parents. He may trump Nick in the son-in-law department, which pisses him off." Her gaze narrowed on something across the lawn. "Why is Maria barefoot and muddy?"

"Because she and my son were chasing peacocks and fell in the mud pit. Hey, girls."

Alexa's best friend and Gen's surrogate aunt, Maggie Conte, joined the group. She wore a daring black cat suit that even Versace's models couldn't pull off. Her cinnamon hair was chopped off at a sharp angle at her chin, and she symbolized chic and fabulous. She had always been one of Kennedy's role models, and was always free with her fashion advice. They exchanged brief hugs.

"Did you bring your yummy men?" Maggie asked. "And why is no one drinking yet?"

Ken laughed. "We got waylaid on the way to the champagne fountain. And I'm solo today."

Maggie crinkled her nose. "Pity. Your dates are usually drool worthy. Has anyone seen Gen? David's looking for her."

Alexa frowned. "She's MIA again. She's so stressed out with her work schedule, I keep telling her to slow down."

"Guess it's the reputation of brilliant surgeons in training. Ken and I were trying to have a talk with her this week, but she kept canceling on us. Is Izzy coming?" Kate asked.

Maggie and Alexa shared a look. "Don't know. It'll be a surprise." Gen's twin was on the outs with the family. Izzy had isolated herself from the MacKenzie clan and driven a wedge between the tight-knit group. A variety of factors was cited as the cause. Drugs. Heavy partying. Abusive men. No one knew for sure what kept her away. Ken wondered if that was another stressor to Gen. She'd ended up picking Kate as her maid of honor, so maybe there was some backlash from Izzy.

"What will be a surprise?" a voice interrupted.

Maggie's sister-in-law, Carina, joined the group. She held a baby under one arm and a drink in the other. Her dark hair spilled over her shoulders in a mass of silky waves. Almond-shaped eyes lit up with an energy and zest no first-time mother with a newborn should possess. Immediately, everyone began cooing and babbling to the baby.

"Gen's twin, Izzy. We're not sure if she's coming or not. Babe, your boobs are huge! Maximus must be one very happy boy," Maggie said.

"Which one? The father or son?" Alexa piped up.

They burst into laughter. Max Jr. was wrapped in a crocheted blue blanket, with one of those tiny knit caps stretched over his head. Dark hair peeked out from underneath, and his sleepy eyes rolled open to check on them, then slid back to slumber. Kennedy itched to bury her nose in his powder-scented skin and cuddle forever. "Hey, I get to have one drink while I'm nursing, right?" Carina asked. "And don't say no, because I already drank it."

"One glass of champagne is fine, sweetie. How are you holding up?" Maggie asked.

Carina rolled her eyes. "I'm fine. Max is a wreck, though. The first few days we were home I caught him just staring at the baby with this wondrous expression on his face."

"Aww, that's so sweet," Kate sighed.

Carina raised a brow. "Yeah, but that's all he did. Refused to change his diaper or dress him or bathe him. He was afraid he'd break something of the baby's. Probably his penis. So I did all the work."

Kennedy winced. "That would drive me nuts. What did you do?"

Maggie and Carina shared a wicked glance. "I left."

"What? You left your husband?" Kate asked.

"Just for the day. Told him Maggie was taking me out to the spa for a massage and a mani-pedi. He freaked out, begged me not to go, but I told him it's time they get to know each other."

Maggie grinned with pride. "Trust me, there's nothing like bonding over a poopy diaper. And it worked."

"Yep. When I got back that evening, he was rocking him to sleep, and Max Jr. had on a clean diaper and onesie. Sometimes you gotta throw the husbands in the deep end and make 'em swim."

Alexa laughed. "You two rock. Nick once told me to hold Lily while he got something, and he actually left the house. *In his car*. Let's just say he paid dearly for that move."

Kennedy laughed. God, she loved this group of women. Strong, sassy, family oriented. They were everything she wanted to be when she finally settled down. One day.

Maybe.

The thought of the man she had shared her most intimate secrets with, taken deep into her body, and refused to acknowledge this entire week haunted her. She missed him. Missed Zumba, and golf, and the sex, God, the sex. She missed the way he spilled stains on his shirt and studied her with all that gorgeous concentration.

But she had to save him.

From herself.

Siccing Mary on him was rattlesnake mean, but she had no choice. By pushing another woman into his arms, she was confirming everything he suspected about her. She could never be the mate he needed and deserved. Eventually, her crappy issues would rear their ugly heads. She'd find something wrong with one of them and break his heart. Better to free him up now. Mary would help him forget.

She pushed the image of Nate firmly from her mind and refocused.

"Why don't we split up and see if we can find Gen?" Kate suggested.

They all agreed. Kennedy filled her glass with champagne and headed inside the house to search. She chatted briefly with Gen's parents, met David's parents, grabbed some celery sticks from the veggie tray and nibbled. She thought she might faint if she caught sight of the steak, so she made a battle plan to stay outside where the air neutralized all those wonderful scents.

The main floor held no missing bride-to-be, so she headed to the second level. The massive open staircase was an architectural dream, with a six-tier glittering chandelier in a rich bronze gold as the main focus. She popped her head into a few rooms, but everyone was outside or on the first level, so she doubted she'd find anyone. She was just about to turn around when a soft creak reached her ears.

She pushed open the door. It was Lily's room. Decorated in happy, bright yellow, a beautiful lace coverlet lay upon the canopy bed, and a huge assortment of dolls and stuffed animals were displayed in every corner. The arched bay windows were open, and the breeze drifted in, filling the room with sounds of laughter from outside and delicious smells from the party.

Gen was perched in the white rocker, staring out the window.

"Uh, Gen?"

She popped up. Surprise skittered over her face, quickly followed by a complete shutdown of emotion. Ken stared at her friend, her gut screaming at high pitch that something was very, very wrong. "Oh, my God. I'm sorry, Ken. I didn't hear you!" Her laugh was forced, and she twisted her engagement ring round and around her finger. Ken noticed the spot was rubbed raw around the band and up to her knuckle. She was dressed impeccably, her vanilla cream blouse and long cream skirt giving her an air of mystical innocence. Her dark hair was caught up in a fancy twist, and diamond studs glittered in her ears. Her eyes, so like Alexa's, were piercing blue. She emanated a nervous, jumpy energy that bordered more on fear than excitement.

"It's okay, sweetie. What are you doing up here?"

She glanced out the window with a half smile. "I just needed a minute alone. I'm meeting a ton of David's friends and associates, which is hard now that I'm being introduced on an equal level. David's been my boss for two years, so it's just a bit strange. I don't want to disappoint him."

Kennedy walked over and grabbed her hands. "Sit

with me for a minute. I want to talk to you." They both sat on the padded bench next to three pink frilly pillows. "Why would you think such a thing? David loves you, and you couldn't be a disappointment to anyone. What's really wrong? We're worried about you, sweetheart."

Gen gripped back with a surgeon's strength. She spoke carefully. "There are a lot of people who expect things from me. I don't want to let anyone down." She lifted her head and gazed at her directly. "I don't want to fail."

Ken's heart broke. Another successful, gorgeous woman afraid of dropping the ball. Life was just overwhelming sometimes. Was David really right for her, after all? Shouldn't her friend be over the moon in love and happy to be planning a wedding? Or was it just societal pressure to have everything perfect?

"There's nothing to fail at," she said. "Alexa, and I, and Kate will help you plan every last detail. You're our family. You need to take a step back and see what you're doing to yourself. Too much pressure won't make you happy, or David, or your patients, honey."

Gen nodded. "I know you're right."

"Have you talked to David? Maybe you can figure something out to slow things down?"

Gen's grip tightened. Her hands suddenly went clammy. "No! No, he's under a lot of strain at work since they doubled his responsibilities. He's traveling back and forth to Manhattan, and he's doing the best he can. It will be fine."

Kennedy studied her friend and took the plunge. "Are you happy with David?"

She jerked back. "What do you mean? I'm marrying him!"

"That wasn't the question, was it? I didn't even ask if you loved him. I asked if he made you happy."

Those blue eyes widened. Seconds ticked. Ken felt on the verge of something hugely important, and she was afraid to breathe and break the moment. Her friend dragged in a breath. Opened her mouth. And—

"Hey, is this where the party is?"

The delicate moment shattered and was abruptly lost.

Wolfe stood framed in the doorway, his head almost touching the top. Gen's face lit up and she raced over to give him a big hug. "'Bout time you got your ass here," she sassed. And just like that, the old Gen was back.

Wolfe laughed and flicked her earlobe. "Nice rocks. Is that what med students get paid in now?"

"Yeah, right. David gave them to me."

"Niiiice," he drawled. "Hey, Ken, I haven't seen you in a while. Things good? Making millions matching up poor schmucks looking for love?"

Ken rolled her eyes. "When are you going to break down and become my client? Really, Wolfe, I would've never picked the last woman I saw you with. Still together?"

"Nah, she only wanted my body. I wanted respect."

Gen snorted. "She was awful. She couldn't even throw a dart."

"Speaking of darts, you owe me another opportunity to get even. You keep canceling on me. I can't drink and aim sharp weapons alone."

"Sorry, Wolfe, I promise we'll do it next week. Wednesday night good? My shift gets out early."

A chilly voice cut through the room. "I don't think that will work, Genevieve. We have the nurses meeting and the charity fund-raiser."

Silence fell. Gen jumped up and ran to David's side, as if he normally had her on a short leash and the daily walk was over. Wolfe's jaw clenched along with his fists, but he forced a smile at Gen's fiancée. "Good to see you, David. Congrats."

David was a powerful presence in a completely different manner than Wolfe was. His suit was tailored in a neutral gray and obviously custom cut. White shirt. Demure tie. Thick blond hair was tamed and smoothed back from his face. Not a speckle of stubble, and his face held the lines and grace of an aristocrat. Kennedy watched in fascination as their opposing male energies swirled and combated with each other on two separate planets. Damn. They did not like each other.

She rose to her feet and walked over. "Hi, David, we met before. Gen's friend, Kennedy. Congratulations."

His smile was impeccable. White teeth flashed. "Thank you, Kennedy, it's a pleasure to have you."

The cool bite of his voice softened as he stared at Gen. "Darling, I'm sorry for interrupting. There are a few people downstairs I really need you to meet—they're on the board. You'll forgive me, right, Wolfe?"

"Sure."

David slipped his arm under Gen's elbow. "I promise you'll have time to hang with your friends in a bit."

"Of course, no worries. I'll see you both later," Gen said, stiffly following him out.

Ken caught Wolfe's expression. Pissed off described it well. Boy, something was going on here. They obviously hated each other, but was it because they were both competing for Gen's attention? Or did the whole subtle put-down verbal challenge mean more?

She decided to talk to Wolfe about it while they were alone, but a toilet flushed, a door opened, and someone trudged toward them. Oh, well, she needed to get in conference with Kate anyway. Where was her champagne glass? She turned and scooped it up.

"Oh, there you are. Hey, Ken, this is my friend, Nate."

She froze. Turned her head. And gazed at Nate Ellison Raymond Dunkle.

Wow. Just . . . wow.

He pulled his own weight next to Wolfe in the "holy hotness, Batman" category. No tats, piercings, or staggering height, but Nate didn't need it. Those moss green eyes shimmered with heat and intensity, and the strong line of his jaw and cheekbones screamed command. Broad shoulders were clad in a hand-stitched black silk button-down. She'd picked it out personally. The fabric shimmered under the light and showed off his lean, muscled chest. The sleeves were rolled up and golden brown skin sprinkled with light hair confirmed his golfer's tan. His spectacular ass was cupped in dark-washed Banana Republic jeans, with a large silver belt buckle. He was completely . . . solid. Energy swirled and tightened around them in a familiar sensual challenge that had been there since day one. She just hadn't been ready to see or accept it.

She still wasn't.

His eyes widened in pure surprise at seeing her there. So this wasn't planned. Oh, no, this was some sort of crazy God universe thing who liked to laugh and torture her. What were the odds? And how the hell did he know Wolfe? She tried to squeak out something, but it took a few times before words took hold. She didn't need to worry. He said the exact thing she would've bet he'd come up with no matter what the situation was.

"Hey."

The worst part was the softening of her heart at the familiar greeting. "Hey."

Wolfe looked back and forth between them. "You know each other?"

"Yes," they both said together.

Nate explained further. "Kennedy is my matchmaker."

"No way. You're hooked up with Kinnections? Dude, you never told me."

"Small world," Nate murmured. His gaze roved over her, hot and hungry and . . . knowing. He knew she loved when he nibbled and bit the crease where her neck met shoulder. Knew the exact pressure to use on her nipples to bring them to a point of pain/pleasure. Knew how to curl his fingers just right when he slipped inside her to bring her quickly to orgasm.

Knew way too much.

"How do you two know each other?" she asked.

"Nate saved my ass showing me how to golf. I'm courting a big client for Purity, and the only way to get close is on the course. Of course, I sucked, and he took pity on me. He's got this scientific thing with figuring out a swing."

"Yes, he's quite the teacher."

Nate remained silent.

The air between them grew heavy and thick with unspoken words and arousal. Wolfe seemed to catch something weird going on, because he kept shifting his glance as if trying to figure out what it was. "Nate's been a wonderful client. I'm excited about his new match."

Nate crossed his arms in front of his chest. "Yeah, Mary does seem perfect. Too bad I'm still stuck on that last woman I was with. Don't you think I need some time to get my head straight? Or convince her to take a chance on us?"

She shook her head hard. "You need to look at the

big picture. Mary is more suited to you; this other one will break your heart."

He took a step in. "How do you know?"

"Because she's a mess."

"Maybe I like messes."

"Maybe you don't know what's good for you because she fogged your head with sex."

Wolfe whistled. "Way to go, Nate."

Nate continued, staring Kennedy down with everything he had. "Maybe she should give me more credit to know what I want and see the situation clearly. Maybe she's so terrified of taking a chance on a real relationship because she's never had one before."

"Maybe she's the only one seeing things clearly and trying to protect you."

"Maybe she's full of shit." He took another step in. His eyes gleamed with a fierce light that shot sparks of fury and frustration. "Maybe she just doesn't want to know the truth."

"What truth?" she asked.

"That I love her."

She gasped. Her heart stopped. Then took off at heart attack pace. The room spun and the glass almost slipped from her numb fingers.

"Uh, dude, when I told you to admit your feelings, I meant to the woman herself. Not your matchmaker."

They locked gazes and ignored Wolfe. "Don't say that," she whispered. "It's not true."

"You don't get to tell me what I feel. You can

throw a bunch of women at me, hide away, pretend this is something it's not, but I'm done with the lies. I love her, and it's not going away. Go ahead and make me date Mary, or Sue, or any other woman you toss in, but it won't change the outcome. I love her."

Her body shook with mini convulsions. He had said he loved her. He thought he loved her. But how could he? How could he know all her secrets and still think she was a good match for him? Men loved her body, her face, her persona. They loved the way she looked on their arm, and her power career, and that she didn't need a man to make her happy. They didn't look into her damaged soul and love the hidden parts. How could they when she didn't even love them herself?

Coldness seeped into her skin and bones. She couldn't do this anymore. He'd already become way too important, and she was slipping under his spell. She had to cut him loose.

"You'll get over it."

The words dropped like stones between them. He jerked back as if slapped, and her heart crumbled into tiny pieces that she feared would never be able to be sutured back together.

"Is she that much of a coward?"

"She's that much of a realist," she said brokenly. "You need to go out with Mary."

Wolfe cleared his throat. "Okay, this is way over my head. Why don't I leave you two alone?"

Nate clenched his jaw. Disappointment, and a

deeper emotion she didn't want to name, emanated from his defeated stance. "No, Wolfe, that's okay. We're done here."

He turned and paused in the doorway. "I'll text Mary and take her to dinner this weekend. Thanks for the advice, Ken. You truly are an excellent matchmaker."

Her knees trembled as she watched them walk out the door. She stumbled to the bench to grab on to her composure, trying to settle her nauseous stomach. What had she done?

The right thing. The only thing. Right?

Feeling faint, she placed her head between her knees and dragged in long breaths. She heard her name being called from a distance, but she didn't look up, just concentrated on getting oxygen in her lungs. When she raised her head, Kate knelt in front of her.

"Sweetie, did you drink that much champagne already? You need to pace yourself better. We found Gen, and she's with David. Are you okay?"

"No. Something happened."

Her friend's face lit with alarm. "What?"

She gulped. "I slept with Nate Dunkle."

"Oh, my God. When? You didn't tell us. Was it good? Are you happy? Is he off the client list?"

Kennedy mashed her fingers against her mouth. "No, it's terrible, well, the sex was off-the-charts amazing, but this whole thing is terrible, I made a big mistake, and now I think I screwed him up. He needs to fall in love with Mary, not me. Oh, please let him fall in love with Mary this weekend so I can go back to my normal life."

Kate sighed, rummaged for her phone, and tapped the screen. "This is too much for one of us. I'm going to Skype Arilyn in so we can discuss."

"But she has the flu."

"She can talk from bed. She probably needs a distraction anyway, she was so upset she couldn't make Gen's party. Hang on."

Ken waited. After a few minutes of back-and-forth texting, her screen flashed on. Arilyn was propped up in bed, her nose bright red, glasses on, her hair a bird's nest of a mess, and a grim expression on her face. "Tell me nothing dramatic happened. Did Gen call off the engagement?"

Kate frowned. "No. Why? Did you suspect something?"

"Gen hasn't been happy lately. I got a bad feeling. What's up?"

"Kennedy has a crisis. She slept with Nate Dunkle."

A coughing fit mixed with a gulp of surprise. "The rocket scientist?"

"Aerospace engineer," Kennedy corrected. "Yes. Him."

"Once? Twice?"

"About fifteen times over last weekend."

"Bitch," Kate murmured. "You need a rest, not an intervention."

"Kate, focus," Arilyn said.

"Fine. But I think my record is twelve. Slade has to work harder."

"Sweetie, why are you panicking? Kate slept with her client and they're happy. Sure, it's against the rules, but sometimes rules are meant to be broken. I can contact the dates you set him up with and straighten out the situation. I'm sure it will be fine."

Kate sighed. "No, Arilyn, you don't get it. Kennedy wants him to fall in love with someone else and already set him up with Mary for a date."

Arilyn cursed. "What is up with you guys pushing the men you want into another woman's arms? I feel like we're doing the Slade thing all over again."

Kennedy shook her head. "No, it's different. I can't have a relationship with Nate."

"Why?" Kate asked.

"Because! I don't do long-term relationships. I get itchy and restless, and I'm a bitch to deal with, and he needs someone sweet and smart to complete his life and give him babies and all that stuff I can't."

Arilyn sniffled, wiped her nose, and glared at the screen. "Back up. You are all of those things. You deserve happiness, too, Ken. Why are you so reluctant to take it?"

"I'm not! I'm being realistic about what I can handle and give back. You guys are always saying I find things wrong with men all the time. I'm not ready for forever."

"Okay, give me a list of everything wrong with Nate and why it wouldn't work," Kate demanded.

Kennedy sniffed. "Too much to name."

"Give me one."

"He loves golf."

Silence. Arilyn glared through Skype. "You went golfing with him and told us it wasn't bad."

"Once was okay. Twice maybe. Not every weekend!"

"Lame," Kate declared. "Next."

"He's too intellectual."

"So are you. You're a complete Gemini—two halves of a coin. You love *Science Today* as much as *Vogue*, and don't deny it."

"He doesn't respect my food choices. Always makes me try unhealthy things."

Kate laughed. "Well, amen, sister. About time to join the land of the living, and salad makes you a cranky bitch. You're toast. You love him."

"No! I don't love him." She moaned and clutched her stomach. "I don't, he's going to marry Mary."

Arilyn groaned. "God, you're just as delusional as Kate was. Listen, babe, we can beat you over the head with the truth, but you need to find it within yourself first. You need to let go of these restrictions from your past finally. You're worth everything, and Nate would be lucky to have you. Trust yourself to love him back."

"No."

"Bitch," Kate muttered. "I knew she'd be the toughest out of all of us. You are meant for Nate. I know this."

"How?"

Kate shrugged and didn't meet her gaze. "I just do."

"I don't want this intervention anymore. My head hurts, I'm in a bad mood, and I just want to drink and celebrate Gen's engagement. Okay?"

Kate and Arilyn shared a deep look over the iPhone. "Fine," Arilyn said. She sneezed. "Take some photos for me and give Gen a hug. Miss you guys."

"Bye, A."

Kate clicked off. Frustration beat from her in waves, but she stood up and offered her hand. Ken took it. "I am going on record to say your plan is asinine and you will end up together, either the hard way or the easy way. But I will drop the subject and drink with you. Slade is designated driver. Now, let's hit the fountain."

"I love you, Kate."

"Back atcha, babe. Back atcha."

fifteen

NATE CUPPED HIS hands around his microbrew and watched his brother trudge into the bar. It had been the week from hell, between endless work hours and coming to terms with the fact that Kennedy didn't want him. Of course, he was the biggest dumbass on the planet. Who else confessed his love in third person? In front of another guy? In code?

He deserved for her to walk.

Connor slid into the booth, and ordered a Coors Lite from the waitress. "Bad day, Con? You didn't even hit on her."

He waited for his brother's easygoing laugh and a crude retort, but Connor only shrugged his shoulders. "Whatever. What's going on with you?"

Besides losing the woman he loved? "Thought we had a breakthrough with a formula, then found out we didn't. Wayne almost cried like a baby. Told him he needed to get out of the lab or he'd go loco. How's the new job?"

"Fine. Same group of guys, so no surprises." His brother snorted. "Not that there's any surprises in my life."

Nate frowned. The beer came, and his brother guzzled it down like water. "What's up? You're not your-self."

Another shrug. "Nothing. Jay caught his girlfriend cheating on him and went nuts on the job. She's a nail technician, remember? Really hot blonde. Told you, little brother. Stay away from those women; they'll nail you and watch you bleed for fun."

Whoa. He wondered if he could talk with his brother—really talk. Wolfe's advice was helpful, but after the engagement party fiasco, he just wasn't sure if he should try to move on or keep fighting. He cleared his throat and tried not to feel like an ass. "Hey, can I ask you something?"

"Sure."

"It's about Kennedy. Do you remember her?"

"Yeah, the looker from your matchmaking agency. What's up?"

Ah, he hated this open-heart, male-to-male stuff. Especially with Connor. "Well, she was setting me up with that girl Sue, remember?"

"The one I met at your place? Yeah. You liked her, right?"

"Sue? Yeah, I liked Sue, but I've been spending a lot of time with Kennedy, and I sorta fell for her."

Connor took another guzzle and wiped his mouth. "Like how? You mean you wanted to sleep with her?"

"Yeah. Well, that's not all I wanted, but we ended up sleeping together."

"Nice! That's what I'm talking about! A little Sue,

a little Kennedy, and you're back in the game, my man."

Nate pushed his hands through his hair and tried not to groan. "No, you're not listening. See, I didn't sleep with Sue. I decided Sue wasn't right for me, but when I say I fell for Kennedy, it means more than sex. It means I fell in love with her."

His brother stilled. His voice dropped to ice. "What are you talking about? You can't love that woman—she's the matchmaker, right? Didn't she try to make you hot shit to find someone else?"

"Yeah. But it got complicated. We ended up spending time together, I got to know her, and I fell in love."

Connor shook his head. "Listen, you need to back off. You spent way too much time with her, and she did this transformation thing, and you got sucked in. Keep your mouth shut, and it will go away, I promise."

"I already told her."

"Shit." His brother drained the bottle and raised his hand for another. "Nate, I saw her, and she's gonna destroy you. She's like a walking supermodel with sex vibes. You don't need a life like we had with Mom, just waiting for her to leave."

"She won't. I know she won't."

"She will!"

They glared at each other. Nate tightened his lips. "I should've known you wouldn't understand. You never had the balls to go after a woman worth anything. You'd rather assume she's gonna screw you over than take the risk at some happiness. God, you and Kennedy are both cut from the same cloth. Can't you just give me some good advice for a change instead of your usual bullshit?"

Connor jerked in the chair. Nate cursed under his breath and opened his mouth to apologize, but Jerry stopped at their table. "Hey, guys, I'm gonna join you. Sorry about the job, Con, but I warned you. Ed was a shoo-in. Ridiculous that they want college fucking degrees to work with your hands. But at least we'll have more time to hang out—you don't need that job."

Nate stared at his brother. "You didn't get the job?"

Connor laughed. Bitterness twisted his face. "I told you. No big deal. I'm not meant for the stuff you are, little brother. Not love, or management. And that's okay. At least I know my place in life."

The bull flying out of his mouth made Nate pause. "That's ridiculous. You can't believe that. Look, when is the next position coming up? Maybe we can—"

"Drop it. I don't want you to mention this crap again. You don't like my advice, fine. Do whatever you want, get your heart trashed. But stay out of my business. Now, I'm gonna get drunk with Jerry. You can stay or go. Come on, Jer."

He left the table, grabbing his beer, and joined another group of construction workers at the far end of the bar. Nate leaned his head against the booth, and closed his eyes.

Overall, this was one shit day.

He stared at the table. Thought about his options for a long time. Then made his decision.

He had a bad feeling his night was going to get even shittier.

KENNEDY PROPPED HER FOOT up and sank deeper into the bubbles. What a crappy day. One breakup, a client who insisted on picking her dates based on looks, and the suffering silence of her best friends. Every look reminded her of their disapproval of her decision. She had no idea if Nate and Mary had hooked up yet and decided to distance herself a bit before reaching out for contact. Things had gotten way overheated at the engagement party.

She breathed in the scent of ginger and sandalwood and reminded herself this was the right move. Every day Nate spent away would give him the distance he needed to move on. He didn't love her, it was just the bonding process getting to him. Sue hadn't been the right match, so that hadn't helped. Maybe—

The door banged. Once. Twice.

Huh, who would be here on a work night? Kate had a key, and would've let herself right in. Gen and Arilyn would've called.

Another bang. More insistent.

A neighbor? She got herself out of the tub, grabbed a long teal robe, and cinched it tight. Her hair dripped but she quickly wrung it out with a towel.

Bang number five.

"I'm coming!" She trudged to the door and looked out the window.

Crap.

She paused. Took a deep breath. And opened the door.

"Hey."

She huffed out an impatient breath. "You shouldn't be here."

He looked terrible. He looked wonderful. He wore his lab coat, and a bright red stain marked two places in the front. Definitely ketchup. His pocket protector was fully clipped and held a pencil, pen, and mini notepad. His hair was mussed but held the wave Benny perfected, along with the trimmed scruff around his lip and chin. She knew now the scruff scratched deliciously when he rubbed against her face, but his hair could be silky smooth when he rested his head against her breast.

"We need to talk. Are you naked under that robe?"

"No. Look, we can't see each other like this anymore. We had good sex, said some things, but we need to back off now. I know you didn't mean what you said last week so let's just forget it."

"Good sex or great?"

"Great."

"I meant every damn word. I'm coming in." He walked right past her and shut the door. The click caused shivers to jump over her naked body. He stood in the middle of her living room, hands on hips, studying every bare inch of skin peeking out from her robe.

She yanked the sash tighter and crossed her arms in front of her breasts.

"Have you gone out with Mary yet?"

He gave a short laugh. "God help me. I tell you I love you, and you try to set me up with a date."

"See! I told you we weren't good for each other. Nate, please. Just go."

"Not yet. I'm here to say my piece, and if you don't want to see me again, fine. I'll leave you alone."

Her heart screamed to grab him and hold on. Her head kept her frozen to the ground. "Go ahead."

"I'm an ass. I told you I loved you the wrong way, but I'm always doing things like this, and if we're together that's not gonna change. I wear my food on my clothes, mutter physics equations under my breath, and am OCD when it comes to germs in public restaurants. I say stupid shit, I'm obsessed with golf, and I fucking love you. I just love you."

Her heart cracked open and crumbled. Tears clogged her throat, and she thought she was dying. It was the most honest, romantic, sexy damn thing any man had ever said to her. He looked at her with every naked emotion clearly revealed on his face. Her soul cried out to run into his arms and never let go. But the inner voice she'd lived with for so many years remained quiet.

"I'll never be able to give you what you need."

The words shattered around them like splintering glass.

He closed the distance and stood in front of her. "Try."

"You deserve more."

Male temper shot from his body. Raw lust shot from his gaze. He studied her for a while, then leaned in. "You lied."

She wet her lips. Shuddered. "About what?"

"You are naked under that robe."

He buried his hands in her wet hair and took her lips.

The kiss burned hot and fast, with no explanation, seduction, or apology. This was another side to him, the frustrated lover desperate to prove something, desperate to claim. She moaned under the sensual assault but couldn't fight back. Her body melted and she wrapped her arms around his shoulders and took it all. As if she knew it was temporary, that she couldn't give him an "I love you" back, so she'd offer her body as the sacrifice.

He ripped the robe from her shoulders. Lifted her high so she was forced to wrap her legs around his waist. His mouth still on hers, his tongue thrust inside as he walked her out of the living room and right into the bedroom.

When he finally slid her down, her feet touched the cool wood of the floor. She heard the bang of a door opening and blinked, trying to get her bearings. He turned her with rough fingers.

The full-length mirror stared back at her.

She kept it on the back of the closet door only to check her final outfit. Her battle with mirrors was legendary, and she normally kept her interactions with them to a minimum. Her mouth opened in horror, the arousal quickly slipping away as she saw her entire naked body on display.

"No." She tried to turn, but his grip was ruthless. His fingers bit into her shoulders and held her still.

"Yes. This is bigger than me confessing my love for you. Bigger than sex. This is about thinking I don't see you, that no one sees you, even yourself. So let's blow that illusion away right now, shall we?"

He bent his head so he spoke against her ear. One hand left her shoulder to cup her breast, deliberately twisting her nipple to a hard point. The tingles shot down her belly and just like that, her body was back up and raring to go. She closed her eyes, but he quickly kicked her legs apart and bit down on her earlobe.

"Eyes open. It's time you see what I do when I look at you. This body you tortured and broke and then healed is beautiful. Look how you respond to my touch, as if you were meant to blossom under my hands."

Kennedy moaned again, caught between wanting him to continue and the horror of seeing herself exposed in every form. He didn't give her time to rationalize or think. Continuing to tweak and plump her left breast, his other hand delved between her splayed legs and played.

Oh, God.

Her lids drifted half shut, but she watched them in the mirror. She grew hot and wet under the plucking ministrations, until her hips rolled in time to try to catch more. Her nipples turned a dark cherry red, like a topping on a sundae, and the whole time his gaze burned and locked on hers, not allowing her to escape his lust. His arms were brown from the sun now, and contrasted erotically with her rosy flesh.

"Look at you. Open and wet and pink from your bath." His erection pressed in the nudge of her buttocks and made its own demand. "If I were an artist, I'd paint you like this and hang it by my desk so I could look at you all day and remember how you're meant for me." His thumb coaxed the nub of her clit to harden further, and her empty channel pulsed for more, needing to be filled by his fingers and tongue and dick, needing all of him.

"Nate," she gasped.

"Yes, you're getting closer. Let it go, baby, and watch me make you come. Look at how fucking gorgeous you are."

His hands slipped deep between her legs, and moved back and forth in a steady rhythm. His thumb pressed and rotated, never giving up the teasing pressure, and his open mouth bit and sucked the side of her neck.

The woman in the mirror was a primitive being bent on satisfaction and pleasure. Her hips rocked and demanded more, her breath panted through her lips, and her nipples stabbed into his hand and begged for relief. She sunk into the depths of darkness and ecstasy, not caring about anything other than giving this man anything he wanted, anything he asked for.

The tension tightened in her belly and he moved faster, bringing her close, holding her on the edge until she cried out, leaning against him, and surrendering to every sensation.

"Nate! Please, Nate!"

"Yes, baby, here you go. Watch yourself, don't look away."

He plunged deep and massaged her clit.

She came hard on a high scream. Her body shuddered as the release went on and on, soaking his hands, jerking helplessly against him. He twisted her head around and kissed her deep, and then he was picking her up again and laying her on the bed. He ripped off his clothes, sheathed himself with a condom, and settled himself between her legs.

"I love you, Kennedy Ashe."

Then he took her, hard and fast, pinning her down with his body with a brute force that rocketed her to another orgasm in seconds. He emptied himself and she hung on tight, tears rolling down her cheeks as she shattered and broke open, never to remain the same again.

They lay quietly together for a while in the semi-darkness. The scent of soap and sex and citrus drifted to her nostrils. She clung to him and wondered if she was strong enough to do what she needed to do.

"This isn't about me, baby. It's about you. I can chase you forever, promise you the world, but until you take the leap with me, I can't win. I don't just love your body. I love your incredible mind, and your sweet soul, and your inner strength. I love the life you built for yourself with your friends and your career. I love every part of you—good and bad—dark and light—and I want to share it all. But you have to let me."

Her lashes were wet when she blinked, but Kennedy knew her answer.

"I can't." He stiffened underneath her. "I'm not trying to punish you, or hurt you. I don't trust myself enough. I can't promise it'll work, or if I'll be able to commit to a long-term relationship, or that I'll do something terrible to free myself. I won't do what your mother did. I won't take that risk. Not with you. Not with your heart."

He was silent. Their breathing rose and fell in the air. Slowly, he disengaged from her on the bed and stood up. She watched him get dressed with slow, methodical movements.

"I won't play this game. I deserve happiness. So do you. But if you've already fated us for doom, we'll never make it. I'd wait for you, but I'm afraid I may wait forever since you seem intent on not hurting me." He gave a humorless laugh. "Which, ironically, you just did."

He began walking out of the room. "You win. I'll call Mary. Good-bye, Ken."

He left.

She knew she'd done the right thing, the only thing.

There were no guarantees, and she didn't do Cinderella endings.

Never had.

Never would.

Kennedy buried her face into the pillow and cried.

sixteen

NATE SAT IN the red chair as Benny whipped around him in a frenzy of scissors. His goatee had already been moisturized and trimmed, brows were waxed, and he'd won a battle regarding his refusal to get a manicure.

As if.

He'd gotten in the habit of seeing Benny every two weeks to keep up maintenance. He also hated to admit they'd formed an odd, grumpy sort of friendship.

Kind of.

"I've been bored to tears this week and need gossip. How's the dating?"

"Fine."

A deep, suffering sigh. "Don't be a mitch. Tell me details. Sex yet?"

"Not yet. We've gone out a few times. I like her. She's nice to my brother. Things are perfect."

"Liar. You're still hot for your matchmaker."

He jerked around. Benny slapped him back to face the mirror. "Do you wanna lose the wave? I almost cut it wrong, for God's sake, stay still."

"What do you know about Kennedy and me?"

The hairdresser snorted but looked gleeful of the

reaction. "I suspected you were hot for each other that very first appointment. The last time you came in, you were all moody and asked casually if I had seen her lately. And when she came in the other day, she was a bitch on wheels. I mean, I told her to eat some damn carbs, but the woman is on a tear. Must be about you."

The idea that she was suffering as much as he was both soothed and hurt. She hadn't contacted him after that night. He'd received a call from Kate, letting him know she'd be arranging his matches from now on, and he took Mary out on a date that weekend. If only he could forget about Ken, he'd be happy.

Mary had a bit of fire, was smart as a whip, and was a witty conversationalist. He clicked much better with her than with Sue in the long run, and their dates were low pressure, getting to know each other. They'd kissed a few times but hadn't pushed for more. The guilt killed him for not being completely open with her about his feelings, but he was intent on moving on. Even Connor approved of her, having joined them once for a drink at the tavern.

Nate hardened his voice. "Her choice. I spilled my guts and she let me go. Game over."

Benny sighed. "Well, there goes my good mood. You're making me feel pity. I hate that."

"Yeah, when you get emotional you lose the British accent thing."

"And now the pity is gone. You are such an annoyance."

"And you're really gay."

Benny snorted out a laugh. "Yeah, but at least I have a lover waiting at home for me. Did you fight as hard as you could for her?"

"Yep."

"Then you have nothing to regret. She's the one who's probably suffering more. I love that woman, but she has issues."

Now it was Nate's turn to laugh. "I know, but so do I. We're a perfect pair."

"Don't fret. At least you look hot. Head right over to Sally and she'll finish you right up."

"I'm not getting my nails done, Benny. Don't try to fool an aerospace engineer."

Benny rolled his eyes and whipped off the cape. "Whatever. But if you ever have your big come-to-Jesus moment, you'll end up regretting not having nice hands."

"As. If."

"Bye, mitch."

Benny blew an air kiss and sashayed off. Nate grinned and went to pay at the cashier. Damned if that man didn't make him feel better.

KENNEDY GLARED AT THE buzzing phone, then snapped it up. "What?"

A pause. "Umm, sweetie, can you come into the purple room, please?"

She let out an irritated breath. "Is it important? I've got a mixer mess on my hands."

"Yes. It's very important."

"Be right there." She replaced the receiver and pushed out of her chair. Damn interruptions. How was she supposed to increase her marriage goal and the marketing campaign for Kinnections if her mixers weren't successful? Her heels clicked on the floor as she walked into the consultation room.

Arilyn and Kate faced her, perched comfortably on the plum cushions. The calming trickle of the water fountain pissed her off, but she tapped a foot and forced a calm smile. "What's up?"

"Sit down, Ken."

"No time. Listen, I think we need to dump the Purple Haze for our mixers. Tony gave me some junk about not including the good wine, and there is no way I'm forcing my high-end clients to settle for a carton that comes out of the refrigerator just to satisfy his mark-up arrangement and—is that chocolate?"

Her eyes widened. Kate held out a tiny square of Ghirardelli dark. Her stomach lurched in enthusiasm, and her mouth pooled with saliva. "Sit down. We need to talk about something, and you really need this."

Her mind clicked through the options of denying herself, but it was way too late. She reached out and snatched it from her friend's hand, sat down, and slowly unwrapped the chocolate morsel. "Bribe accepted. You guys look super serious. Did someone die?"

"Yes," Arilyn said gently. "You."

Her mind jumped with confusion, but the heavenly scent of butter and cocoa drifted up, and suddenly she couldn't care less what the conversation was about. The first bite slid over her tongue and melted. Her body heated and the image of Nate feeding her while she was naked on the chair slammed into her vision, and tears suddenly threatened. What a big baby. She had to get herself together. Work was definitely the answer. She'd squeeze in another mixer. The more people who found love, the better she would feel. What was Arilyn saying? "Did you say I died?" she asked.

"Your heart did. Sweetie, you're not going to like this conversation, but it needs to be done. Three weeks have gone by since you kicked Nate out of your life. Besides being a bit, er, difficult and—"

"Bitchy as hell," Kate supplied.

"Temperamental," Arilyn corrected. "You're working nonstop and staying way too late. You're not eating properly either."

"Yes, I am. I'm not starving myself. I've had the perfect amount of protein, fat, and calories to sustain a healthy, balanced diet."

"You haven't allowed yourself enough sugar or carbs to make you happy. I'm not talking about health or maintenance. I'm talking about joy."

Kennedy took another bite of the chocolate. Her temper spiked. "I have no time for this touchy feely stuff. I appreciate your concern, and I'm sure I'll get over it. I did the right thing, and at least I sleep well at night knowing he'll be happy."

"Screw this, A. I told you she's hard-core and she doesn't get subtle. I'm taking over now," Kate announced. She jabbed a finger in the air at her. "Listen up. Slade had the same screwed-up ideas about our relationship. Believed he was doomed for failure, and that his crappy experiences proved we were never going to make it. So what did he do? I told him I loved him, and he walked away from me. Just like you did with Nate. Slade gave himself this bull about doing what's best for me, but meanwhile, he was a little coward who didn't want to take the risk."

"I'm not Slade."

"No, you're not. You think you don't deserve Nate. Screw that. You deserve happiness. You deserve him. You deserve a life. Is this what you think it's about? Work, sleep, loneliness, and martyrdom? You're not doing anyone any favors, and it's time to stand up and go after what you want."

Kate's voice softened. "You have food issues. Body issues. Perfection issues. So, what? Does that make you unworthy of loving someone who wants to love you back? Love has nothing to do with perfect. It has to do with flaws, and overcoming failure, and fighting for what you want. You have always been the strongest person I've ever known. You used to go after what you wanted. Until now."

Arilyn cut in. "Happiness doesn't just tumble into your life, sweetie. You have to grab it."

She stared back at her friends as a tiny flare of

hope burst to life. Were they right? Was it as easy as making a conscious decision to leave the past and her insecurities behind and let herself be happy?

It was then that her friend brought out the knock-out, championship punch.

"I felt the touch, Ken. With you and Nate."

The air left her lungs in one swoop. The room tilted, and she grabbed onto the arms of the chair to keep from falling. "What did you say?"

"That night we did the role-play in the bar? I touched both of you and got electrocuted. That's why I fell."

"Impossible," she whispered. "It can't be."

Kate bit her lip. "I'm sorry. I know we all made a pact I'd never tell either of you if I felt the touch with any men. I hate the idea of manipulating Fate or your feelings. I'm not supposed to get involved because it's up to each lover to choose the other—touch or no touch. But I couldn't let you walk away from this. Nate is your soul-mate. He belongs to you."

Kennedy moaned and wrapped her hands around her stomach. In seconds, her friends were by her side, hugging and supporting her weight as the knowledge crashed over her.

She was meant to be with Nate.

Kate had never been wrong. Her touch was special, though they always joked about her being sort of a witch, they'd never doubted her ability to make a love match.

They were meant to be together.

The knowledge helped cement all the backed-up emotions the past three weeks had thrown at her. She'd been so wrong. So cowardly. Even after he'd stripped her barriers in front of the mirror, she'd still run away and ended up hurting the only man she'd ever loved.

But it was too late. Wasn't it? The floodgates opened, and all her frustration and rage and pain poured out. She jumped from the chair and paced back and forth, muttering vicious curses from English all the way to the zingers in Italian she'd learned from Maggie.

Arilyn waited in semishock. Kate looked impressed by her vocabulary.

"Why can't I do anything the normal way? Girl meets boy. Falls in love with boy. Girl is happy. I'm twisted. I made him be happy with someone else on purpose!"

Kate murmured in sympathy. "I know. I tried to do the same thing."

"I have to do something! Go to him. Tell him. Beg his forgiveness."

"Go," Arilyn said.

"What if he doesn't want me back? What if I hurt him so badly he'll never forgive me?"

Kate squeezed her hand. "My mom once told me there are no guarantees in this life, but if you don't try, you'll always be empty. Tell him how you feel, sweetie. That's all you have control over."

Kennedy nodded. "Yes. Thanks guys."

She tore out of the office.

"HEY DUDE. MIND IF I hang out here for a few hours?" Connor asked.

Nate straightened his jacket and threw on a touch of cologne. He'd gotten much better at not overdosing. "Sure. How come you're not at the bar with Jerry or the apartment?"

His brother looked away. "Jerry went out with Ed tonight. Haven't seen you in a while, so I figured I'd drive up. Sorry if I busted in."

"Nah, I'm just meeting Mary over at Mugs for a burger. Gonna be an early night, so why don't you stay? We'll hang when I get back and watch *Breaking Bad* on Netflix."

"Cool." His brother studied him with a weird look on his face. "You like this girl?"

"Mary? She's nice. We're having fun."

"What about Kennedy?"

Nate flinched. He still wasn't able to hear her name aloud without a bodily reaction. At least he had finally learned to control his automatic erection. "What about her?"

His brother dragged his foot and seemed uncomfortable. "Well, one minute you're declaring love for her, and the next you don't mention her name."

The tide of emotion that swept over him caught him like a fierce right hook. God, he missed her. Her laugh, scent, walk. Missed being in her presence and arguing with her. But that was over. And he was moving on.

He squared his shoulders. "She wasn't into me. I'll get over it."

"Yeah, you'll get over it. Trust me, bro, much better to commit to a woman more like you. Mary's nice. And she's . . . safe."

"Yeah." Damn, this whole conversation was depressing as hell. If he didn't fire up some sparks with Mary quick, he was going to have to tell her it wasn't working. Maybe he just needed a little more time. Get over Kennedy. Keep it slow and steady. It'll work out. If not, he'd date someone else, again and again, until he met the right one. At least he felt more comfortable in his skin. "Gotta go, I'm late. See you when I get home."

He headed toward Mugs.

KENNEDY DRAGGED HER PALMS down her skirt and hesitated outside the door. Eating crow was not her favorite thing, but she'd crawl on her damn knees if he'd forgive her.

His car was parked outside. But when she knocked, it was Connor who opened the door, and his expression told it all. Pure dislike and judgment. Uh-oh. What had Nate told him? Everything? Pieces of it? Maybe she should start by apologizing to his sibling first. Oh, God, she sucked at this whole thing, so she opened her mouth and said the first word that came to mind.

"Hey."

"Hey." He didn't budge. "Nate's not here."

"Oh. Oh, okay. Can I come in for a minute?" He didn't look happy, but he let her in. She didn't have the patience to sit, so she paced back and forth in his small kitchen. "Do you know if he'll be out long?"

Connor walked to the refrigerator, grabbed a beer, and kept his back turned. "Probably. He's out with Mary."

Ouch. She breathed through the panic that she was too late and definitely knew Connor was majorly pissed at her. Time for some truth. "I'm not sure how much Nate told you about us. You mean the world to him, and I was hoping we could talk. I'd like to explain what happened. Maybe get your advice?"

He tipped the beer back, swallowed, and faced her. A shiver wracked her body. Pure ice mixed with disdain gleamed in his eyes. She was in definite trouble. "No need to talk, I'll give you my advice right away. You did a good job making him over. Also did a good job working him over. You almost broke him, you know that?"

"I'm so sorry," she whispered. "I made a mistake. I need to make it right."

"I called it from the beginning. Beautiful women think they rule the world. They take what they want with no thought to hurting someone, and then leave you in a broken pile at the door. Nate wanted to believe it could work. I warned him, but he took a chance and look what happened. Why are you back? To screw with his head some more?"

She began to shake. "I swear to God, I never wanted to hurt him. I got spooked. I'd never fallen in love before. I forced him to leave so I wouldn't break his heart later, but I realized all this time, I was just afraid of him leaving me. I was a coward. I need to tell him the truth."

"It's too late." He set his jaw as if making a decision. "He's involved with Mary now. They're sleeping together."

The blood drained out of her as if a vampire had feasted and left only the shell. Too late. She was too late. She felt his brother's gaze trained on her face, as if judging her reaction, but she didn't care any longer. Her voice barely worked.

"Is he happy?"

"Yes. Don't ruin it by coming back into his life. Just leave him alone."

She managed to nod. He was right. Nate deserved his own brand of happiness, and if he had found it with someone else, it didn't matter. Not the touch. Not her own broken heart.

He was sleeping with her.

Nausea lurched in her gut. She had had her chance, and she was too late. The least she could do was not swoop in and destroy something fragile, something that could be good for him and make him happy. Happier than she could.

She moved in a fog. Her hand paused on the doorknob. "Connor?"

"What?"

"I love him. He deserves . . . everything."

Then she left.

NATE GOT TO THE restaurant and grabbed a table. Mary still wasn't there, so he ordered his Darth Maultini. This time, the bartender didn't question him, and he realized he was making Verily his home. Weird. He'd lived with his brother for all that time, closer to work and on the edge of Manhattan, but it never felt like home. Just a nice spot to rent.

Genevieve's bungalow was warm and filled with a joyous vibe he'd gotten used to. The entire town had cast a spell on him. He loved taking a walk in the evenings and stopping for ice cream, or to people watch at the dog park. He'd purchased a gorgeous piece of art at the local gallery, and started to make casual acquaintances at the Purple Haze and Mugs. He even craved getting out of work on time, or at least, mostly. Wayne was getting a little pissy at his sudden longing for home, but he was playing with formulas and doing research outside the lab for the first time in his life.

Now if only he could fall in love with Mary.

A shadow fell over the table. "Hi, Nate." Her smile was easy and warm, and he automatically stood up to kiss her, but she turned her head at the last minute so he only snagged her cheek. She slid into the booth and clasped her hands on the table that he'd already wiped down for excess crumbs. "How are you?"

"Good. You look pretty." Her short blond bob was chic and sleek, framing a round face with bright green eyes. She was slim and fit, and favored more casual clothes such as jeans, T-shirts, and comfortable shoes. Much more his type. Much better than a fashionista who'd always outshine him in public events. This woman was more his match.

"Thanks." Her gaze darted around the place, and he caught nervous vibes. Was she getting impatient taking it slow? Should he up his game tonight? They'd stuck to kissing and holding hands, never needing to go further, but maybe she was questioning his intentions? He remembered a *Glamour* article that said men needed to make a move by date four or the woman lost interest. What number was this? Six? Crap, he was way behind.

He slid his hand over and grabbed hers. She jerked a bit, laughed, and then busied herself with the menu. Yeah, this was heading south fast. Maybe he'd invite her back to his place and text his brother to leave. Nate fought back the nerves jumping in his stomach. He was good at sex. It would probably bond them and get him to the next level. Right?

His dick remained silent.

Nate cleared this throat. "I ordered you a glass of the Merlot you like."

"That's so sweet." She looked up from the menu and sighed. "You're a wonderful man. Do you realize that?"

"Thanks. Listen, why don't we skip dessert and head back to my place after dinner? Spend some quiet time."

She dropped the menu and closed her eyes. "We need to talk."

He clearly remembered at least four blog posts on the worst things a woman could say was "We need to talk." He tried not to panic. "Sure. You can tell me anything."

"I've had a wonderful time dating you. Truly, when we met at the mixer, I thought we'd be good together. But I can't see you anymore."

Huh? He stared at her and tried to gather his thoughts. "Did I do something stupid?"

She laughed and squeezed his hand. "No, of course not! See, I met someone at work. And though you and I have a good time together, I don't think there are the sparks needed to start a long-term relationship." She bit her lip. "I hope you're not mad. I truly believed nothing would happen with this man, but he let me know how he feels, and I need to take a chance. We decided to date monogamously, so I'm going to pull myself out of Kinnections."

Her eyes sparkled with the flush of that first excitement of meeting someone who clicked with you. Someone who got you in every way. Someone you wanted to spend every spare moment with, and whom you missed, and who made you feel alive. Nate waited for the deep disappointment to hit for losing the woman who could've been his mate. Instead, relief sunk into his whole being and settled to stay.

Mary wasn't for him.

He laughed then, because it was too damn ironic.

"No, I'm not mad at all. In fact, I'm happy for you. You're an amazing woman and he's a lucky guy."

She smiled. "You are one hell of a catch, Nate Dunkle. I hope the next woman in your life sees that."

"Yeah, me too." They chatted for a bit more, and then he kissed her on the cheek and watched her disappear.

And the question pulsed through his mind. What next?

Maybe . . . nothing.

He sipped his drink and went over his options. If he was going to have a shot at happiness with someone else, he needed to get over Kennedy. Dating other women and hoping to forget wasn't helping. Maybe he'd take a break. He liked his new home. Enjoyed his new friendships. He was confident to approach women now and open to possibilities. Kennedy had given him all those gifts, but until his heart was free to give again, he was only going through the motions.

Yes. He'd pull out of Kinnections. Forfeit the fee, take some time to heal, and go back on his own terms. He couldn't be involved with Kate or Arilyn when he'd only be hoping to catch a glimpse of his real matchmaker. Distance and time was what he needed.

Nate paid the bill and walked home. The spring evening was lively with crowds, mingling in and out of the shops and filling up the outdoor cafés. The moon was full tonight, a beautiful orangey disc hanging over the Hudson. The Tappan Zee Bridge spread deep and long, with twinkling lights against the black sky. He stopped to chat a bit with a few residents and when he reached the door, he felt positive about his decision.

His brother was propped up on the sofa, beer at his side, chips on the table, *Breaking Bad* on the big screen. "Hey, you're home early. Everything okay?"

Nate joined him on the sofa. God, he was tired. "Yeah."

"Date good?"

"Nah, she broke up with me."

His brother cranked his head around. "Are you kidding? Why?"

He shrugged and grabbed a few chips. "She met someone at work. We didn't have any chemistry. Blah, blah, blah."

"Dude, that sucks. Wanna go out and get drunk?"

Nate laughed. "No, I agreed with her. I'm actually relieved. I'm gonna take a break from the dating scene for a while. Get my head together."

His brother gave him a strange look. "I think that's the wrong move. You need to get laid. Get out there and date someone else. Don't stop and don't look back."

"I'm not like you. It's not that easy."

"This is about her, isn't it? Your matchmaker? You're still pining when you should be celebrating you got rid of her. She's toxic, man."

He shook his head. "No. She's just like you, Con."

His brother popped off the sofa with his mouth open like a guppy. "What? What the hell did you just say to me?"

Crap. What a night. But it was time for some hard truth, and he was tired of skirting the real issue. "She's like you. You both got damaged from the past. You're both afraid to trust. Hell, neither of you thinks you deserve a real relationship, citing bullshit excuses like you don't want to be tied down, or have a long list of people you've already prejudged and declared guilty. Look at you, for example. No cosmetologists, no beautiful women, no women who are too smart and who'll judge you. It's ridiculous. Kennedy did the same thing. Told me over and over we weren't compatible, or that she'd end up breaking my heart."

"She would break your heart!"

"How do you know? Because she's beautiful? Because she'd leave me for someone better one day, like Mom did? You both drive me crazy! There's no guarantees here. Bottom line is you have to be willing to go for it. Kennedy couldn't. I hope one day she does, because I think I'll love that woman till the day I die. But you? You still have a shot. Get your head out of your ass and do something with your life."

Rage poured from his brother's figure. Connor grabbed him by his shirt, dragged him off the couch, and shook him like a dog showing dominance. "Fuck you! I tried and didn't get that supervisor job. I'm not a college-educated brilliant scientist, and I never will be. This is all I got!"

Nate shoved him away and fisted his hands. "Fuck *you*! Who said this is all you got? Mom? Dad? Me?

You? Decide what you want, and you go after it. If getting a supervisor position means a college degree, go back to school."

Connor pushed him back, and got in his face. Spittle flew from his mouth as he growled, "Fuck you! I don't have the money."

Nate took the first punch. A nice, clean arc connecting with his brother's jaw. "Fuck you! You sacrificed and put me through school and raised me. You don't think I'd pay for your education and anything else you need? Why can't I finally give something back to you?"

Connor held his jaw, lowered his body, and sicced him with a powerful uppercut that snapped his head back. Little birdies began to fly, and then the world steadied. "Fuck you! I'm not smart enough to go to college."

Nate bent low and head butted him in the stomach. His brother gasped for air and fell back. "Fuck you! You've always been smart, but you never had the chance to show it. You're a natural at management, and a business degree would give you everything you want. Pussy!"

His brother straightened and stepped in the ring. "Who you calling a pussy?"

They stopped talking and started punching. Nate used everything he was taught and added some new moves, but Connor was the master and blocked most of the serious jabs. Finally, they both fell back on the floor, panting for breath, adrenaline pumping and filling up the room.

It was beautiful.

His muscles let go, and he laid his head back on the floor, catching up on his oxygen and staring at the ceiling. He sensed his brother was doing the same. After a while, Connor's voice drifted up. "Would you really put me through college?"

"Yeah."

A pause. "You think I could do it?"

"I know you could."

"The guys use this local community college that gives discounted rates. I could still work, go to class at night, and take the accelerated weekend ones to finish earlier."

"You already checked into it, huh?"

A sigh echoed. "Yeah."

"Good. Register this week."

"Okay. Where'd you learn that 'right hook, swipe the knee at the same time' move?"

"Took what you gave me and tweaked it a bit. A bit of science helps."

"Nice. Hey, Nate?"

"Yeah?"

"Do you still love that matchmaker? If she wanted you back, would you go?"

His heart died a little, but he was used to it, and figured one day it wouldn't ache so much. Maybe. Maybe not. "I love her. But I don't know. It would depend. She needs to take a hell of a leap for me to believe she'll stick. Because I won't survive losing her a second time."

"I hear you."

They lay in silence for a while, then slowly got up. Retrieved their beer. And started watching *Breaking Bad*, side by side.

seventeen

KATE PEEKED IN her office. "You okay?"

She forced a smile. "Hanging in there."

"Ladies' night. Mugs. Friday. Gen's coming."

Ken raised her brow. "You believe her?"

"David's out of town at a conference so I think she'll sneak out. Jane and Arilyn are in."

"Okay." She tried to keep her voice from sounding lackluster, but her energy was low these days. The knowledge that she'd lost Nate for good would take her a long recovery time. But she was making some changes. She'd gone back to her therapist, and the sessions were helpful. All that time she'd gotten her body back to being healthy, she'd forgotten the other important half. To love all of herself, good and bad, fat and skinny, smart and not so smart. They were delving deep, and though the work was painful, a weight began to lift from her soul.

Three weeks had passed since she officially lost Nate. Both Mary and he had withdrawn from Kinnections, and she hoped he was happy with her.

Kate spoke quietly. "You're going to be okay, sweetie. We'll get you through it."

"Can I ask you a question?"

"Anything."

"What happens if you let your soul-mate go? You sensed we were meant for each other. But what if it doesn't work? Is one doomed to spend the rest of her life searching for something she'll never find?"

Kate shook her head hard. "No. You cannot think like that. My mother explained about the gift. It doesn't guarantee a happy-ever-after. Two people may not be meant for this time around. You can have many people you love in this lifetime, Ken, I swear to you. And we don't know the future. The most important part is you didn't turn away from it. You tried to tell Nate the truth. You took the risk. That's the key. Understand?"

Silly tears threatened. She was so frickin' emotional lately. "Yes. Thanks."

"No problem. I came in to tell you there's a client waiting. I tried to help him, but he only wants to talk to you. Heard you were the best."

Ken swiped at her eyes and laughed. "Well, he's right about that. You can send him in."

"You got it."

She straightened her desk, adjusted her cocoa brown jacket, and put her game face on. The pen dropped from her fingers when she came face-to-face with Nate's brother.

Fear cut her apart piece by piece. "Is Nate okay?"

"Yes, he's fine. Just wanted to talk."

The breath left her body. Thank God. She'd take the emotional hit of being close to his brother as long as Nate was safe. "Sit down."

He unfurled his long, bulky length into the seat. He tried to hook one ankle over his leg but bashed himself into the desk, so he settled for shaking his foot back and forth as if he were about to face the principal in elementary school. "Got something to ask."

"Go ahead."

"Do you still love Nate?"

Her body froze but she forced herself to speak. "Yes. I will probably always love him."

"I lied."

She cocked her head and studied him. His hand began to pound out a rhythm against his knee. "What do you mean?"

"He wasn't sleeping with Mary. He never did. They were dating, and I didn't trust you. I lied to make sure you didn't bother him again."

A small smile broke over her lips. "I don't blame you. You're his brother, and you wanted to protect him. I would've lied, too."

He stopped rocking and tapping and met her gaze. The hazel eyes that were once filled with accusation now seemed softer. More forgiving. "I made a mistake. I never told Nate about you coming to see him."

She shrugged. "No reason. He's with Mary now, he's happy. That's all I wanted for him. They both withdrew from Kinnections, so things must be working out well."

"He's not with Mary anymore."

The breath whooshed out of her lungs. A terrible

hope sprang from deep within, but she held it back. "What are you saying?"

He muttered something under his breath. "Nate loves you. He never had a relationship with Mary—they didn't connect. Mary found someone else, and Nate decided to take some time off from dating. He's trying to get over you, but it's like he's haunted all the time. Unhappy. He goes through the motions. Meets me and the guys for drinks, but he's like a shadow of himself. I think I was wrong."

Her heart pounded so hard and so loudly she swore his brother heard it. "About what?"

"About you. I think you got scared, like you said, and freaked out. I think I judged you because you remind me of all these women who have hurt me, starting with my mom. But I don't want to do that anymore. Who am I to judge you? We all make mistakes. I'm a walking mess, but Nate's putting me through school now, and I want more. Don't you?"

"Yes," she whispered.

"Good. You need to go see him. Get him back."

Her hands trembled as she pushed her hair back from her face. "I'll need to prove he can trust me. You think he'll forgive me?"

"Yeah. But you gotta come up with something good. Something epic."

The hope let loose and sprouted. She had another chance. "I have to think."

"Maybe you go see him in a raincoat, and you take

it off, and you're naked underneath. Then you say I'll do anything to get you back."

She rolled her eyes. "Dude, are you serious? That's so lame and overdone. Next idea."

Connor glared. "Would've worked with me," he muttered. "I know! We deliver a big cake to his lab, and you jump out of it in a sequined bikini while the song 'I Apologize' is on in the background and beg his forgiveness."

"Never gonna happen. Can you come up with an option where I wear actual clothing? It needs to be an emotionally epic moment, not physical."

"I think you're going in the wrong direction here."

"You're gonna be a real pain in the ass as a brother-in-law."

They looked at each other and shared their first real laugh.

And then, suddenly, she had it.

"I know what to do. But I'll need to recruit help."

"What's the plan?"

She relayed the basic details. His eyes widened and he finally nodded. "That's a good one. Even though you're not naked."

"Thanks. I'm making the call."

She reached out to grab the phone to talk to Wolfe.

NATE CHECKED HIS WATCH and decided to wait another five minutes. Wolfe was rarely late. He hoped he showed. Since the fight with his brother, things had settled a bit, but loneliness and thoughts of Kennedy still ravaged his mind. He was looking forward to a good game to test his skills and some male conversation for distraction.

The phone buzzed and he slid it out of his pocket. "Standing me up?"

A low chuckle. "Sorry, man, I got caught up in a project and can't make it out."

"No problem. I'll miss kicking your ass, though."

"I'm closing in on you, buddy. Shaved off two strokes in my game and closed my big deal. It was a beautiful thing."

Nate grinned. "Damn, huge congrats. I knew you could do it."

"You made it possible. Also realized there's an untapped market in the hotel industry on the golf course. I left something for you in the office. Show Ron some ID and he'll give it to you."

"ID, huh? The plot thickens."

"Enjoy. And don't call me back with any bullshit. I can't return them."

"Now I'm worried. I guess I'll thank you in advance, then."

"Welcome. I found you another partner, too. Should be in the office waiting for you."

"You think of everything. Now go make some money, for God's sake."

"Check in with you later."

Nate hit the button and slid the phone back in his pocket. Pride surged through him for his friend's accomplishment. He headed to the office, showed his license to Ron, and got escorted to the back room. There in the middle of the room lay the most magnificent golf clubs ever created.

He leaned over to inspect them. Shock held him immobile. His hand trembled as he ran a finger over the solid platinum and gold finish. Son of a bitch. The HONMA five-star custom set golf clubs were extremely rare, and crazy expensive. Trump played with them. How the hell had Wolfe managed?

As if his friend anticipated the question, Nate's gaze snagged on the small envelope taped to the bag. He reached out and opened it up.

> Nate,
> Thanks for everything. I sent a video clip
> of your swing and got these custom
> made in London. Of course, I got my
> own set, so watch out. The student
> eventually surpasses the teacher.
> > See you next week.
> > —Wolfe

It was a while before he was ready to actually slide one of the clubs out and hold it in his hand. The metal glistened, and the handle fit in his hand like it was meant to be there. Emotion clogged his throat, but he fought it back because he knew Wolfe would groan about getting all mushy and refuse to acknowledge his gratitude. He was damn lucky to score a friend like that.

The door opened. "Nate? Your partner is waiting out here for you."

"Coming." He hoisted the clubs onto his shoulder, still bedazzled, and walked out of the office to the main fairway. Then stopped short.

"Hello, Nate."

Kennedy stood before him.

Holy crap. She was gorgeous. Thick waves of hair fell past her shoulders, streaked with candy caramel color. The tennis dress thing was different from the last one she wore. This dress was shorter, and in fire-engine red. Her bare golden legs went on forever and ended in a pair of scarlet golf shoes.

His voice didn't work. He kept trying, but it got stuck halfway up his lungs and caught in his throat. His dick seemed to work fine, though. It rose to full staff salute and pushed painfully against his pants. This was not happening. Was it? Was he dreaming or was he just completely stupid to think she ever secretly loved him at all?

He quickly ran through endless physics equations to calm his mind and be able to walk without highlighting his arousal. "What are you doing here?"

Her tongue shot out to dampen glossy pink lips, showcasing that one crooked tooth he was so crazy about. "Golfing. Wolfe couldn't make it."

Temper warred with his sick desire to spend time with her. "And you're okay with this?"

She blinked. "Sure. Aren't you?"

He grit his teeth. No. No more games and pain and

hoping for something from her she wasn't able to give. "No, I'm not. Are you trying to deliberately mess with my head? Why are you here, Kennedy?"

She flinched, and suddenly the fake calm dropped from her face and was replaced by truth. Those whiskey eyes filled with longing and a hint of—fear? Was that even possible? What was going on? "I need to talk to you," she murmured. "To explain. Some things."

His heart leaped with hope. He squashed it like an annoying gnat. "I think we've said everything we need. I can't do this with you anymore. I'm going home."

He turned and prayed for the strength to reach his car. To drive away and heal from this woman who stole his heart and turned his world upside down and didn't want him.

"Wait!" She jumped out and blocked his path. Twisted her fingers and looked up from thick dark lashes with pleading, puppy dog eyes that walloped away his breath. "Please, just give me a chance. Play three holes with me. If I win, you listen to everything I have to say. If I lose, I'll walk and never bother you again."

He looked at her in astonishment. "Are you kidding me? That's the most ridiculous thing I've ever heard."

"I triple dog dare you. Three holes. You owe me that."

He owed her? Was she kidding? Pure temper

warred with his survival instinct to get away and save himself. She wanted to challenge him to a game? Fine. But this time he was playing for keeps. On his own holy ground of the golf course, Nate intended to finally finish this relationship and not look back. On his terms.

"Be careful what you wish for, Ken," he growled under his breath. "I've finally had enough."

The woman had the guts to smile at him. "So have I. Let's do this. This time I brought my own clubs."

He smothered a humorless laugh. Damn her to hell. But he realized this was the only way to end it. Once he won, she'd leave him alone, and maybe he'd finally be able to get on with his life. It was a poetic sort of finale, but more like an opera where everyone died at the end rather than a romance novel.

"Fine. We won't need the cart. Follow me."

He grabbed her clubs, refusing to allow her to carry them up the hill, and trudged off. She kept up, but he refused to look back. All he needed to see was that perky rear barely covered by the ridiculous dress. How could they make such stuff to play golf in? It wasn't decent. What would happen if she had to bend down to get one of the balls?

Smoke steamed out of his head, but he reached the first hole, released her clubs, and got his head in the game. "Ladies first."

She took her spot in the tee box. Glued her gaze to the ball, shimmied a bit back and forth while the red skirt swung in rhythm, drew back, and socked the ball with a perfect arc. It landed nicely on the edge of the fairway. Usually, she commented and chatted nonstop while they golfed. This time, she remained quiet, as if this game was actually important to her.

Nate knew the feeling.

He yanked his emotions under wrap and set up. His approach shot was flawless, and he watched as the ball landed right by the tee, set up for perfect par.

She frowned. "Nice shot," she offered.

He glared. "Thanks."

They trudged to the fairway and finished up.

Score: Four strokes for her. Three for him.

The second hole she upped the stakes, with a gorgeous powerful line drive that got it close to the green. How on earth did she just happen to have the perfect natural swing that no one in his life had ever possessed? Was she wearing red panties to match the dress? Would he find out if she bent down? He actually smelled her, the scent of bare skin and arousal, spice and musk, and all woman. His brain pingponged between lust and golf, but he swore to win and managed to knock the ball right to the green. Then wrapped it up quickly while she fumbled on the final putt.

Score: Four strokes for her. Two for him.

"It's over," he said quietly. "You'd have to get a hole in one and that's impossible."

"I can do it."

Frustration singed his nerves, and he clenched the club around his fingers. "It's over," he said again, more forcefully. "Besides needing a hole in one, I'd need four strokes handicap."

She stuck her chin out, got on tiptoe, and spoke right in his face. "I'm not a quitter. We said we'd play three holes."

He grit his teeth and swore. "This is ridiculous and unnecessary. Fine. Let's go."

He marched to the third hole and she kept pace. The rolling green hills spread before them, and sun streamed over the land like a gift from the gods. Birds sang with Disney cheer, a light breeze caressed the skin, and he'd never been so fucking miserable in his life. Last hole. He should've known she'd never give up, except on herself.

Except on love.

She seemed quieter and more reflective as she took her stance, glancing back over her shoulder at him. Her swing connected at the sweet spot, and put her right onto the green.

But it wasn't a hole in one.

He didn't say anything. They both stared at the ball, lying on the green, and something heavy pulsed in the silence. When she finally turned her head, those haunting amber eyes held the glimmer of tears, but nothing fell. "I lost."

His heart tore and bled, and he wondered if he'd die right here on the golf course. "Yes."

"But I can't play by the rules. Not now. Not with you."

He let out a primitive cry that he bet cavemen had

originated when their women had beaten them to the ground, literally and figuratively. "Don't," he tore out. "I can't—I can't take it."

She lifted her hands in the air in pure supplication. Raw emotion ravaged the graceful lines of her face, and for the first time, he glimpsed all the hidden corners of her soul, naked for him in the blinding sunlight of the golf course. "I love you."

"Oh, crap. You're going to kill me." He spun away and tunneled his fingers through his hair. "Now you decide you love me? We get on the course, you see me again and remember what it was like, and think you want me back?"

"I came to see you weeks ago. You were out with Mary, and your brother answered the door."

The pain was replaced by ice. So much better this way. It hurt less. "Why?"

"I came to beg your forgiveness. To say I love you, that I believed in us, and a real relationship, and I was stupid and scared. You deserve more, I know you do, but I had to try and tell you the truth."

He jerked and studied her face with an unrelenting stare. "You were so intent on this big declaration, huh? Then why did you leave? Why didn't you stay and fight for me?"

"Because Connor told me you and Mary were sleeping together. He asked me to stay away from you, that you were trying to build a relationship with her. That you had a shot at happiness."

"We never slept together. Mary found another guy

and quit Kinnections. I've been trying to get over you."

"I know," she said softly. "When you both pulled out of the agency, I thought it was because you were together."

He tried to sort out the puzzle. "Why now? Why weeks later did you suddenly decide to waltz onto the golf course?"

"Connor came to see me. He told me the truth. We had a long talk, and I confessed it was me who was scared the whole time. You were right." She drew a shaky breath and tipped her face up. "I gave myself excuses that weren't real. Tried to push you away by pretending I'd hurt you, that it was for the best, that I didn't deserve you. But I do. I deserve love, and I deserve not to be a coward, and I need to try. I will give you everything. My heart, my soul, my life. I will never leave you. I will love you for as long as you let me."

His breath stopped. He gazed at the woman he loved before him, face pleading, and saw the truth in her eyes. She didn't want to run any longer. She loved him. All of his dreams came down to this moment.

His eyes burned and he lurched forward a step, his mind reeling. He ached to drag her into his arms, forgive her, love her, but that tiny piece of fear still clung because he knew that this time there was no turning back. Something white fluttered in front of him, and he looked up.

What the hell?

A massive white banner opened up in front of him. Dozens of people clutched the material, holding it up proud and straight as the breeze tried to grab hold and shake it. Inky black writing scrolled over the clean, bright surface, flashing the words that seared right into his brain and straight to his gut.

I Love You, Nate Dunkle. Really . . .

Her voice floated, soft and husky behind him.

"Connor and I decided I needed to do something epic. I understand if you don't want to take another chance. I can only tell you what you taught me."

He turned and looked into her face.

"You taught me to be brave, to open myself to joy, and to be a full person. You reached in, saw every broken part of me, and loved me anyway. You are my everything. But most of all, I learned I *am* perfect. For you. With you. I don't want half measures anymore. I don't want safety. I want you. Only you."

She waited. Her humbleness and vulnerability made her even more beautiful, sketching out the lines of her face, softening her eyes, and giving him . . . everything.

He jerked her into his arms and took her mouth. Drank in her sweet taste, and softness, and strength, as the sun streamed hot and bright and a cheer went up from the top of the hill from all the nameless, faceless strangers. He kissed her for a long, long time, and when he finally broke away, he knew his life would never be the same.

"I still won," he said.

She laughed, the sound rolling over the green and in his ears like a sweet melody. "This time. But I got you, so I'm the real winner here."

He dove his fingers into her hair and kissed her again, long and deep and hard. "I love you, Kennedy Ashe. Let's go home."

The words had never sounded more perfect.

epilogue

KENNEDY SIPPED HER tea and leaned back in the seat. "I still think my 'happy ever after' ending is a tad better than yours. After all, you just got recliners."

Kate rolled her eyes and poked her in the upper arm. "Heated, leather, massaging recliners. Golf course endings are like airports. Overrated."

Kennedy gave her famous pout. "What do you think, Arilyn? Whose is better?"

Arilyn sighed and finished doctoring her tea. "Both are beautiful, and quite satisfying. Now stop acting like children and try this scone thing. It's outrageous."

Arilyn broke off three pieces and Kennedy nibbled with enthusiasm. Eating was an amazing thing, and she was beginning to embrace it a bit more easily. The melty sensation in her chest was becoming more familiar. At first, she thought it was a wonderful kind of indigestion. Kate had finally set her straight.

It was happiness.

"Well, at least Kinnections is booming," Kate said. "The clients are pouring in. Do you think it was that story leaked to the city paper? I wonder who could've done something like that after it was discussed and agreed we'd keep our personal lives private?"

Kennedy focused on chewing. It wasn't polite to answer with a mouth full.

Arilyn shook her head in disapproval. "We know it was you, Ken. That damn sharklike marketing gene of yours is gonna kill us."

"Where's Slade when I need a defense lawyer? I plead the fifth. And I didn't notice you crying me a river when our list shot up after the story broke."

"Fine. Then you won't mind if we film a video of your own relationship journey, right? That will get us tons of exposure."

"I can't. If mine is publicized, people will begin to think we're a matchmaking agency that steals the clients for ourselves. Could be bad PR."

"She has an answer for everything," Arilyn said.

"We can always say it was the love spell," Kate joked.

Kennedy and Arilyn shared a glance. "I forgot about that. Kind of hard to track, though. Gen was already engaged, and you have the touch."

"Do you remember the qualities you requested? Does Nate have them?" Arilyn asked.

Kennedy sputtered a laugh. "No one would have all the traits you dream about. Plus I was drunk. I doubt . . ." she trailed off, her mind sifting through the list. "Huh. That's weird."

Kate got a funny look on her face and placed her tea down on the table. "What?"

"Nate hits every one of my dream requirements. Even the ones I thought weren't possible to achieve."

Arilyn looked nervous. "We shouldn't have done the spell. I knew it. We opened up a portal or something."

Kennedy shook her head. "Listen, don't get spooked. So, the list was right. Doesn't mean the love spell works. Tell you what, A, if you find the man with all the traits you requested, then we know for sure it's valid. There's no way you're not gonna settle with a man who wears organic cotton, doesn't eat meat, owns dogs, teaches yoga, and practices tantra in the bedroom."

Arilyn looked away. "You don't know what I put on my list," she said quietly.

Kate raised a brow. "True. You gonna tell us?"

"No."

Kennedy laughed. "Thought not."

The red door slowly opened, and the tiny Japanese woman exited. Her gleaming white robe was tied with a bright scarlet sash. Her bare feet floated over the bamboo floors as she walked toward them, a tiny smile resting on her lips. Kennedy couldn't help the slight tremble of both anticipation and nervousness before a session with Ming.

As Nate well knew.

Her lover trailed behind Ming in a dazed cloud of peace and relaxation. His skin was damp, and he smelled deliciously of citrus and soap. His gaze scanned the room and locked on hers.

Nate smiled. "Hey."

Her heart squeezed with emotion. "Hey, baby. Good session?"

"Not sure right now."

Ming gave a delighted cackle and gently pushed Nate toward her. "He good boy. Much better this time."

Kennedy snuggled into his arms, warm and snug and safe. "This my woman," he slurred.

Kate laughed. "He's punch-drunk, Ken. Gotta love a man who can't hold his muscles through a Ming session."

Ming reached out a hand and pointed to Kate. "You next."

Kate bit her lip. "Umm, can Arilyn go first?"

"No. You get married soon, no? You need cleansing."

Kate shuddered and slowly stood up. "Okay. I think."

Ming's sharp gaze swung to Arilyn. "You drink more tea and wait. You have man?"

Arilyn nodded. "Yes, I have a man."

Ming frowned and jumped up and down in temper. "Your man no good for you. I feel this. You need to refresh aura for right man."

Arilyn's mouth dropped open. "No, I don't! I'm—happy."

"You lie. I speak with you later." Kennedy buried her face in Nate's robe and tried hard not to laugh. Ming was a massage therapist, healer, and psychic, and no one ever knew what type of session they'd have. Her humor was short-lived when Ming focused all that concentration on her. "You marry this man?"

"Not yet. One day. Right now, we're happy the way things are."

Nate tugged at a wayward curl. "Yes, we're getting married. As soon as I convince her," he said with an amused grin. They had decided to move in together and had settled into a happy routine, inviting Connor to join in on their eclectic family and encouraging him to pursue school.

Ming nodded, pleased. "She hard case, but you strong. You don't give up."

His face softened. "I never will," he whispered.

The man said the damnedest things. She knew they were both right. She'd break down and say yes, but not for a while. It was too much fun to let life take her in this direction, enjoying every second of the incredible gift of Nathan Ellison Raymond Dunkle.

Ming turned to Kate. "We go now."

Her friend gave a desperate look back and stepped into the hallway. "Bye, guys. Wish me luck."

The door closed.

Arilyn shook her head. "I'm happy," she insisted. "Ming is wrong."

"I believe you, babe. No worries. It'll all work out in the end." She looked up at the man she loved and smiled.

"It'll all be . . . perfect."

acknowledgments

AS ALWAYS, I must begin with my thanks to the team at Gallery Books, especially Lauren McKenna, the coolest editor on the planet. Girlfriend, thanks for saving this book and especially for Ming. It was epic.

Thanks to my agent, Kevan Lyons, for her guidance.

Huge thanks and smooches to the Probst posse for their support, cheerleading, and help with naming my hot geek hero!

To my childhood friend, fab assistant, and gym supporter, Lisa Hamel-Soldano. If you weren't around, I wouldn't have a posse or be able to make a deadline, so thanks for keeping me sane.

To my amazing, kick-ass husband who cooks and helps me in every way possible, and keeps me laughing at every turn. Love ya, babe.

This is a nutty business. My author friends are the best and deserve a special shout-out: Aimee Carson, Wendy S. Marcus, Abbi Wilder, Catherine Bybee, Megan Mulry, Alice Clayton, Elisabeth Barrett, Jen McLaughlin, Jenna Bennett, Jen Talty, Bob Mayer,

Ruth Cardello, Kathleen Brooks, Melody Anne, Janet Lane Walters, and way too many more ever to name here without creating a separate book. Thanks to all of you for the inspiration, support, and laughs. Bring on the conferences!